Dedication

This book is dedicated to the giants of inspiration that walk my particular earth and who I shall always look up to:
Lindsay Smith, Pascal, Olivia and Darcie.

PROLOGUE

Autumn. S.W coast of England. Recent past. Early morning.

Pilgrim stumbled onto the pebble beach of the deserted cove, her feet bloodied, clutching a torn coat about her slim body, her long hair plastered to her face from sweat. Moving unsteadily to the shore's edge she stopped, allowing the cold waves to lap over her bruised ankles. She gazed out through crystalline blue eyes over the steel coloured water as the wind buffeted her pale aquiline face. Rimmed indigo clouds reached out over the sea where a solitary boat bobbed back and forth in the distance. Pitiably, she still yearned for a normal life.

She shivered, not from cold but from exertion. She'd left them dead – what did they expect? Lifting and turning her wrists inward she gazed down through tears at the blackened bruises. She'd been so careful these forty years. Who'd given her away? Why ask the question? It could only be her – there was no one else. There couldn't be anyone else; she'd had to accept that. Then what had she said or done to give herself away? She mentally flicked through the last few clients requests that'd been made to her secret storage facility – The Vault. 'La Petite Ingénue' – a priceless painting by the French renaissance artist, Solière. She tracked through her memory of the surveillance of the Principle and meticulous research to authenticate its provenance. Nothing there, it had run like clockwork. Before that, there had been the fragments of the crown that had once encircled the imperial brows of the Ottoman dynasty? Nothing there – she had checked and double checked – she always did. Then what?

She'd been vigilant to the point of obsession when it came to keeping herself to herself. Ritualistic in her daily life, in and out of humanity like a thief, never striking up conversations as she travelled, no verifiable details on file.

So they knew about her – but they didn't know all – even she didn't know all. The harsh memory of their indifferent brutality metered out on her body began crushing her. Pilgrim unleashed her anger, opening her mind, allowing all those forces which lay menacingly on the fringes of her consciousness to rise up in retribution. Embracing them, her mind became molten as the heat of unfettered fury hit her, coursing white hot as it melded with her soul. Her vision blurred as she stared forward unseeing, her eyes iridescent, began to spark and fleck.

Altered and lost, Pilgrim, was oblivious to the sudden drop in the wind, the immediate hush of the sea as the surface flattened to glass, drew back and began sharply rising up the cliff face. Gaining momentum, it surged forward, losing its steel patina and folding to inky black. Nautical flags fell limp and all wildlife cowered. The small fishing boats, prone on their sides in the harbour, lifted under the incoming swell, straining against their moorings as the massive wave entered the quay.

Pilgrim choked back a cry as her anger subsided, her plight mocking her. As quickly as the natural environment had become ominous, those changes fell away. The sea flushed to its former hue and resumed its slow rhythmic brush against the shoreline. The wind picked up, moving along listless clouds and causing the tattered flags once again to snap against their masts. Exhausted, she lifted her coat sleeve to brush away her tears.

She needed a friend - maybe Hansford – no, he'd already shown he wasn't interested in friendship. Looking up, she watched as a seagull heading in from the distance, arced toward shore. Pilgrim followed its flight as it swopped overhead. She would find a friend. Turning, she began slowly trudging up the beach. As she did, the bullet hit her, searing through her back, throwing her forward onto the shale.

CHAPTER ONE

Present day.

> *Being her, she couldn't have done anything else. There had been a veiled life unlived with the freedom of choice. Decisions had been made centuries before, making that impossible. However, there is an imperceptible pattern of balance unseen by our short lives. Mother Nature always addresses inequality and things were about to change.*

Henry Baxter

From this angle I can see tomorrow. It glints and smoulders with possibilities of all things to all people and yet its presence is never in the moment. This benevolence is our gift. Cling on to it; you're going to need it!

Chassé!

I am ecstatically happy. No, that's not good enough. It doesn't convey the pounding of my heart, the quickness of my fingertips on the keyboard, which can barely keep up with the flood of emotion clogging any coherent thought that I need to put down on paper. Breathe … softly. I feel as if my soul is uplifted.

I am certain that I am finally and blessedly free. I can draw the arc to complete the circle of my life and what I believe to be the purpose of my existence. I can purge my consciousness and share with you the single, most important discovery of any age. I have at last been given permission to write!

You will find no answers, neatly tied resolutions or apologies, just the facts plain and simple. There is no escape here, either written on these pages or after. Tread therefore with conviction or don't tread at all.

I suppose one of the most important aspects of this work is to draw your attention to the curious fact that our most recent generations have been exposed to all manner of media saturated by the supernatural, more so than in the past, that is unless you feel it necessary to point out the Romans, Greeks and Egyptians. I now firmly believe we are on the threshold of the most astounding human evolutionary leap of any age for which we are as prepared as we are ever likely to be.

When I look back and tell you about the inauspicious beginning, after the events that have followed to this day, I am compelled to remind myself that we live not only in a wondrous time, with the greatest opportunity for creative thinking, which forms the core in realising our destiny, but are discovering the symbiotic relationship we share collectively that runs through everything, not just on this planet but across the solar system. Your initial reaction to this stunning piece of news may be a momentary pause – just like that.

Even now, after I have had time to digest the information and reflect somewhat on those people, with the truth of who they are and what they are capable of, I am thankful that we have a sacred weapon incorruptible by man.

You may ask yourself why, after all these years, am I finally divulging what I know, and to you, and why on earth should you be the slightest bit interested? I should stop at this point and ask you to consider, are you interested in truth? Do you have the kind of imagination and intellect that allows you to extrapolate information, pertinent to forming, not just a hypothesis, but enabling you to believe? Do you love yourself enough to fight for your survival? An inane question I agree, if you're sitting in a comfy chair with things you trust and know surrounding you, but I have to ask you these questions as I have been forced to answer them for myself. For those of you reading this sentence, you are beginning at the same point of consciousness that I was at all those years ago. I wanted to write sooner but it was impossible. It was not that I didn't ask and at the most advantageous of times, but you must understand, my business partner, Pilgrim, forbade it. I cannot say her name in my head without the enormity of what I must impart bringing me to the verge of tears, not of sadness but of peace. Because the moment we arrive into this world of ours we will not feel its presence again until the day we die. So why now? The reason is simple - sufficient time has passed and Pilgrim, not always right but definitely wise, has given her consent for me to write down some of the events that have occurred to us. Actually, now that I can begin, there is excitement but also a genuine fear that comes with revelation. So for the first time I, Henry Baxter, take up the mantle of scribe!

There is not much to say in the way of my physical attributes; I would be every investigative police officer's nightmare if given a description of me. I am of medium build and height, have a fair complexion and grey eyes with a little padding underneath. My remaining hair is kept short

3

and grows on my head like a monastic skull cap. I prefer to be clean shaven and my lips are meagre. Interestingly, I do like to smile, more so than before, and I have the teeth to pull it off admirably, so I do have one saving grace. The remainder of my features are so nondescript as to be termed 'usual'. Now that I've put my physicality to paper I feel somewhat surprised. Not at myself, you understand; surprised because how could a person looking like me possibly have lived anything but an ordinary life? Equally surprising is the truth of the matter, you will shortly discover, is that my life now is anything but ordinary. Perhaps it's me, but, if I hadn't been writing this book, I would have thought the kind of person living the life I am must have something noticeable about him, that makes him stand out from the crowd. But I digress. At this juncture, it is perhaps best if I take you back to last spring, when I was approaching forty, a dyed-in-the-wool UK expat living on the Upper East Side of Manhattan.

I had been working for the 'Great White' (otherwise referred to as 'G.W'), a banking executive on Wall Street, as his personal valet. Some may consider this a humble role, those who have no real knowledge of the art of a practised and proficient gentleman's gentleman and, in all honesty, it can be irksome when the culmination of one's expertise boils down to picking up the used undershorts of your employer. However the perks infinitely outweigh those boorish moments. If you choose carefully, your employer will be fair and interesting; you'll travel the world in first class style and meet on intimate terms those people featured so much in the media. Despite my years in service, I should have known better. I freely admit I took the position for no other reason than that it offered more money than I had ever earned. In accepting the situation, I lied to myself, embracing the affirmation my unique skills as a personal valet were certainly worth every cent my new employer was willing to pay. There is nothing quite so irritating as the self-absorbed, hence we were a pair. He had created a religion out of his life by the reverence in which he held his practice in the art of accumulating wealth and the homage paid to acquisitions. I, in turn, looked down my nose and onto my very ridiculously expensive shoes. I make no claim to being either smart or perfect. Real life was hastily stuffed to the back of my mind and hedonism took precedence.

That morning I went about picking up various pieces of underclothing strewn across the bathroom floor along with the half used bath towels, through the cloying aroma of tropical flowers, and opened the windows, not to the chirping of birds and a bright sunlit morning but to the honking of impatient horns, the blasphemous shouting of vendors trying to circumnavigate vehicles straddling the sidewalk, and the bang of the front door downstairs which could only herald one thing: the arrival of Patrick. Without much impartial discussion on the matter, Patrick would certainly have been pegged as a diva of the first order and, as if to confirm my suspicions, when we first met he corrected my pronunciation of his name; he informed me the pronunciation was to be Patrique. Never mind the fact his Irish accent was very much in evidence and he walked as if waving an invisible flag, planted firmly between the cheeks of his buttocks. Patrick, you see, was the house manager of this luxurious three storey townhouse, in which passers-by would attempt to catch a glimpse of life beyond their means. The only thing I saw him manage in the three years I spent there was to adeptly dodge any physical labour and employ a gullible patsy – you've guessed it, me– to do all the work. I could hardly complain at my own naivety.

My mental salve was the remuneration which was at least three times the amount I could have earned in England. Yes, I concluded, I could be bought. I had decided upon a term of three years to give my life some meaning before the bell tolled forty.

It was on that morning three years later that I committed myself to leave Manhattan and not return. I didn't have a plan, just the certain knowledge that, forty or not, money wasn't everything. You can think like that when you've squirreled away pretty much every cent you've earned since arriving on the island, and utility bills are as remote in the conscious mind as a bitter winter in north Finchley. So it was on the last hour, of the last day, after having given a month's notice, I was disappointed, but not surprised, when my employer called to inform me a package would be arriving within the half hour. I was to sign for it and place it on the hall stand. It would be collected within thirty minutes of its arrival and I was to hand it over with no further ado. I had hoped he would wish me every success for my future, but the dismissive click from the other end signalled the close to another chapter in my life.

Moving my modest suitcase to the side of the entrance hall and checking the electronic clock above the little used and pristine stainless steel cooker that was sometimes admired but rarely used, I suddenly realised, once I stepped over the threshold of this house, the rest of my life was mine to reclaim. The sudden surge of relief and euphoria gushed through me and I clenched and unclenched my fists in an effort to abate my excitement. Then had come the sound of the front door buzzer. It was half-past three, EST, and the moment my life began.

Looking back, with a colder eye, I should have known there was something out of the ordinary in the transaction. To begin with, he arrived on time, *he,* being the stereotypical courier. The package, which was handed to me with a nod to initiate pen to paper, was the size of a well-wrapped spectacle case in regular brown paper, fastened with fine waxed cord which in itself was unusual, and with a type of knot I have since come to recognise with extreme caution. Sure enough, before the hands could reach four o'clock, the buzzer sounded and the package was collected by a similar courier. I was oblivious to the fact this simple interaction would send ripples through the rest of my life.

I did not return directly to London. The chill in the air on the east coast of America was quite enough to jog my memory of wiping the condensation covered windows and the moroseness of the British native waiting for signs of the first spring buds to form. Instead, quite contrary to my sense of order, I decided to take a jaunt around South America, though it could not have been described as a holiday as that would imply it was a leisurely break. As soon as the currency exchange cashier began to count out pesos, in a manner that reveals a person unfamiliar with any foreign realm, I was compelled to offer a fixed smile. And so the die was cast.

Of course, I had travelled extensively on an international level in my capacity as a personal valet. However, my well-heeled shoes had only trodden the finest hand-woven carpets on private Gulf Stream jets to the gilded foyers of some of the finest hotels in the world. I had considered my travel experience a precarious one if room-service was not available on a twenty four hour basis. Now my determination to live life, as opposed to observing it, meant I should jump in with both feet and with my eyes wide open, if there was to be any possibility of salvaging my remaining years and developing myself into the type of human being I could be proud of. This higher goal would require becoming financially independent, courageous and unselfish. Grand ideals indeed if, like me, you knew you were beginning at the opposite end of the spectrum.

In retrospect, the change in language, culture, weather, food and, more importantly, perspective, couldn't have been more agreeable to me. I flew from JFK to Lima in Peru, where I spent a couple of days mentally adjusting to my choice of destination, and then stepped down into Chile, where I sought to admire the architecture of the fine universities at Santiago, before finally crossing over into Argentina, where I intended to visit Cordoba and leave via Buenos Aires. By then, spring should definitely have arrived in London.

It was whilst admiring the relief facades of the famed Jesuit University that I clumsily backed into a lady as I was trying to capture the sight with my travel camera.

"I must apologise, I am so very sorry." Realising my reactionary faux pas, I babbled, "Con permiso", which I couldn't help but voice with an Italian intonation. Before I could embarrass myself further, much to my relief, the lady in question answered in the most eloquent English.

"Please, think nothing of it. It was quite my fault for passing behind you when I could see you were moving back to take a better shot."

She smiled and, turning away, lifted a perfunctory wave as she disappeared down a side street. Despite the shortness of our meeting, her image was seared indelibly on my mind's eye. Firstly, she had an aura about her something akin to magnetism, as I felt compelled to watch her. This was a strange phenomenon, an alchemy of the mind as she wasn't any great beauty. I don't say that in a malicious or derogatory manner. Simply put, I would not have described her as pretty or beautiful; her cheek bones were too pronounced for that. Some might have called them aquiline – I called it 'in need of a square meal', especially given her above average height. Her eyes were stunning. They're the kind of sparkling blue you see in butterflies and large, maybe a little too large for her pale face. The look she had given me made me unsure of myself. It appeared cursory on her part but left me feeling vulnerable. With her dark auburn hair that swung about her slender shoulders, she leisurely walked away.

The following day I had quite dismissed the whole incident. I had been waiting at the reception desk in my hotel, preparing to leave, when there had been an odd occurrence. At the time I had genuinely believed it was simply a coincidence.

As I stood checking my bill for discrepancies, a package the size of a shoe box was placed on the desk by the bellboy. It struck me immediately as similar in wrapping to the package delivered to the house in Manhattan. My curiosity forced me to take a closer look and to my surprise I saw the same unusual knot, which I now know is called a 'Monkey Fist', made with the same flaxen cord. Perhaps you can imagine how intrigued I was. My concern was abated by my immediately deciding that the unusually dull paper and rare fastening was merely the marketing ploy for some exclusive product. Why else would my former employer have taken an interest? As I counted out bill upon bill of pesos, I reminded myself that I was no longer gainfully employed and the upcoming time for exchanging pesos into pounds sterling was going to be a painful one. Still, I was comforted in the knowledge that I had at least two years' salary in my bank account in England. With my hotel bill paid and the courtesy car ready to drive me to the airport, the desk manager confirmed my suitcase was stowed in the trunk. Walking past the pink marble colonnades toward the sun-drenched entrance, I turned to look back, to remember in the years to come, how splendid it was and how different I knew it would be in contrast to wherever I might find myself in the future.

That moment became frozen in time because, appearing out of the dining-room and now dressed in a flowing azure kaftan, strode the woman I had bumped into. I had stood transfixed in the lobby, thinking I must have been within her peripheral vision, but she took the brown paper parcel and walked forward to the outside terrace and never once glanced in my direction. It has, since that day, when I mentally stumble upon that memory, to be among the most singular occurrences, given the catlike perception which I now know her to possess.

There is nothing like returning to London. After having spent some time away, you definitely feel as though you're home. The pleasant familiarity of the soft rumble of conversation between those city folk, accompanied by the slosh of vehicle tires passing through the dirty rain-filled gutters, and the quietened sound of your tread on well-worn flag stone, reminds you that this is where you belong.

After my initial short-lived nostalgia, I set about looking for somewhere to live. The thought of going back on the books of servitude rankled with my new found freedom. I gave myself one year in which to decide what to do with my life and act upon it. I initially toured the great museums, and indulged my love of all things culinary by taking a six week gastronomic course for beginners entitled 'The Chef's Apprentice.'

The twelve months passed more swiftly then any I had experienced in my forty years and as my forty-first birthday came and went, marked only by my landlady pushing a birthday card under my bedroom door, I made a decision; something had to be done. Money was running low, London was more expensive than I remembered plus there were no work prospects in sight, and even less companionship to be had. It was at breakfast the following morning, as I manoeuvred a well done kipper past a croquette of bubble and squeak on my breakfast plate, that my landlady piped up.

"Oh dear, oh dear, oh dear." Tutting to herself from behind the daily scourge, she had drawn a sharp breath. "I don't know what the world's coming to. All those people that died in Caracas."

"Caracas?" I had questioned absently.

"Yes. You must have read about it at the time. `Bout two years or more. Thousands dead in that slum. Not a mark on `em, and no explanation."

"Really."

"Deary me, Mr. Baxter. You wanna read a paper occasionally."

"No, thank you."

"Anyways, as I was saying, after millions spent on research they've come to the conclusion it was an accident.

'Pollution and squalor.' Well, no surprises there then!" She chortled uncharitably.

I imagined foolishly she would stop and allow me to get back to my tired kipper but no such luck.

"Well, I never! All the years I've been in hospitality, I've never seen it this bad. You know people just don't know how to get along with each other these days."

"Something wrong, Mrs. Stillon?" I asked affectedly, purely for her benefit.

Hunching forward, she offered conspiratorially, so as not to be overhead by the other few diners.

"It says `ere, more women are now choosing to live alone." She continued reading verbatim: "The percentage of unmarried and childless women has increased by fifteen percent in the last ten years." She continued in the most serious tone, "There's this new executive living complex with its own gym, restaurant, bar and library, already with a waiting list of people trying to become tenants. Isn't it awful?"

Not having strictly paid attention to the way in which Mrs. Stillon's mind worked, I ventured, "Awful, why awful? That's good news for you, surely? More people looking for long-term accommodation."

She stared at me as though I had said something most unpleasant and then, as if explaining to a particularly stupid person, she shook her head.

"No, it's not. When my mother left me Holly Lodge, 'Margret', she said, 'it's like `aving a big family. They'll come and stay, find love, marry and move on – just in time for the next lot, but more importantly, you'll never be alone'."

I must have looked nonplussed as she hurriedly continued.

"Well, I don't mean you, Mr. Baxter, no, not you. You're what they call a confirmed bachelor. It's not you I'm talking about. If a woman came in `ere you're likely to run the other way." She chuckled to herself as she folded the paper untidily. "No, me and you 'ave a lot of years `afore us an' thank God for that; now my Malcolm's passed on, I could do with someone to talk to. You sit there and I'll bring you out another kipper; it's on the 'ouse!"

It was the wink she gave me, as she pendulated her generous proportions through the swing doors into the kitchen with three cats chasing her heels, which made my decision final. Today I was going to move out!

Not knowing quite how Mrs. Stillon would take the news, I waited until she had left to go shopping to pack my few belongings, leave a note and two weeks' pay in lieu of notice, and closed the heavily green painted door behind me.

Depositing my suitcase in a locker at Waterloo Station, I bought the *Times* and began studying the classified ads. Before long, my eyes had become accustomed to the small print and abbreviations as I began to identify those notices which might be useful to me. I don't recall how long I sat there, only that the amount of coffee I had drunk was beginning to have an adverse effect on my internal system. As I folded the paper and rose with the intention to tuck it under my arm, my eye caught an ad that began:

'Large comfortable six-bedroom house in north Finchley, two large rooms available for rent. House has one other tenant and efficient live-in housekeeper. Reasonable terms for full board and lodging.'

13

I pulled my mobile phone from my pocket and called the number. Following a slight hesitation, the voice of a woman answered. As she said 'Hello', the hair on the back of my neck stood up. I couldn't be sure until she repeated herself - but surely I must be mistaken?

I agreed to meet her at the house in question at six o'clock that evening. During the half-an-hour walk from the tube station to the top of Bow Lane, I had already chastised myself and worried slightly at my state of mind. I couldn't stop her image, and those questioning eyes, from appearing in front of me; I carried the worry up to the moment I knocked on the front door and it was opened by the lady I had bumped into in Argentina.

She looked at me wryly.

"I was wondering when you would see that ad."

CHAPTER TWO

With some trepidation and despite my confusion, I couldn't help but like the woman before me, so I entered the house. Her straight auburn hair was drawn back accentuating those cheekbones and a mouth that was fuller than I remembered. The blue kaftan had been replaced with black jeans, a plain white T-shirt and a pair of soft loafers minus the socks. She hadn't done or said anything to put my mind at rest, as it whirred anxiously with all manner of unlikely scenarios. She seemed oblivious to her own magnetism, compelling me to follow her lead through the front door and along the spacious hallway.

The house was meticulously kept and my eyes scoured the surroundings in the hope they might be able to shed light on the reason for this strange and unforeseeable event. At the end of the hallway, passing the bottom of the stairs to the left, stood a jardinière was the largest aspidistra I had ever seen. Following her, I continued until we came to a spacious reception room to the right, which we entered. It was both bright and airy. Large French doors spread open leading out onto a cobbled patio where various brightly coloured pots stood to attention, overflowing with botanical perfection. Obviously, someone in the house had a green thumb, but I didn't believe it was the lady escorting me. I couldn't imagine those delicate white hands plunged into soil.

"Please, take a seat,' she said, smiling reassuringly. 'I won't be a minute, I'm just going to see if Mrs. Cotterill the housekeeper, has returned."

'Ah, the green thumb,' I thought. As she left, I realised neither of us had introduced ourselves. I heard her light tread outside and strained to hear any other voice but, all was silent. Looking about the large room, it was obvious it had seen little structural change since its Victorian construction. A large carved-oak fireplace surround with a decorative wrought-iron inlay dominated the end of the room. Evidence showed, from the smudge of ash on the grate and the unmistakable aroma of cindered wood, that it was still in use. On the back wall facing the French doors, rested a large dark green leather Chesterfield which could very comfortably have seated four adults, along with its accompanying ottoman and two sunken chairs, one of which I claimed. An ornate silk screen, depicting various colourful birds and fauna, hid a grand piano behind which, stuffed to the gills from floor to ceiling, stood a bookcase of epic proportions. If this room was anything to go by, the remainder of the house must be both expansive and comfortable. I panicked, as I suddenly realised someone's 'reasonable rent' was probably far beyond my meagre savings or prospects. I had a word with myself, to remind me, these were very unusual circumstances. It was not that abnormal occurrences didn't pique my interest – it was just my 'pique-o-meter' had become somewhat blunted by my years in service. Living with the eccentric demands and whims of previous employers, and their outrageous life styles had desensitised me. My apprehension as to whether I could afford the rent was put aside as I heard the turn of the door handle and a leap of anticipation coursed through me. She entered wearing a look of relief.

"Mrs. Cotterill will be in with tea shortly. It's occurred to me I haven't introduced myself. My name is Neath A. Pilgrim." She had hesitated, as if she hadn't been sure about the use of her name. I had looked directly at her and was reassured by the warmth I saw reflected in her eyes. I wondered at the reason she would be so precise; was it habit?

"Although I should point out no one calls me Neath. Everyone…," she hesitated again, "calls me Pilgrim, other than Mrs. Cotterill who calls me, Miss Pilgrim." She hummed an unexpected self-conscious laugh.

I stood as if on command and proffered my hand which she gently shook.

"Henry Baxter," I announced with more confidence in my voice than I was feeling.

She shook my hand purposefully.

So, it is, to this day, for it was never meant to be any other way, that we address one another in a formal manner but with the easy-going camaraderie of soldiers in arms, as 'Pilgrim and Baxter.'

Suddenly; overtaken by myself; I spluttered, "We did meet, briefly, in Argentina, didn't we?" The worry in my voice made me sound like a self-conscious school boy. Not the impression I wanted to project at all.

"Yes, we did - briefly," she answered, smiling.

The look in her eyes made me believe she had read my mind. I suppose my awkwardness was blatantly evident to even the most unobservant person. Before I could ask my next question the door opened. I could barely contain my desperation at wanting to ask her what the meaning of all this was. She was clearly the orchestrator of my presence here today and had admitted as much. But why?

Mrs. Cotterill entered quietly and deliberately. She was a lady of approximately sixty years of age who, by the straightness of her backbone, even though the tea tray she carried looked heavy and cumbersome, had the demeanour of a person who stood for no nonsense. Thankfully, and to my great relief, she smiled at me. As she placed the tray on the table there was some thought behind those bright eyes which told me I was being measured. Pilgrim, who never missed a thing, confirmed my suspicions by whispering to me, once Mrs. Cotterill had left the room.

"Mrs. Cotterill is a very good judge of character. She obviously approves of you, otherwise she would never have smiled."

There would have been the inevitable cigarette she'd light and I can't remember how much cake I ate, only that I had to stop myself for fear that little would be left on the plate and my appetite construed as greed, not hunger, when it was most certainly hunger.

Pilgrim had excused herself and left the room to make a phone-call. In her absence, Mrs. Cotterill had returned and begun to clear away, when she suddenly stunned me with an unexpected question.

"Would you be the same Mr. Baxter that was the personal valet to a Mr. Stenmore?"

I had been surprised and taken aback by her question and in the momentary absence of a reply she had continued.

"An exacting man, with a penchant for automatons and head of Crisid bank in London. It's rumoured to be the most exclusive independent bank in the world, isn't it?"

"Yes, yes it is, by all accounts. But how do you happen to know Mr. Stenmore?"

"My sister was the head housekeeper at Fernley – where you both visited - before she passed away. I believe Mr. Stenmore was there to make a purchase for his collection?" she asked.

"Yes, he was. Well, it is a small world Mrs. Cotterill."

"Smaller than you think," she had stated cryptically, before continuing, "then you must also be the Mr. Baxter, who protected that poor child at Crainlee Hall. Horrible business that. It seems to me the more money people get the crazier they become. Well, certain people."

Mrs. Cotterill, waited for my response, but I was frozen, not in fear, but by something from my past that I kept locked away and would never divulge to another living soul. She continued slowly, watching my reaction. "I take it from your lack of response, it was you?" She took a moment's pause before adding, "my hat's off to you. I remember reading about it. It was all over the papers for weeks. Shocking; he must have gone clean off his head; what was his name?"

Somewhere from the depths of my soul, I uttered the name that had remained at the forefront of my mind everyday but had never passed my lips in over a decade, "Mr. Phelps." I uttered.

"Not so much killing his wife and that other man, but butchering them. How you stopped him from murdering his own kin I don't suppose I'll ever know. What were you doing there in the first place?"

Stung by the memory, I instinctively closed my hands and drew my arms closer to my body, where the defensive scars from an eight inch filleting knife, wielded by Mr. Phelps, had slashed in frenzy years before. There had been two children and their cries and horror stricken faces still ruptured his dreams occasionally.

"It was a brave thing you did, and then to testify against him in court, and him being so high up in government. Whatever happened to him anyway? Probably rotting away in prison where he belongs – 'diminished responsibility', my foot! Just the establishment covering up for their own. More maniacs in Whitehall then you can shake a stick at!"

She paused and I saw something in her gaze akin to pity.

"You must have breathed a very rarefied air in your time?" she remarked contemplatively.

"It's true I have worked for some unusual people." I replied lightly.

"Unusual people!" her laugh was genuine and spontaneous. "That's the understatement of the year. Now I begin to understand Miss Pilgrim's interest in you."

"I'm afraid I cannot talk about any of my previous employers--confidentiality agreements. You understand?" I buffered. I was beginning to feel the scrutiny of Mrs. Cotterill tighten like a vice around my answers. That unassuming congenial manner had melted away and I was reminded of her quick analysis of me upon my arrival. I believed her interrogation, for that is what it felt like, had been prompted by her protectiveness of Pilgrim. I tried to reassure her.

"In my previous professional capacity I have worked intimately with geniuses whose profiles never enter the public domain, but I've also worked with garden variety eccentrics, the self-absorbed, and the psychotic. I have never once revealed a secret confided to me, either inadvertently or otherwise. In short Mrs. Cotterill, I can be relied upon."

Mrs. Cotterill had stopped placing items on the tray. Pushing the tray forward on to the table she left it there and began straightening the room in a most methodical fashion, whilst continuing our conversation.

"Perhaps," she had answered casually.

"May I ask Mrs. Cotterill, how long you have known Miss Pilgrim?"

"I've been her housekeeper for several years now," she answered quietly. Turning toward me she gave me the most searching look.

"And my real name isn't Mrs. Cotterill. We've all been called Mrs. Cotterill. She hates to think anyone would leave her. The original Mrs. Cotterill died in harness and was hired by her grandfather to look after her, following the death of her parents."

I was completely at a loss at what to say in response to such an awkward and revealing piece of information. Mrs. Cotterill, or whoever she really was, surprisingly, looked at me with kindness. She continued while she busied herself tying back the heavy curtains.

"Like you, Mr. Baxter, I've worked for some unusual people, and asking me to go by the name of a much missed person in her life, whilst odd, didn't bother me. After all, I'd previously spent three decades being called Cookie."

There was an easy amnesty between us and I believed I had passed muster in her eyes.

Upon Pilgrim's return she laid everything before me. I listened to some of her history, the unique position she had carved out for herself in life, and the reason I was there. She needed a business partner.

As I have chosen to embark on this path of putting pen to paper, perhaps more for my own benefit than anyone else, I should tell you what it is that Pilgrim does to earn money. She is the guardian of secrets and the only one to do so to my knowledge. These are not secrets one might hear in general terms; you'll find no sordid intrigues here. These are physical items their current possessors wish to keep hidden. I say 'current possessors' to cover death and the inevitable sinuous change in territorial boundaries. Pilgrim's unbreakable rule is: nothing illegal, nothing alive. I was later to learn a tracking device hidden in the casing of a large quantity of class A drugs that had almost revealed the location of her business, hence rule one, and an unfortunate incident with an undetected stowaway who remained encased after a prolonged absence resulted in rule number two.

I had wondered at the time, how she would have reacted if I had divulged some of my unfortunate professional experiences in return. The fact I hadn't, reinforced my instinct I had been right not to do so. Uncannily, we had one thing in common. Pilgrim keeps the tangible secrets of others whilst I guard those that must never be exposed.

Over the years I have learnt that Pilgrim had cultivated her life, which was inextricably bound by her work, through the bequest of her grandfather, who had been a tunnelling engineer at the turn of the century carving out London's Underground railway. I believe that it was from him that she had inherited her aptitude for numbers and her problem-solving skills, although she also has the remarkable ability of foresight, which I found at first disturbing.

Her father had been the Head Porter at the infamous Loxton University for five decades where his position enabled him to take advantage of reduced fees for her further education. Loxton, whose name is synonymous with those eccentric leading academics and the seriously gifted, has a reputation for turning the unteachable into the pioneers in their field. Pilgrim, didn't do very well amongst that venerable society, having left after the second year of studying Astrophysics and Chaos Theory. It had not seemed to have been to any great detriment in her life, but actually the opposite, as it was around this time she had developed her own unique career. There was little money remaining in the family and no relatives. So it seemed fitting that the only thing she had to show for the last two generations of hard workers was an old cast iron ring with four large rusted keys from her grandfather, and a black leather-bound pocket book containing the promissory notes of errant students from her father.

Not being a person who can tolerate the everyday routine most of us are yoked to endure; she had taken a position teaching maths to the children of a wealthy family in Chelsea. One day, shortly after she had witnessed a scene resulting in her employer throwing a phone through a plate glass window, she had been prompted to ask if she might help, hoping he would divulge the reason for his agitation. He had stated, without revealing the exact nature of the problem, his need to hide some sensitive papers for a short period of time. He had then given an account of the precarious financial circumstances in which he found himself. It's extraordinary the information employers are happy to share, particularly to those in their domestic staff, without any consideration to its sensitivity. For Pilgrim it was the beginning of a future she could not only live, but also enjoy.

Upon the death of her grandfather, her last relative, she had attended a meeting with his solicitor, Mr. Buttercluck, who had given her a letter written in her grandfather's hand and the accompanying iron keys bequeathed to her. The sealed letter had been succinct and to the point. Located within the London Underground labyrinth were two large cavernous rooms with cathedral ceilings held aloft by stone columns reaching up to a ribbed Vault tower. There had been no explanation as to their original purpose, just an addendum stating they had been built and never used and didn't appear on any maps. The letters P.T.O appeared at the bottom of the letter and showed a rough plan indicating the entrance to the first chamber. Her grandfather had left her the means to pursue her own direction in life, not on a financial level, but by providing her the minimal shelter and warmth at no cost.

Pilgrim could barely recall the chain of hurried events as she had snatched up the letter, left London's commuters behind, and located the cobweb strewn entrance off a disused narrow corridor off London's Tube line. The key had fitted perfectly in the lock and with some manoeuvring had finally clanked open. Using a torch to locate the ancient electric light switch she had stood in awe as the antique lights finally fizzed and pinged into life to reveal a vast room, more befitting in style to an ecclesiastic interior; she aptly named it *The Vault*.

Since then, The Vault had become synonymous with secrecy and discretion to those clients dotted across the world. She has never divulged anything other than an email address; the remaining logistics are handled by us with complete confidentiality, for a fee.

From then until the present day, there now exists seven such Vaults of varying sizes spread across the world containing items of extreme importance to their owners. Some are worth billions and would be at the top of any government's wish-list, whilst others have a negligible financial worth, but a value in human terms that renders them priceless. Such as a fragment of stone tablet from Byzantium times that would turn some religions on their head. The variety of items can certainly be described as eclectic and their storage can cost the client, from millions, to nothing. Some items are stored because of the potential they hold to wreak destruction in one form or another. She's always been sensitive to the frailty of innocence.

Having provided this rudimentary information I should tell you of the Black Pearls, and the reason for Pilgrim's initial interest in me. Of course it had begun with the parcel that arrived just before my departure from that sterile residence in New York. I now know my former employer desired to keep something hidden. This fact surprised me, as I believed he didn't have the wit to procure such an service. I have been wrong plenty of times over the years in my summation of a person.

It is naive in the extreme to suppose even a non-descript item will not be researched, or have its provenance scrutinised. I had imagined these terms and conditions could place her in extreme danger, however I was soon to learn that Pilgrim does not need fear anyone. Indeed, such was the case with the 'Papal Vial'. However, I digress. Pilgrim, as I have mentioned, has a remarkable faculty for numbers. Each parcel, and there are now thousands, are assigned a unique numerical sequence, never to be repeated, all of which are stored, not in a ledger, neither written nor typed, but in her head. At will she can recall packages from twenty-five years ago and tell you their identifying number and contents. And so, naturally after the parcel from my ex-employer reached her hands, she opened it.

Held within an oblong Perspex box, nested in white foam, in a line of six separate round indentations, sat the blackest and most luminous pearls; or so they looked at first glance. As Pilgrim later stated; no natural pearl ever looked that perfect, and why would someone go to the trouble and expense of having fake pearls stored? Using impervious gloves and tweezers she had examined them under a microscope. They were found to be perfectly spherical with a hard outer shell, approximately the size of a large pea and weighing as much, but with nothing else to signify. Not being able to identify what they were, or the possible reason for their storage, Pilgrim scoured the papers, the Internet, and also observed my employer over a period of time.

In an effort to establish the extent of my involvement with the pearls, she informed me she had been observing my movements for a few weeks. To my enormous pride she hadn't taken long to reach the conclusion that I was, that is to say, am, a trustworthy and honest person.

It wasn't until some days later, after exhausting all possible avenues as to what the pearls function could be, that Pilgrim happened to hold one up to the light and suddenly became aware of a mechanism contained within which moved when her breath was upon it. Being in the age of unprecedented technological innovation, she realised that here was an area she had not investigated, and thus it was necessary to establish if there was any contravention of her rules in this matter. The first thing she did was to seek to identify what those mysterious spheres actually contained. She was helped in this discovery by the then-budding university nanotechnology guru, Professor Shelby Haines, who has since gone on to have such a distinguished career. Professor Haines' assurance of complete confidentiality concerning the spheres was guaranteed by a certain promissory note made during her Loxton days. Its contents were never divulged to me. All I witnessed was Pilgrim destroy the scrap of paper that looked as if it had been torn from a jotter. We had been standing next to the open fire at Bow Lane, when she had thrown it into the fire where it was quickly consumed, and its secret leverage with it.

After a few private informal chats Pilgrim had learned that the spheres contained technology of an unknown generation. The Professor pointed out that their external design would not be compatible for any technology today, or the immediate generations. Therefore it wasn't a stretch of the imagination to conjecture the pearls were intended for hardware yet to be developed.

Pilgrim recounted her conversation with Professor Hines.

"The Professor stated there is normally a practical application intended for such things."

As we sat drinking our tea, she continued, "practical applications lead to money and the more refined the application; the more money is anticipated in return. Therefore, I knew the answer could only come from the client, as he had to know their worth, otherwise why hide them? Their designer should be relatively easy to track down. Usually all designers in my limited experience are notoriously suspicious of everyone, especially those learned colleagues in their immediate circle. However, there was no one to ask without arousing interest, so I took the unusual step of opening the client's e-mail the week before the collection of the parcel." She finished, her eyes locking on mine, watching for my response.

It wouldn't be the last time I'd remark at Pilgrim's algorithmic mental agility which had never come across a door, virtual or otherwise, she couldn't unlock. However I couldn't pretend to approve.

Noting my seriousness, she frowned. "I'm wondering if you would be kind enough to help me with something." Her voice bore the tenor of innocence.

The way she had asked the question, so matter of factly, made me believe she wanted me to perform some mundane action or another, like handing her a book from the bookcase. I agreed with equal composure.

Her quiet smile should have alerted me. She stood up and walked out of the room, disappearing into the hallway. Not knowing what I was meant to do, I stood but hesitated in moving further, until I heard her impatiently call me. Following her out I was puzzled to see her buttoning a coat.

"Sorry. I should have mentioned we need to pay a visit to Du Calls." she announced seriously, straightening a long black Russian coat with a deep hemline in faux fur with cuffs and collar to match; which she pulled up in anticipation of the blustery outside weather. Her ensemble was finished with a pair of black leather gloves. "Is that OK?"

"Yes, certainly." I gave one of those involuntary answers one gives when unsure. But it was at this point my trepidation melted away and my curiosity took over.

We left the house and rounded the car in the drive. I slowed as I eyed her and the car. There was something she should know but I didn't have the courage to tell her. I should have but I didn't. Perhaps she need never know; I can't drive.

"Why, - Du Calls?" I distracted myself.

"I've arranged to meet someone. Jump in," she instructed.

I opened the passenger door of an older style silver Jaguar, which despite its age had retained its classic pedigree. During our journey she explained we would be meeting a person whom she thought would be able to shed light on the purpose of the spheres. However, we must first stop at a pub on the way to collect some insurance.

I remember thinking, 'If this has anything to do with firearms, this is not going to work out.' It's not that I'm against the use of firearms, I believe they have a time and place; I just couldn't envision any purpose for which I might ever have occasion to use one. As it turned out the reason for our visit to the pub was more extraordinary than I could have imagined.

We arrived at the The Hind, whose sign depicting a stylised galleon on a choppy sea, swayed back and forth in the wind and rain. It wasn't yet afternoon, but the oppressive coal grey clouds conjured up a far later hour. We entered that rustic inn packed with all those that had been blown in by the weather. The volume of noise was almost deafening, what with people shouting their drink orders over the crush at the bar, and the remainder heatedly debating one subject or other. The humidity created by damp clothing and a roaring blaze in the grate, thickened the atmosphere while I curiously observed the twizzled wisps of damp as they leached from coats close to the hearth. I followed close behind Pilgrim, hoping we would not be confronted in any way, as I wouldn't have been sure what to do. We headed straight for the end of the bar.

Sitting on his own customised stool was a middle-aged man of diminutive stature, dressed in a three-piece suit with a crimson silk cravat, patent leather shoes, holding a beautifully crafted silver-topped walking cane with its head of an anvil at his side. I didn't know what to make of him; his appearance was in direct contrast to his surroundings. He gave an almost imperceptible bow of his head and stated with a serious tone:

"Pilgrim."

Without saying anything to him, but giving a similar nod in response, we passed directly behind him and through an old wooden door that automatically slid open and shut behind us. Walking up a small spiral staircase that creaked and groaned, we came to the top where Pilgrim pulled back a heavy velvet plum coloured curtain and entered a room very much in size like the one we had left below. There was no carpet, just the plain and unvarnished floorboards that looked by their state of wear to be original to the building. One of the most surprising aspects was the amount of light in the room made possible by what can best be described as the stern of a galleon ship with all its mullion windows in a sweeping curve. Sitting at a plain wooden table was a man of considerably advanced years with a shock of white hair sprung like a halo around his head. He was dressed in clothes that would have been more appropriate to a hard day's work in the garden.

"Pilgrim," he said with a hint of admonishment in his voice.

"Monsieur Cailliaud, may I introduce Mr. Baxter." Pilgrim stated as she removed her gloves and coat.

"As what?" he asked tersely.

"As my work colleague," she answered in a measured tone.

She didn't look at me and I didn't look at her, given the presumption of her statement, so we both looked at Monsieur Cailliaud expectantly. It was obvious any continuation of our meeting would be decided by his accepting me, or not. His blunt continuation was my cue to breathe a mental sigh of relief.

"Let's get on with it then," he huffed.

He walked back to the table and opened a briefcase. Inside, filling the entire compartment, lay a block of what looked like gelatinised soap. It had that soft opaque look and I was surprised when Pilgrim stepped onto a dark metallic slab lying on the floor and rested both hands on to the block. To my astonishment her hands began to gradually sink until the substance covered her fingers and palms up to her wrists. During these unnerving minutes Monsieur Cailliaud was watching her intently.

"Just a few more minutes and you'll be finished." He was already stuffing the Racing Post newspaper into his jacket pocket when he addressed me. "So you've been working with Pilgrim for how long?" He lit a cheroot and inhaled deeply, finally leaving the smoke to exit in plumes and languid swirls. "Well?" he prompted.

"It seems longer than it actually is," I answered, convincingly, I thought. His answer was a harrumph of dismissal as he turned back to Pilgrim.

"You'll be fine for four hours; obviously the more contacts you make the more time you lose."

With Pilgrim's hands now out of the strange substance and with nothing to show they had ever been in contact with it, Monsieur Cailliaud slammed the briefcase lid shut and bent to pick up the metal slab. In doing so, he jumped back and cursed, as if the metal had burnt him.

"Putain de merde!" he shot through gritted teeth. He clutched at his chest momentarily. I at once saw the fear in his eyes, quickly replaced by anger.

"This is the last time. The plate is over charged. The plate is meant to charge you, not the other way around, dammit. You could have killed me."

 Pilgrim stood in the centre of the room, her arms held down at her sides but away from her body.

"Je suis désolée," she offered innocently, as she pulled on her coat and gloves.

"Of course you are. Incidentally, he'll be the death of you," he uttered derisively, lifting his chin in my direction; before he had retreated down the steps from which we'd come. I couldn't do very much other than stand and stare at Pilgrim. When she remained silent, I finally gasped:

"What the hell was all that about, and what the hell's going on?" But before she could answer, a stream of incoherent thoughts and fears came blurting out of me. "I can't be a party to anything illegal you know. I've never been in trouble in my life and I'm not about to start now. I don't know who you are, who these people are and even what I'm doing here. As much as I want to rent a room from you, I don't think this is going to work," I finished, absolutely exhausted.

"You have nothing to fear. I grant you, what just took place is unusual – but it is not illegal. As I mentioned before, I needed to obtain some insurance," she stated matter-of-factly, raising an eyebrow in my direction to underline her point.

"Yes, well, I stupidly thought you must be referring to a gun or something like that, or some big guy with tattoos and missing teeth!"

She stood still, prone in the same position, looking at me as if for the first time, with a quizzical expression clouding those distinctive features.

"You're quite the oddest person,"

"I'm odd! I'm odd!" I spluttered.

"Is that a question or a statement?"

"You don't see me sticking my hands into some mucous jelly thing, which isn't just odd, it's creepy and strange, which also goes for your friends!"

"They are not my friends. They are work acquaintances."

"How very clinical of you. Whoever they are, they're weird!"

"True, they're not exactly main-stream. They are however exceptional at what they do."

I had now calmed down sufficiently to be able to think,

"So why don't you tell me what it is they do and I'll think about whether I want to get a taxi away from this place."

"Monsieur Cailliaud is a scientist."

"He's not exactly selling brushes out of that briefcase is he?"

"Mr. Baxter, please."

Her authoritative use of my name immediately calmed my nerves.

"I realise bringing you here could have been a mistake – but now I don't think so. If I've read you correctly you have an unusual capacity to absorb and adapt to situations which most would consider out of the ordinary. As this was your first, I think you handled it very well."

There was a silence in which we were both sizing up whether we could work with one another. I'd made up my mind, so I asked, "So what was that *stuff*?"

"Professor Cailliaud was, rather is, an electromagnetism specialist in relation to the human body and in his down time he studies mathematical probability."

"Is he any good?"

"The bulk of his income is earned by it. Don't let his dishevelled appearance fool you. He owns most of the original Park Lane building footprints, but chooses to live in a rented basement in Whetstone."

"What?" I asked, totally confused, before adding, "you and your crazy friends."

"What he has done is provide me with four hours in which my body will give off and provide a camouflage, for want of a better word. Contained in that gel are trillions of microscopic metal particles, all of which occur naturally in the human body. When I placed my hands in the gel I drew an invisible layer into my hands that will distort my electromagnetic signature, and finally be absorbed into my body, with no real after effects."

"But why the metal plate?" I asked, completely fascinated by the unbelievable event I had just witnessed.

"The plate increases the volume of polarity in the body to draw up the particles in the gel. Its secondary function is to scramble any electronic devices one comes into contact with."

"Such as?" I asked with some trepidation.

"Such as, listening devices, recording devices, that sort of thing. If I stand too close to a computer I can wipe the hard drive clean. The whole thing wears off in four hours, or less."

"So who is it we're meeting at Du Calls?"

I was dreading the answer. Seeing the look on my face, Pilgrim suppressed a smile and said with affected brightness.

"You'll love him, he's great." But in a more serious tone added, "just don't tell him anything about yourself."

CHAPTER THREE

Du Calls hotel is situated in London's Mayfair and is the current place to be seen for the nouveau riche. The imposing black and white marble lobby was just as I remembered, having accompanied my ex-employer two seasons prior. I recalled him bellowing at me through the clouds of steam from behind the bathroom door.

"Just think of it Baxter, no New York, no Long Island, you'll be able to meet up with old friends, maybe visit some relatives?"

This would have been not only a nice gesture, but also a sign that my employer knew a fundamental fact concerning my life. As it was, he didn't and it wasn't.

Being the shy retiring type, I had lived a solitary existence, up until I met Pilgrim. My only living relative in the world was a maiden aunt I hadn't seen in many years. In truth, at the time I didn't have a single friend in the world. There were certainly acquaintances amongst my former peer group, but none of them had graduated to friends. I'm not sure how I had become so isolated, but it had happened leaving a hollow where I imagined love might live. I avoided at all costs peering into that place for fear I would fall in and never find my way out again. Maybe it was then, and not after, G.W and I returned to New York, that I decided to quit. I know I felt a steely determination not to re-enter such a position that magnified my seclusion – but what was I going to do for money?

Pilgrim was accustomed to any society and wore its mantle as if born to it. She breezed through the pillared entrance of Du Calls and strode toward the front desk as if she owned the place; all eyes were upon her.

"Miss Pilgrim to see Professor Wexler," she stated, with just a hint of warmth in her eyes. The desk clerk nodded to the bell boy.

"Jones will escort you, Miss Pilgrim. Professor Wexler is waiting in the Chancery."

I followed her resolute light pace and we soon entered a large subdued room, lit only by the cut-glass standard lamps. At its centre on the back wall a roaring fire was ablaze, crackling in the grate behind a large ornate metal screen. The room was obviously meant for quiet conversation and was overlooked by seventeenth century oil paintings of austere people with powdered wigs and ridiculously small hands, gazing out to infinity from their gilt frames. Large leather sofas lined the walls and the effect created was one of sumptuous intimacy. As we neared a table by the fire, a gentleman arose, for there was no mistaking his character either in dress or manner. He had a broad forehead and grey hair combed back. Large brown eyes set deeply beneath bushy white eyebrows, gave him the appearance of peering out at the world from under a cliff edge. He was over six foot tall, as we both looked up as he stood. With his hand outstretched in welcome, he greeted Pilgrim.

"Miss Pilgrim, I'm delighted to see you after such a long time." His eyes twinkled in the curious way of a man containing his excitement, but with whom British propriety forbids anything but a warm handshake.

"Professor Wexler, may I introduce my colleague, Mr. Baxter." She turned slightly toward me and although she was smiling, it didn't show in her eyes. I felt a sudden need to be on my guard. He shook my hand and gestured for us to sit down. A waiter arrived and asked if we would like anything to drink. I followed Pilgrim's lead and declined, although I certainly felt a cup of fortifying tea would have been welcome.

"Unfortunately, we cannot stay long. A previous engagement," she offered, by way of explanation.

"Then let's get to it," he enthused.

I momentarily imagined all these professors must lead frantic lives, that only afforded them minuscule amounts of time before they were off to some other strange clandestine meeting.

Pilgrim drew an enlarged photograph of the sphere from her coat pocket and passed it to him. The photo had been backlit and revealed the outline of the mechanism within.

"Do you recognise this?" she inquired pointedly.

He took a long hard look.

"No."

"Can you theorise as to its function?" she asked, revealing concern in her voice.

"Well..." he began seriously, "I would say given its obvious complexity, it was some form of transmitter. What's its size?"

"About the size of a pea," she answered.

"A pea!" he exclaimed, obviously taken aback. "You have the original with you?"

"No, the original is not available." She must have sensed I was looking at her but chose not to look at me. I looked back at Professor Wexler, as he quietly laid the photograph on the table and turning, stared into the fire. Pilgrim then looked at me with a quick frown prompting me to remain quiet.

After some little time, Professor Wexler began slowly and deliberately.

"If, I was to hypothesise and we were, let's say twenty or thirty years in the future, I would say this is a transmitter which by its outside design and size, suggests it's intended for ingestion." He looked at both of us as if appraising whether this was information we were already aware of, or if it was entirely new and unheard-of concept. "Its purpose would be to either effect a change in behaviour, or to transmit information regarding the condition or functionality of internal organs, or to kill. Although I feel the latter unlikely as a post mortem would certainly find it," he finished, with more than a little excitement in his voice.

I know this revelation shocked me more than Pilgrim, as she continued as if he had simply stated the sky was blue.

"Not if the shell and its contents degrade after contact with moisture," she proposed.

"Much would depend on the digestive time of the host," he mused. "Let's say, this is not intended for animals, or to kill, or to affect behaviour, although…," he hesitated. "I would feel happier if you could assure me this wasn't being funded by a government. If this did emit an electrical charge subcutaneously and was implanted, as opposed to ingested, one would expect an immediate and energetic response."

"Which would mean what exactly?" I blurted out, desperate to hear some word to allay my feeling of dread. These were the sorts of ominous conversations I listened to on television, when you knew with certainty things were not going to go well for the leading characters. Looking at Pilgrim, I had expected some reaction, even a consolatory smile, but her face might as well have been carved in stone. Her countenance was one of impartial attention and nothing more. I recalled her words of warning concerning Professor Wexler:

'Don't tell him anything about yourself.'

As if reading my thoughts, unnervingly his cold eyes fell upon me, appraising me momentarily. Thankfully, he then continued the conversation.

"It could be used for stimulating a hormone release, for example adrenalin, or inducing a different mental state, you've heard of shock therapy which precipitates states of euphoria. These sorts of applications would be useful, let's say if you wanted people to behave collectively in the same manner, at the same point in time." Again he looked at us expectantly.

"If you're referring to the military," she confirmed his thoughts as he nodded in agreement. Pilgrim stuck out her lower lip, which I had come to recognise as the precursor to a contradiction, "then we would not be having this conversation." He began to disagree, when she cut him off. "I believe, Professor Wexler, your ideas as to its purpose are believable, and I value your opinion." She stopped briefly before continuing. "However, I think we're at the beginning of its development and not at its end. I must therefore reiterate my request for your silence and discretion."

"Of course, you have no need to ask." He obviously thought a lot of Pilgrim by his immediate agreement. I wondered if his compliance might be the result of another promissory note – but I rather doubted it. With our meeting at an end, Pilgrim rose to shake his hand, and I in turn, after which we promptly left, with me feeling both slighted and relieved that he hadn't taken any interest in me.

As we pulled away from the hotel I fell quiet. It's in my nature to have my everyday actions bolted firmly in routine. I felt uncomfortable; as exciting as my excursion had been; I was at sea, not knowing exactly what was to become of me and the very serious matter of a place to live, and work that would enable me to pay for whatever financially conservative lodgings I could afford. Pilgrim must have sensed my uneasiness and suggested we go for a night-cap at L'améthyste; *the* city club, where she is a member.

I had of course heard of L'améthyste and seen the entrance occasionally, in the media, as the backdrop to some highbrow luminary. Its reputation was as a retreat for London's intelligentsia. Situated on the bank of the Thames east of Vauxhall Bridge, its Corinthian columns stood either side of a pair of impenetrable black doors adorned with ornate brass fittings. As Pilgrim nodded to the liveried doorman I thought it was hardly surprising he had the build of a prize-fighter, given the fact he had to open those massive doors many times a day. Once past the doors the interior opened up revealing a stained glass dome that cast a kaleidoscope of soft hued light upon the polished granite floor. Sweeping graciously from the left and resembling a giant cornucopia lay a white marble staircase, stretching to the first and second floor. We made our way to an imposing desk at which sat an elderly man with a ready smile and a fresh gardenia in his button hole.

"Miss Pilgrim, very nice to see you."

Pilgrim leant forward, signed in to the ledger and added my name as a guest.

"Thank you, Mr. Myler," she said warmly.

With an almost imperceptible lift of his chin, a young uniformed girl, sprang up walking forward to open a large oak panelled door to his right, stepping aside to allow us to pass through. Moving forward we found ourselves in a long corridor brightly lit by ornate wall sconces. Through the windows I saw pendulous orb lamps hanging between the colonnade arches outside. The long wood panelled corridors passed a number of closed double doors, whose rooms behind them suggested they must have substantial proportions. We finally stopped outside a door with a highly polished round brass handle. Opening it and walking in, I was surprised to find a room which despite its size and impressive furnishings was very cosy.

"Here, take a seat," Pilgrim offered. "What would you like to drink?" Seeing my hesitation she said, with bemusement, "I don't know about you but I could kill a large gin and tonic."

"In that case, I'd like a whiskey, if I may."

I was relieved to finally have something to drink, although I have to say by this time, which was half past nine by the solemn chimes of a French style black and gold clock on a pedestal standing next to the long bar, I was absolutely famished. I had already considered where I would sleep that night and had decided upon one of the cheaper hotels by Waterloo station, but if we didn't hurry up it would be necessary for me to take a taxi back and knowing the price of a taxi after 9 p.m. I wasn't exactly pleased. The drinks were served by an amiable young man with a ready smile and pleasant manner. To my relief the measures were generous and as I lifted my glass I thanked Pilgrim for a very interesting if somewhat perturbed evening.

"You're certainly welcome." Pilgrim said, with a note of curiosity in her voice. She had wanted to add something else but had decided to wait, when she then changed her mind and begun suddenly.

"You know, Mr. Baxter, I think we can be of service to one another. You need a place to rent and Mrs. Cotterill needs…more to do. Plus I am also looking for a caretaker." By her intonation it was meant as a question.

I was slightly taken back, but also relieved as I needed to have these issues resolved immediately. Still there was the question of money. How much does a caretaker earn – not much? – I thought. And what about the lodging – that wouldn't be cheap? How could I have known Pilgrim had read my consternation as accurately as if I had stated it outright to her?

"Let us begin Mr. Baxter with the question of your employment. Would I be right in saying you no longer wish to seek a position as a personal valet?"

She was looking at me with a look of innocent curiosity which belied the fact that she knew the answer and was walking me pedantically through the process of realising and accepting the role I would play within her organisation.

Such was Pilgrim's foresight; I have yet to meet a like intellect. Although as I write this text; I cannot suppress the name, Dean Stephmoure, from rising in my conscious. I cannot begin to explain, nor do I want to, concerning the vapid guise he cunningly employs to achieve his ends. A man whom God has abandoned and as a God- fearing man, I do not choose my words lightly. He walks the earth still to this day, his foot leaving a charred and sterile print. No, I will not say any more about him at this point. The time will come and you will learn that it is not violence and death we truly fear but the absence of hope.

Getting back to that day with Pilgrim, I should laugh at the way I had acted, but I cannot without being concerned at my utter lack of intuition. As she had foreseen, I readily agreed to the rooms offered at such a reasonable charge. I had naively believed it was just the accommodation I was accepting. In actuality I had consented to change the course of my life.

That time seems veiled in innocence and when I glance back, not over years, but to those crystalized memories that skim like pebbles across my consciousness, serving to remind me I am mortal, I understand I can never live any other life than this.

"I like you Mr. Baxter and I can tell you, I have never said that to another living soul. I know we will work well together."

She paused to study my reaction. I was of course flattered and curious as to the nature of the work.

"You need a caretaker, for what exactly?"

I experienced an unusual surge of courage at this point in our conversation. It was obvious she possessed a strong personality and was extremely intelligent. In all honesty I understood the foundation of our relationship, of how we would regard and work with one another, was being forged as we spoke. I had made my decision never to be in a servile role again, it no longer suited my personality and explained my reticence in securing a similar position. This conviction instantaneously became so firmly entrenched in my psyche it felt like an impenetrable shield. I had no qualms about ensuring Pilgrim understood I expected to be treated as a working partner, not her employee. Being more assertive in my responses than I was accustomed to, but which I felt compelled to apply, now all I had to do was tell her.

"I have no wish to be a 'caretaker'. However, I will be your partner."

There was a momentary pause before she surprised me by replying:

"OK. That should work, but we each play to our strengths, agreed?"

"Agreed!" I breathed a sigh of relief.

"I have a location here in London," she paused and the weight fell on her next words, "where I have stored a number of very valuable artefacts. Their monetary value varies from zero to priceless. I need someone I can trust." The perceptible earnestness of her last word was left to resonate off the walls of my mind as if she had shouted it.

"But how do you know you can trust me?" I countered.

"I've done my research and concluded, if you agree, that we can form a working partnership which will benefit both of us." She took a large sip of her drink and for the first and last time I witnessed a flicker of uncertainty in her eyes which disappeared before I registered it consciously.

Predicting my next question she continued; "How else would I have known you're in London, if I hadn't followed you from Argentina? You've been observed since New York. I know where you've been living and how you've been living. Your regular trips to the museums, the pair of new brogues you took an interminable time to select." She stopped short of other revelations as my face no doubt wore a look of incredulity.

"It has all been performed within the realms of propriety, Mr. Baxter. You will appreciate that the true nature of a person cannot be identified by the figures and dates on a piece of paper. My business is steeped in secrecy therefore it has been necessary for me to take these steps. I should point out, you will be my first and last partner and will have considerable scope. The items are of immense importance to their owners; I could not employ anyone else. I should also mention in passing I have waited a considerable time for the right person to present themselves."

"I am a trustworthy person," I stated with all seriousness. There was a pause in our conversation which filled me to bursting with all manner of emotions, none of which I could articulate but left me knowing I would not be used or be a party to anything underhand. Pilgrim read my thoughts correctly.

"As you do not know me, I can give you the contact numbers for the Commissioner of Scotland Yard, Madden. The Secretary of State, for Foreign and Commonwealth Affairs, and more besides, if it will satisfy you as to my character?"

"It will not." I stated firmly and quietly.

She didn't show surprise, indignation or anything in between. "Whom then?" she asked matter-of-factly.

"I will take your word for it…" I paused, adding, "If you are prepared to give it?"

"Then you have my word; I am a trustworthy person," she added seriously, her smile spreading slowly.

I knew she finished short and the measure of her would come rarely, but each time at a price that cannot be exacted by any coin.

"You see, Baxter, I need you to be my conscience."

CHAPTER FOUR

Pilgrim had not been mistaken in recognising that she swayed near the edge of the moral precipice at times. What do I mean by that? Well, there is no doubt she has a brilliant mind. However, that does not automatically exclude her from making errors in judgement, not only about people, but more importantly, about whether we should accept an item for storage or not. Very occasionally she exhibits the kind of rationale normally excused in the young when they have acted without considering the consequences. This is in complete contrast to the majority of the time, when she assesses each risk more predictably. As for myself, I have very little ambiguity as to what I consider right and wrong, for Pilgrim these two rarely exist to her way of thinking. As she has stated before, 'what is wrong for the general populous on one day, may be acceptable practice on another; their tolerance is determined by circumstance alone,' and maybe that is why, very occasionally, she has trouble in identifying the line between that which is morally acceptable, and what is not. I'm not saying I own morality. I just have to go with my gut instinct and a set of values which I believe make for a happier society.

A good example occurred not so long ago. A package was requested for storage which eerily turned out to be the intact body of a twelve year old child. An only child, who had died quickly and tragically after a rare illness. His parents, bereft beyond all reason, had made the decision neither to bury or cremate, but to preserve. After some ill-advised and no doubt very expensive private consultation, they had convinced themselves a hermetically sealed saline bath with a self-correcting Ph. would maintain the integrity of the body; until such time science caught up to bring him back. Upon learning of the request for storage, I immediately said no.

Pilgrim was not so sure. None of her rules were breached. Technically, he wasn't alive and a genuine need had been established, as there was certainly nowhere else his remains could have been stored, as options such as cryogenics were never likely to fulfil the expectations of their users. We definitely argued about that one, and the bulk of my objection was based on my firmly entrenched moral stance, whereas hers was based predominately in fact. She finally conceded after I pulled the only card left in my hand; she had specifically hired me, in her words, 'to be her moral compass'.

"I'll give you this one Baxter, based only on the fact there are no verifiable and independent tests, to satisfy myself, as to whether their science is sound. The last thing I need is another decomposing corpse on my hands."

 "And what if the science was sound?"

"Then we would not be having this conversation."

She had reached the door and was about to leave, but her high-handed attitude rankled me and I called out.

 "I don't agree. Are you saying science will have the final decision regardless of my thoughts on the matter?"

She had turned back slowly and studied me briefly, I could tell by her expression of 'fait accompli,' that she was finding it a challenge to relinquish responsibility to me. She conceded reluctantly.

"You're right of course. I cannot expect you to manage your role competently if I interfere. I agree the body should be cremated or buried. Not to alleviate your indoctrinated religious beliefs but because, undoubtedly, science will one day bring back the body to a functioning state, but not the soul."

"Then, why did you even consider it?"

"Because it doesn't breach any of my rules."

"Now I understand why you need me."

"Need you?!"

"Yes, need me! Those were your words," I replied sharply. "Obviously a smidgeon of common-sense remains in your vacuous conscience, otherwise I wouldn't be here, and just in time. Lord only knows, what else you've stored? It doesn't bear thinking about."

"Are you quite finished?" she asked, with a perceptible drawl.

"Yes, I believe I am."

In retrospect, I am stuck firmly to my beliefs. I don't mind people questioning them but at the same time I don't want them torn down – which might suit others but would not suit me. I am bound to live in my society, as fragile as that veneer may be, in my spot in time until I expire, and I want to live as harmoniously and with as much dignity and respect for others that I hope for in return. Enough of that – you get the picture; cogent otherworldly woman meets moral rhinoceros with rather nice shoes.

So, the morning came when Pilgrim smiled over the remnants of our breakfast with "When you're finished we'll visit the London Vault and I'll show you around." She laid her linen napkin on the table and rose from her chair heading toward the door, calling over her shoulder. "Wear something in dark colours. Ten minutes. OK?"

"Sure, ten minutes. No problem."

I had scuttled out of the dining room and up the stairs to finish my toilette. Dark colours? Something to do with looking inconspicuous, I concluded.

Once ready we stepped away from the warmth and comfort of the house into a wind that whipped around us, chilling the end of my nose. I dug my fingertips as far as they would go into my fleece lined gloves. Looking up at the disgruntled sky I was not surprised it was threatening to rain and perhaps even thunder. Those stalwart trees lining the avenue that must have been lazily bobbing their chartreuse canopies in deference to those balmy days only weeks before, now lashed their ochre leaves, agitated by a biting wind portending the coming of Winter.

"This weather doesn't look very good. I wouldn't be surprised if we don't have a bit of a storm later on," I ventured, pulling my neck into the collar of my coat like a startled tortoise.

Pilgrim didn't answer but stepped toward the waiting cab. She looked to have the freshly scrubbed face of a younger woman. The weight of time's veil had not been drawn across her features so heavily. Her eyes sparkled, her lips were pursed in a mischievous smile and I worried momentarily what might lie ahead as she held the door open for me.

"Jump in Baxter."

"Where's the Jag?" I asked, as I entered and sat down. I had to wait a few moments before Pilgrim reluctantly replied, whilst looking out distractedly at a nondescript landscape.

"It was towed," she answered matter-of-factly.

"Towed – why?"

"No car insurance."

The idea that something as straight forward and legally necessary had bypassed Pilgrim's memory revealed to me those fundamental requirements we all had to deal with in life, were apparently beyond her.

"So, when do we need to collect it?"

"We can't – it's impounded."

"Impounded?"

"Let's just say it's not the first time."

I decided to leave the whole business, as it was obviously a source of some embarrassment to her. I longed to tell her my own secret but I couldn't coerce myself in enough time before a doubt crossed my mind and stilled my tongue.

We drove for twenty minutes to Barnet and caught the Northern Line into the city. After a couple of changes we got off and followed the swirl of drab clothed commuters until we reached the bottom of an escalator and passed behind it. Tucked away against a grimy wall stood a large riveted steel door. It reminded me of those industrial sized fridges with no hinges or handles in evidence. It looked impenetrable. Standing in relief, it was bolted to the frame of the escalator itself.

Placing her left palm along its edge the door surprisingly exhaled open. Pilgrim stood back to allow me to pass through. Despite the monotonous trundle of the

53

escalator ferrying worn commuters from the bowels of the earth to the light of the day outside, no one gave us a second look.

With the door closed behind us, a narrow passageway stretched out in front, dimly lit by dirt encrusted bulb and saucer lamps from above. A few thick black cobwebs lay in swags between the light fixtures. I followed Pilgrim as if I were walking the plank, when I noticed how much warmer it had become.

"Is it usually this warm down here"?

"Yes, it's the hundreds of machines they have. It works quite well for our purposes. Not exactly fresh air; but perfectly breathable and perfectly dry."

I had my doubts as to the breathable part. It seemed to me the air was thick with the distinctive odour of mechanical oil – and the burnt ether of diesel, a culmination of all the engines and machines needed to operate the Underground. I imagined people must get used to it but I wasn't convinced I would. After all, that was why we were down here because this dismal place was going to play a large part in my daily work life. A feeling of unease came over me. I was no longer sure I had done the right thing. To counteract my reservations, I forced myself to recall the light airy rooms and magnificent cooking of Mrs. Cotterill. As balm to the soul, I felt comforted I was doing the right thing.

"Not far now, it's just up ahead. There's a bathroom to your left," she indicated with a wave of her hand, "but no cooking facilities. Of course, if you need to spend hours down here, I would recommend asking Mrs. Cotterill to pack a lunch for you. I only enter the Vault to store or remove items for clients. Despite you thinking we were not noticed entering here, we most certainly were. Any anomaly will be picked out by the seasoned commuter and stored, if not consciously, than unconsciously." Pilgrim suddenly turned to me adding seriously; "Never come here in anything other than dark coloured clothing, and soft soled shoes. Oh, and hats are recommended, but should be in a dark colour with no decoration and never bring an umbrella. For some reason people pay particular attention to umbrellas. A person's choice of umbrella says more about them than they realise, fascinating!"

We continued and reached the end of the passageway which culminated at a large gaping black void, outlined by a surprisingly ornate stone arch, spanning twenty feet above our heads and whose height hinted at something unusual beyond. A small amount of light thrown from the last lamp fell onto the black rock floor beneath our feet. I stopped in my tracks as Pilgrim reached into the dark and listened to her hand flutter against the wall in search of the switch. Flicking it on, lines of strip lights buzzed and pinged into life showering their cold white light far off into the distance.

"Bloody hell," was all I could utter. Stretched out away in front was row upon row of stacked boxes and crates of varying dimensions. It looked like the Manhattan skyline in brown paper and wood, some the size of a shoe box whilst others looked large enough to hold a sarcophagus.

"Quite." Pilgrim replied.

"How many are there?"

"Four thousand, six hundred and twenty-two." She had unbuttoned her coat and was removing her gloves when I proceeded to do the same.

"Although the Vault is difficult to see from this angle, imagine two football fields, because it is roughly the same size, and then there are avenues between to fit a forklift. You'll notice all the packages have a number on the outside in black felt pen."

She picked up one of the smaller packages and showed it to me. The number 2961 was hand-written on the wrapper.

"The number identifies the package with the person and its contents. The person who owns the package might not be the person who has asked for the package to be placed here. It depends upon the circumstances."

I was going to ask a question to show, if nothing else, that I had been listening, even if I was already having difficulty in deciphering how her particular numerical inventory process worked. I knew if this was going to be a success, it would be imperative to understand the procedure fully and that meant asking basic questions; I placed my ego on the backburner.

"So, a client asks to store a package. You agree. You collect the package?"

"Not necessarily, actually, hardly ever these days."

I felt it was 'game on,' so despite not fully knowing the rules, I picked up the proverbial racket.

"Ok, let's say the package is collected. You then ascertain what's in the package?"

"Yes."

"Then you identify the owner of the package."

"I identify the owner of the contents of the package," she corrected. Advantage. Pilgrim.

"And then, providing everything is above board, you store it?"

"Not necessarily. It depends on the circumstances."

"Okay," I finished, still none the wiser and two points down.

"Let me give you examples which will identify the rule of thumb for those packages accepted and those declined."

We were strolling along the main avenue of the Vault, where two cars would have fit quite comfortably. It was obvious some packages had been there for a considerable time. Their paper worn and their corners frayed, despite the fact they were obviously seldom moved, if the thick layer of accumulated dust was anything to go by.

I glanced at Pilgrim from the corner of my eye. She had invoked a kind of stillness in me that I only now became conscious of. Behind those glacial blue eyes a razor sharp mind was disseminating and collating information, of that I was sure. Having sensed my observation she picked up the conversation where we had left it.

"Firstly, we are not talking about a question of money here. There are - ," she hesitated, "a small number of packages, not all of them here, which are stored at little or no cost to their owners. You see, Baxter, it's a question of what is the right thing to do? I have to admit my ethical line has become worn; tainted after so many years by human corruption in its subtlest form. That particular shellac is impossible to buff." She turned and smiled with genuine warmth toward me. "When you deal with clever people, you'll be surprised what you believe is plausible. There is nothing more persuasive than the person who has great intellect and conviction, and nothing more destructive if they are predisposed to carnal weakness, and there is none as strong and prevalent as possession. Our history is littered by those notorious leaders who began their ascent well, only to fall after acquiring power and wealth. It requires a rare and exact psychology to continue to rise, allowing and promoting the mind to pursue ideas beyond its parameters." Seeing the look of confusion on my face she added quickly.

"Every machine needs calibration occasionally. What I mean is I'm not as astute as you might think. I've been taken in by people. I make mistakes and sometimes they're big." She threw me a compensatory half smile. "Now back to my examples. Firstly, let's say a certain foreign potentate was hedging his bets, due to an uncomfortable skirmish located at the border between his country and the next. Lying along the disputed boundary are valuable remains of both archaeological and international importance. Those items are requested to be stored. However, after identification, I cannot be certain to whom they belong, and then the real purpose, for their storage becomes ambiguous. Will they be used to hold a nation's religious beliefs to ransom? You understand Baxter, how the question can arise as to their use, never mind their ownership?"

"So, in such a case, you would refuse storage?" I added quickly, glad to have secured a foothold on exactly what would be expected of me.

"Yes."

"But wouldn't they just go elsewhere?" I conjectured.

"Mine, is the only safe, completely anonymous vault of its kind, in the world," she breathed solemnly. "There is no other place like it, that can guarantee complete anonymity and I have the track record to back it up. There is no government, tax body, army or person, however well connected, that can influence me."

"And if you were taken and tortured?"

"That's been tried."

The icy diamond look in her eyes was enough to convince me. I choose not to pursue that line of conversation any further.

"What about a Swiss bank? They're well known for keeping the personal possessions of others a secret."

"They used to be, but not anymore, especially given the fact they've been forced to open their files recently."

"And your second example."

"Imagine, you're asked to store a small package. The package consumes one eighth of a millimetre in depth, the contents of which are a recorded conversation between a certain female politician plus a would-be president, and a man of Asian lineage. The conversation is brief and to the point. The fear of one is the doctrine of the other. What is clear is that if this conversation entered the political domain the bedrock of several countries belief system would crumble. You appreciate that sometimes it is better to kill an ideal, than kill a dream."

"So you're saying in this case, the package would be stored?" I asked, subconsciously filing this information for private review.

"Exactly."

My brain tried to simultaneously absorb the implications of the information, which I felt sure were real examples and the moral decisions I was soon to shoulder. I was overwhelmed, as I committed to further fortifying myself.

"I would be obliged if you would outline the duties for me."

Pilgrim continued as if we had been discussing her wardrobe choices for the following day.

"Specifically, to manage the Vaults. I will supply you with a request. You then identify the client, I'll show you how to do that, you then arrange for collection and transportation of the package, then comes the tricky part; ascertaining exactly what the package contains. It may look perfectly innocuous to us to begin with, for example something of great financial or historical worth, - a crown, a famous painting – I've even had a set of fingerprints belonging to …" she faltered; "well, perhaps that's not appropriate at this juncture. You will have to learn to put aside your personal 'oohs and aahs.' That reaction will wear off very quickly. You should be thinking: is the reason for storage valid? You will be able to determine this by research. I'll show you later what I use to answer such questions. Providing, up to this point, you and I are in agreement, we store the package. You will not be required to number them; that is my particular area of expertise."

She rasped the word 'expertise' and I half expected the forked tongue of an asp to flicker out. My imagination was taking over a purely factual conversation, or Pilgrim was exerting some sort of influence over my thoughts, or more than likely, the whole bizarre situation was beginning to take a toll on me. I longed for the sanctuary of my newly acquired rooms, but quickly quashed my visions of a comfy bed.

"Did I hear you say *Vaults;* and if they're large packages from abroad?" I was thinking of a certain sarcophagus shape.

"I have a small number of other Vaults dotted across the world. They are kept in very similar circumstances to this. There is the Vault of a cathedral, a library and interestingly, one that was once a bank, plus an area under a famous fountain, another on an island. There is also one special item that is stored on the International space station."

"You're joking?"

"No, I am not."

"I suppose that avoids any embarrassment with Customs and Excise?"

"If a client chooses to move a package themselves, onto a particular continent, it becomes their risk, not mine."

"They'll find it a bit difficult to move it from the International space station!" I quipped.

"That person happens to be me." She stated seriously without emotion.

Her sudden change in mood put me on my guard. I reminded myself there was a lot I didn't know about

Pilgrim. She pulled out a slim gold cigarette case from the pocket of her coat and opening it, offered me one of the Black Russians. I was surprised; hadn't she been *observing* me. She must have known I didn't smoke. She read my thoughts.

"You're going to need to develop at least one vice Baxter, otherwise I shall begin to worry about you."

"I prefer to pick my own vices thank you."

She lit the cigarette and inhaled deeply.

"And what are your vices, other than the obvious?" I asked.

Her cool eyes were observing me, but she broke from her assessment.

"Oh, you know, the usual, tobacco, alcohol, and I also have a weakness for glass, it's my favourite medium,"

"Really." I responded more interested in her reactions than the information.

Pilgrim continued to explain the storage process, whilst I listened.

"Any large packages, those that cannot be carried by hand, are delivered by train. You appreciate the simplicity and privacy?"

"Yes, of course. So, you own a train?" I asked the most simple question I could in an effort to keep up with all the information and suppositions that where tumbling around in my head like a psychological washing machine.

"Yes, I do." she answered, slowly. "It's quite special, one of the earlier underground models. It was never decommissioned; had just been relegated to the cleaning and maintenance division when I acquired it. It's rostered for the weekends." Pilgrim's voice was fading away until it became barely a whisper, "LT Rail Red made by T. R. Williamson with Enid Marx Moquette, Brent upholstery with matching green leather hand-rests." Continuing on her trip down memory lane she finished: "I miss those bobble straphangers." This was the first time I had witnessed Pilgrim accessing those extensive mental archives of hers. It was worrying and fascinating at the same time.

"Now take a look at this." She had snapped out of her reverie and was pulling a large piece of brown paper from between two boxes. Tapping the dust off it she turned her nose up and moved her head to one side to avoid the airborne cloud of dust erupting from its surface. Opening it, she laid it out across the nearest flat surface. The paper was covered liberally in thousands of numbers scattered un-sequentially, some shown horizontally whilst others had been scribbled down vertically. I realised at once it was a map and record of the numbered packages. Its complexity was astounding. I began to notice many areas contained numbers superimposed upon others rendering it almost illegible.

"It's a bit of a mess, isn't it?" I couldn't help wonder why she had bothered with such an unreadable document.

"Yes, well I've never been very good at keeping things 'just so', hence Mrs. Cotterill. I put this together when I realised it was necessary to find a trustworthy person to help me. I myself do not need to have the locations of the packages written down. It's all up here." She tapped the side of her head. "But I do understand the packages should be documented with their positions and numbers, for your sake."

I gingerly took the paper by the corner allowing it to dangle.

"When exactly did you put this together?" My ex-valets' instinct for all things starched, pressed and clean was bristling with disbelief.

"I can't remember exactly, but I do remember I stopped recording the numbers, oh, it's got to be, well, it must be, well, that is, it must have been about twelve years ago."

"I see." This job loomed before me like a giant mail room, packed to the rafters, a week before Christmas and I was the only member of staff. She observed my look of consternation and offered a balm.

"It's not a big deal. Forget this paper."

With a flurry of hands, she ripped it into several pieces. I stood aghast as the only map to this maze fell like confetti to the ground.

"You're better off putting together your own system." She stopped, lifting her forefinger to gain my full attention, "However, you may not move or mark a single package. Is that clearly understood?"

"Yes, clearly."

"Well, if you're satisfied, we should be off."

Pilgrim had already begun to turn and head back toward the way we had come, when I found my voice.

"Sorry, can I stop you there."

"Well, what is it?" She instantly turned, the impatience in her voice most discernible.

"I'm not sure I can do this work. It's not the location, although I will be living like a virtual mole. It's not the fact the place smells strongly of diesel, I suspect after time I will come to ignore it. You're asking me to manage this, Vault, but I'm not able to move or mark the packages? That just makes this job impossible."

"So, have you thought about how you would like to make things work here?"

"Yes, I've had some ideas but they don't meet your requirements."

"Okay, let's hear them!"

"To start with, if there is anything of value in this place it must be saturated with this mechanical odour in the atmosphere. We need to get rid of that. We need to put in an air purifier. No one is going to notice the noise from another machine down here. Plus, this place is filthy. I'm not even going to collect the pile of crud that would accumulate on my finger if I were to run it across any surface in here. Now we come to the packages. Some of them are seriously in need of a new wrapping. More importantly, I cannot catalogue the packages if I can't move them."

Pilgrim had a look of contemplative boredom on her face.

"Yes, to the air-conditioner, I'll have it fitted. Yes, to cleaning this place up; frankly it needs it. Yes, to new wrapping, but over the old wrapping, and *I* will be writing the numbers on the packages. This, in turn, will involve you moving them. Here is what you will need to do. As the numbers of the packages and their relative position will remain the same, for every hundred you catalogue, once completed and stacked you will call me to take a look."

At the time the request seemed merely that of an attentive curator. Of course, nothing is ever what it seems where Pilgrim is concerned.

"How are you with a gun?" she asked, matter-of-factly.

CHAPTER FIVE

I vaguely remember those days directly following my first visit to the Vault. I recall feeling excited, overwhelmed, and with an eager anticipation causing me to clap wildly, as a way to vent some of the excitement; of course, I only clapped in private. I realise it was a lot for me to take in, but at the time, at those moments of introspection, I believed I was managing very well. Thankfully Pilgrim spoon-fed me her organisation a mouthful at a time, so I didn't mentally choke on the intricacy of the whole thing. It turns out she was quite determined for me to succeed and for that I shall always be grateful. I learnt, that although we were the only two people directly involved with the business, there was a small collective employed to provide transportation, information and logistic help. Some of these people knew very little about Pilgrim, whilst one in particular I later learnt, was on a first name basis with her.

The following day, after our visit to the Vault, a brief and to the point conversation took place at the breakfast table. At least she had the decency to wait until after I had eaten.

"The thing is, Baxter, this line of work has two parts, the boring administrative part and the 'certain amount of danger part'. It's because of the 'certain amount of danger part' that I believe you would be better off knowing how to handle a firearm. Nothing better says, 'touch me and you're dead', than the business end of a gun-barrel."

"Naturally, but I don't understand how such a situation could arise?" I commented, before the face of Mr. Phelps flashed upon my mind's eye and I appreciated there were events one could never prepare for.

"I'm sure most people who have been the victim of a violent crime thought exactly like you, before it happened. If you have no objections I would like to turn you over to a friend of mine, Major Coal. Retired to civilian life and teaching certain people how to handle and use fire arms."

"Certain people? What does that mean?"-

"Major Coal has been handling firearms since he was a boy reloading for his father in Luanda. He taught me."

"Did he? I've never seen you with a gun."

"No. I prefer a sword." She finished slowly.

"Fine, set it up." I answered despondently, feeling overwhelmed and without an ounce of control over anything, apart from my choice of pyjamas at night. It was going to take some management to train Pilgrim not to be so heavy-handed.

I looked down at my toast carefully buttered with the thinnest smear of home-made marmalade and realised I wasn't hungry anymore.

Misinterpreting my mood, Pilgrim stepped away from the table and stopped by the door.

"Baxter, I've come to recognise a rather disagreeable habit of yours; you tend to sulk when circumstances seem beyond you."

Looking directly at her, I stood up and walked toward her as I replied "Just the one?" I had breezed past her and sought the solace of my rooms.

Meeting Major Coal that same day was not as intimidating as I'd thought it might be. He was a very courteous man, who had survived three much publicised wars and countless military skirmishes relatively unscathed. We understood one another from the first, and I felt a keen affinity based on our mutual need for order. It was decided I should begin the following week. I would be tried and fitted with a gun to suit my aptitude and personality. In the interim I was to take a few practice shots from a variety of hand guns he had selected.

I don't know if you've ever fired a gun, dear reader? I had never fired a gun and the experience was a mixture of terror and seriousness. Once I had been instructed on how to hold the gun, aim and breath correctly, I felt much more comfortable.

Upon my return to our lodgings, I entered the drive just as a man, I had never seen before, was leaving. He was middle-aged with a practised military bearing. His thick dark hair was cut neatly to the nape of his neck, but an unruly curl of ashen hair lay at his left temple. He walked with an economy of movement that hinted at a physique kept in top condition. As he neared, my valets training automatically calculated his height at approximately six feet four and weight in the region of one hundred and ninety pounds. I smiled and nodded as he passed. Dark brown eyes glittered from under slate grey eyebrows set back from a nose which had been broken more than once and now sat suitably arranged. A clean two-inch scar ran from the right-hand side of his bottom lip to the left of his chin. Obviously, he was not the warm friendly type, as he chose to ignore my subtle greeting.

I entered the house to find Pilgrim pacing up and down in agitated excitement, her hair piled up untidily on her head, finally grinding her cigarette in the ashtray with such vigour I believed she hadn't heard me enter.

"You'll need to put your coat back on Baxter. I have just received some additional information regarding our mysterious spheres."

She lifted a note of paper from her pocket, holding it up between two fingers for my attention. Catching my coat on the way out, I followed after her into a waiting cab, where she hastily closed the glass privacy partition.

"What's happened?"

"This has happened," she answered seriously, handing me the note.

Your spheres are not transmitters they are receivers. They exceed the amount of 16 TB of information, so far as we can measure. It would be the equivalent of a life time worth of experiences. Not just the visual memories but the smell, touch, taste and sound plus more.

Not like anything we've ever seen.

H'

"Who is 'H'; was that 'H'?" I asked perplexed. Sitting back in my seat, I continued breathlessly, "I suppose this means we're not going to store the Black Pearls. Is 'H' the man I just saw leaving?"

"We'll discuss that later. However, think about this Baxter; your Wall Street banker intends these high-tech spheres to be stored covertly. Intelligence espionage? I

70

could understand money, numbers, or pretty much anything in relation, but spheres are an unusual choice for a banker, wouldn't you say? Therefore, they must equate to money. In turn, the spheres themselves are throwing up all kinds of red flags. They're designed to receive information, but they're also designed for ingestion. So, then, we don't have an answer for the next question, which is, 'why?'"

"You haven't met GW; I find it improbable in the extreme that he is anything other than an intermediary."

"Perhaps," she ruminated.

Pilgrim sank back into the leather upholstery with a look of determined study on her face. I, for my part, decided the problem was so intriguing I wouldn't be able to think of anything else. As we were driven into London city, I observed the well-ordered Victorian and Edwardian houses, with their tightly clipped privet hedges peter-out and the larger, stalwart buildings of London's metropolis begin to rise from her grey stone pavements. I experienced a momentary feeling of uneasiness, suggesting familiar things might be coming to an end.

"Perhaps they're designed to record the sounds of the body and meant for medical use?" I conjectured.

"Sounds of the body?" She looked at me with wry amusement. "No, I've learnt they cannot have any practical use in that sense. Are you talking about resonance and ultrasound? Is that what you mean?"

I could only listen as she continued.

"By definition a receiver has to be triggered to accept information, effectively turned on and turned off. That means a secondary device has to be used in conjunction with them."

"The on-switch," I guessed.

"Precisely, but in order for us to discover it, we need to establish the spheres' purpose and for that we need a creative intellect."

Pilgrim's eyes narrowed, as she appeared to be considering some point.

"If I'm not mistaken she will be on her second martini by now."

"Where did you say we're going?" I asked, wondering if we were likely to miss dinner. For some reason I now couldn't think of food without the friendly face of Mrs. Cotterill popping up. Invariably, I recalled her lowering some sumptuous dish or other, onto the perfectly starched white cloth of the dining room table.

"Baxter!"

I was yanked out of my reverie.

"I said, L'améthyste. Are you OK?"

"Yes, I'm fine, just wondering about the purpose of those spheres." I lied, and then added fervently, "And he's not, 'my Wall Street banker.' "

A silence descended on us as we each found ourselves deep in thought. I was racking my brain, trying to think who 'H' could be.

"Isn't a written note a bit low tech?" I asked.

She ignored my question.

Arriving at L'améthyste was always a finger squeezing moment of excitement for me. Guaranteed never to allow a single self-absorbed person past its inner Lalique doors, it had favoured and courted the humanitarian intelligencer of each era. These were the people who levelled the playing field for us mere mortals, they ensured life on earth was tolerable for most species, including us bipeds, and to that end it had developed some unique function rooms. Whether you were rich, poor, counted royalty as your closest friends, or came from the most remote reaches of the globe with zero connections, L'améthyste was not concerned in the slightest. Membership was by invitation only, to those who had earned a reputation for the betterment of the planet and its variety of inhabitants, and who lead by example. Membership to L'améthyste is the aspirational benchmark for many a president, king, queen or mere prime minister, because membership guarantees office, support and continuance and, as a consequence, pedigree.

As Dr Mary Congo, so named by the orphanage she grew up in, at Mbandaka, Africa, which is acknowledged as one of the poorest and most violent places on earth (and sadly she has the facial scars to prove it); the woman who discovered and gifted the malaria vaccine to the world, stated at her inaugural dinner.

'Becoming a member of L'améthyste has given me the opportunity to brandish my scientific discovery, to sever the political and economic heads of the Congolese Hydra and resurrect my humanity. My will be done.'

Who would you bump into? Who would Pilgrim nonchalantly introduce you to? Even now, after all these years, I always associate it with the most vibrant, gregarious, interesting and down to earth people it has ever been my pleasure to meet. Although, I myself am not a member, I'm well known to them by association through Pilgrim and she had informed me the rooms upstairs carry plaques of the surnames of some of the more illustrious patrons. You might think my head is easily turned and I suppose for those I admire it is. However, it is not as easily turned as it once was. Familiarity has a well-documented tendency to lean towards the banal. Even the most luminescent and distinguished cast a mortal shadow. Maybe, I've just become a little jaded over the years?

Passing through the sumptuous lobby of L'améthyste, Pilgrim and I headed straight for the art deco bar. Seated in the corner by the open fire. With a fine clay pipe resting languidly between pale pink lips, sat a lady-, whose study of the back of her hand caused me to wonder what might be observed there to hold the intellectual attention of one of the finest minds of our times - Dame Fitz Baderon. Head of the world organisation in neuroscience, with more letters after her name than the alphabet, she stood and smiled as we entered.

"Neath, how lovely to see you, no one mentioned you were in town?" Dame Fitz Baderon had a distinctive, plummy drawl edged with the soft warmth of the Welsh lilt; she greeted Pilgrim warmly on both cheeks. Turning toward me, her opalescent green eyes stood in dramatic contrast to her olive skin tone.

"You must be, Mr. Baxter?"

She held out her hand which I took, giving a cursory bow.

"Dame Fitz Baderon." I nodded over her hand.

"I prefer to be called Helen, socially. Please won't you join me?"

Removing our coats and handing them to the porter we sat down beside her as Pilgrim ordered a refresher for Helen and the same for herself. The waiter looked at me expectantly, I asked for a whisky, to which he responded by standing perfectly still, I was at a loss to know what to say, so I repeated a sentence that had been said to me many years before.

"Why don't you choose your favourite and I'll see what I think, thank you."

There was the slightest, almost imperceptible hesitation before he left. I decided to store his mental query until later. The inquisitive eyes of both ladies were upon me. Helen spoke up stating with a tinge of curiosity in her voice.

"I see, Mr. Baxter, you have an innate ability to blend seamlessly into your environment. Your adaptive qualities will prove invaluable to you, if you decide to remain with Pilgrim."

"My allegiance has to be earned and once given, is non rescindable." I inclined my head as a mark of respect.

She took a deep draw from her pipe and exhaled white smoke past those puckered rose lips.

"You mustn't mind Helen, Baxter; shes bored now she's won every prize going. What's going to be next, another Noble Prize?"

"I don't think so; all that hand shaking and nodding has made my chiropractor a rich man. Besides, who wants to travel to Norway in winter? No, I think I've just got to wait it out and see if something interesting comes up to hold my attention."

"Well it just so happens." Pilgrim smiled, as she handed Helen several photographs of the spheres. "What do you make of these?"

After the waiter had returned, Pilgrim and the Professor discussed the spheres, whilst I sipped the nectar of the gods. I didn't want to appear gauche by asking the waiter the name and origins of the whisky he had selected, so I took his name to thank him. Anticipating, that upon my next visit I would certainly ask for him, and being the excellent waiter, he undoubtedly was, he would remember instantly the whisky he had served me, therefore saving me from revealing I was ignorant in such matters. It's true to say I knew all of the finest single malts that dominate the market; however, the amber caramel swirl with flecks of fire that had leapt to life in my cut crystal tumbler was definitely off-carte. I must confess, I moved quickly to the periphery of the conversation, as they discussed between frowns and raised eyebrows, the possible evolution and purpose of the spheres. I had just finished when Pilgrim stood, saying seriously.

"I hope we've got enough time."

We hastily said our goodbyes and left, to the worried expression of Helen.

Leaving L'améthyste, Pilgrim almost ran down the steps. I had to pick up the pace as the doorman hailed a taxi.

I opened the door of the taxi for Pilgrim and followed her in.

"Heathrow!" Pilgrim instructed the driver.

"Something the matter, other than the obvious?" I was beginning to feel a nervous knot form in my gut. I was rarely wrong about the implications of such feelings.

"The clock has just begun ticking, Baxter. We need to be in Edinburgh at this moment and as we are not, in the time it will take us to get there, I need to make my presence felt. Therefore, it means running our quarry to ground, but not out of the country." Pulling out her mobile phone she made a call. "I need help. Know anyone in Edinburgh? Thanks, I need some eyes around the Royal College of Surgeons and some ears in room 394. I'm sending two photos."

Late that afternoon, Pilgrim and I, arrived at the Royal College of Surgeons in Edinburgh. It appeared to be a fact that Pilgrim had hitherto unknown resources at her fingertips. We arrived in a private jet, at a small landing strip just outside of the capital on a surprisingly warm afternoon. Although the wind was sharp the air was clear for tens of miles. I had asked Pilgrim on the plane for the summation of Helen's thoughts concerning the spheres. The upshot was she recognised the handy-work. However, it didn't fit in with their possible use, which meant it had been commissioned, but by whom?

Plus, there must be a second if not third person involved in its design and manufacture, as she was unaware of just one person with the intellectual capacity who could be responsible for its entire development.

A sleek black sedan with tinted windows sped us to our destination. As we pulled up on the opposite side of the street, Pilgrim's phone beeped at her. Looking at the screen, and then at me, she ordered. "Let's go in."

I took a few glances about me as we ascended the stone stairs, expecting to see someone, given Pilgrim's conversation on the phone prior to our arrival. I wasn't unduly disappointed when I didn't see a single person I would have described as 'loitering with intent'.

Walking through the regal atrium, Pilgrim seemed to know exactly where she was going. I obediently followed. We took an elevator to the third floor and proceeded down a long corridor until we stood looking at a plaque which read, *Department of Biotechnology and Genetic Engineering*. Not bothering to knock, she opened the door and we walked straight in. It was obviously a laboratory, filled with what looked to me to be very sophisticated high tech equipment, with not a Bunsen burner in sight. The sole person, who was sitting at the back of the room, was wearing something very similar to a NASA space helmet with a gold visor. As we approached he stood up, removing the helmet. I don't know what I was expecting but I certainly felt relieved as the friendly face of a young man appeared of no more than thirty years of age. A fan of bright ginger hair puffed out like a ripe cotton flower that had just popped and I wondered how he'd been able to accommodate it in the helmet. He was tall and wiry with an open countenance and dark brown eyes. Taking a pair of glasses from the counter with a green tartan frame, he placed them neatly on his nose and smiled even wider, now that he could evidently see us more clearly.

"May I help you?" he politely asked in a broad Scottish accent.

"We've come from Dame Fitz Baderon. My name is Pilgrim."

At the mention of her name, a momentary flicker of recognition played across his features.

"Dame, is she now? You Sassenachs and your titles. You'll not find me in any bureaucratic yoke. You're Pilgrim?" he asked, as if making certain.

"Do I know you?" she asked quietly.

"No, we've never met. *Helen* called me to let me know you were on your way up. I'm very pleased to meet you. I'm Professor Ankerville Cromartie."

He stepped forward holding out his hand to Pilgrim. The gesture seemed normal enough but there was an aura of reticence about the movement which immediately put me on my guard. Pilgrim, however, seemed perfectly at her ease. Following the line of her gaze, I watched him, as she began to talk of the reason for her visit; a photograph she would like him to take a look at. I mentally put my finger on it; he was fascinated by her. There was obviously something he had been told about her, probably from Helen. He was observing her. Why?

"May I?" He took the photograph from her hand almost immediately handing it back to her. "Well, you've come to the right man."

I think we were both taken aback that such a young man could be responsible for the Black Pearls.

"So this is your handy-work?" she asked.

I could tell from the little I knew of her she was restraining her enthusiasm.

"Yes, it is," he answered proudly.

"Can you tell me what they are exactly?"

"What *they* are?" The frown and look of disquiet in his eyes, was worrying.

"There are six," I stated.

79

"*Six*, but that's not possible. I only created one," he uttered confused.

"You're obviously funded, Professor Cromartie. Therefore someone further up the line has duplicated your work – five times, so it seems."

The dazed expression on Professor Cromarty's expression was not helpful.

"Professor, we need to ask you some questions in relation to the Pearls."

"The *Pearls*? Oh…I see. May I ask what your interest is?"

"We're here because someone might be using your research to further their own ends and Helen thought you were the best person to talk with."

"Of course. The *Pearls*, as you call them, are in fact a protein shell. It's my field of research."

"A protein shell? What is a protein shell, if you were to explain it in its simplest form?"

I was hoping she would ask that question.

"A protein shell is," he hesitated, trying to find the best words to describe so complicated a concept and item. "Well, it's a layer formed of a specific DNA sequence, repeated over the surface of the shell. The word 'shell' just means outer layer. It doesn't necessarily have to be spherical."

"That's it?" she sounded disappointed. "What is it meant to do? Or more specifically what is the purpose of the one you designed?"

"It's rather clever actually; I won the Cronus Prize for it. I designed it to be able to take on a spherical form, hence it's a hexecontahedron, part of the remit for the challenge. It was a one off, but very versatile. Its unique biotechnological engineering gives it the ability to map the DNA of the host and morph it into the shell. No rejection once ingested." He finished, very pleased with himself.

"Or detection either?" Pilgrim added darkly.

"Exactly." He chirped, pleased that Pilgrim had grasped its basic principles, but oblivious to her veiled reprimand.

"Are you aware it contains a mechanism of some kind?" she asked pointedly.

"No," he uttered with uneasy curiosity. "When you say mechanism, you mean an autonomous functioning part?"

It was clear from the blush that was diffusing his face; he didn't have any knowledge of anything that might be contained inside.

"What are we talking about here? Who would be able to design a mechanism to be placed in something like this?" Pilgrim asked firmly.

"I really couldn't say," he answered, obviously both confused and with an underlying tone of anger to his voice. He was clearly taken aback by the news, as he continued. "I don't know anyone who can design and construct a device to fit into something so small without compromising the shell…unless it was organic on a subatomic level?"

The sudden concern in his voice was beginning to make me feel nervous.

"Do you know what is inside?" he asked cautiously.

"It's a receiver." Pilgrim answered resolutely.

"A receiver? Then you're in the wrong part of the world. You should be on the Pacific Rim. Nanotechnology; I'd say you're looking for a specialist, heavily funded, non-institute. A receiver?" he added contemplatively.

"Why, non-institute?" I asked, in an attempt to keep his mind focused.

"Because otherwise, I'd know who it is. Mine is a particularly small field of research. We're talking about just over a handful of people who could realistically pull that off."

"Names." Pilgrim demanded.

"There'd be no point. I'd know if any of them were involved. This person must work out of sight of the general halls of academia."

"You'll supply them anyway. Can you hypothesise as to its use?" Pilgrim asked seriously.

"No."

"Professor Cromartie, how many other scientists were involved in the Cronus Challenge?"

"Six, from different countries, but if you're thinking any of them could be responsible for this, you're mistaken. I don't want to blow my own trumpet, but I was only ever the real contender for the prize."

He seemed perfectly truthful and without any feeling of insecurity or pride in his voice, just stating the facts.

"So, it therefore stands to reason this person potentially thinks more creatively than you and has more funding. May I ask what the prize consisted of, that you won?" Pilgrim asked.

"Or someone who is just plain smarter and not funded?" I juxtaposed.

There was a moments silence as the implications of such a person existing sunk in.

"I won a rolling fund of 1.2 million pounds Sterling," he stated flatly.

I whistled my shock at the enormous sum of money.

"Yes, it is an impressive amount. However, the fund is paid out, only, for further research and staggered every three-year period. If, I make significant progress in my research, the fund is topped back up at the end of the period, and if I don't, it isn't."

"Interesting." Pilgrim stated.

Pilgrim seemed somewhat distracted. Though, whilst this new information was pertinent, it didn't seem to me to shed any new light on the matter.

"That's a curious way of putting it," the Professor quietly added.

It was clear we had gone as far as we could. We said our goodbyes, throwing lines at him as we left. "You've been a big help," and, "We'll let you know what happens."

I remarked to Pilgrim, how uneasy he had become after she had asked about the mechanism.

"Yes, you're right, Baxter; but I believe he was only telling us a partial truth. Perhaps he has heard of something on the scientific grapevine but just wasn't sure it's a match."

"Mmn," I answered, in the affirmative.

Leaving the relative warmth of the Royal College of Surgeons, we buttoned our coats and took the brunt of the wind on our backs as we crossed to the car.

"We're not going to Asia, are we?" I asked nervously.

I didn't feel able to make a lengthy journey and then scout around for someone we had no clue how to find.

"I don't think that will be necessary." She held up her finger for silence. Pressing her finger to her ear she scribbled on a writing pad she'd laid on the roof of the car. Pulling what looked to be a piece of foam from her ear, she dropped it into her pocket.

"No, not as far as Asia, but we'll need to take a trip to France post haste."

"France; why France?"

"Because Professor Cromartie has just made a telephone call and I have a small errand to run."

I was driven back to the airport, after which Pilgrim took off for goodness knows where; informing me she wouldn't be long. I detected a hesitation in her, which I interpreted as meaning; perhaps it wasn't a suitable destination for me to accompany her. As her car disappeared into the distance, dark ominous clouds began to form above the airport and I felt the frustration and helplessness, of one that is a party to current events, but has little influence over them.

CHAPTER SIX

As any bureaucratic boffin worth his weight in paperwork will tell you, France is unequalled in the covertness of administrative forms. A condensed document will not suffice, as it might be interpreted as being of minor consequence, or even worse, virtually unimportant, which in turn would reflect its lack of gravitas upon its official. Such laxity cannot be afforded in so cartesian a society. Therefore, reams of paper with abundant suffixes and addendums must be brought to bear, for the sake of the vexed Gallic reputation. A person sporting a sheaf of paperwork under his arms, need only add purpose to his step and a look of brooding to his brow, to be deemed as one whom shoulders great responsibility, and therefore of considered importance, and the bigger the sheaf, the more important that person must be. Such is the cultivated burden of the uninspired.

It was therefore of paramount importance for Pilgrim and I, not to create a single ripple across the French government's clerical pool.

"If you're asked, Baxter, we're visiting old friends of the family, who live in the local area. Throw the name, Marchon out there if you have to. Fortunately, by your own admission, your language skills are not brilliant."

"Pilgrim, I don't like lying, and to be perfectly honest, I'm not very good at it either. This whole business makes me very nervous. Official bodies and all that, plus they are French. They've no doubt got a whole series of instructive manuals from the dear old Republic, on how to deal with foreigners that don't tell the truth. Probably land up imprisoned on one of the colonies doing hard time."

There was a momentary stillness from Pilgrim, quickly followed by her raucous laughter. It was so unexpected, from one so obviously in control, most of the time, that it quite took me by surprise, and I suddenly burst out laughing too.

"You know you really are the funniest person, Baxter. I had no idea you could be so dramatic."

My laughter died. I wanted to vehemently deny such an inaccurate label, but for that moment I saw the truth of it and laughed again at my over-reaction.

As we circled over the long plateaus of Franche Comte, with their bright yellow swathes of rapeseed, we finally came to land at Dole's municipal airport. I discovered Dole, to be a bustling medieval town. I had thought how wonderfully green and lush this area of France was and so conveniently close to Switzerland. The airport, although modest, lacked nothing necessary to the ardent traveller. In my opinion Dole is a jewel in the crown of France, with its own smaller name-sake, Notre Dame church. Sitting majestically above the town, it looks down onto the Doubs River, with its traditional blue and white boats tethered to the grassy banks. Despite the emotional storm that was soon to follow, I shall always remember it that way.

Our small private jet taxied to a stop and as before, a car was waiting upon our arrival. I noticed the impressive heraldic shield of the Jura County, with its gold lion on a blue background, and felt sure I had seen it somewhere before. I then remembered a postcard that had been wedged into the frame of a notice board behind the desk of Professor Cromartie; it had displayed the identical shield.

I had discovered we were to visit the Pasteur Institute, so named after Louis Pasteur, who was born in Dole. The institute is a veritable hive of activity, for all things microbiological. Situated opposite Notre Dame church, some hundred feet below it, it stands in relief to the cascades of the Doubs falling behind it.

"So, you think there will be someone there that can help us?" I asked hopefully.

"I'm counting on it," she answered, raising an eyebrow.

After ten minutes we reached the centre of Dole. Running parallel to the river, we pulled down into a long drive lined with large Camellia trees, whose recent moult had left curls of pale brown bark lying on the grass, as if from some enormous pencil sharpener. Passing through an impressive carved stone arch, we entered a large gravelled courtyard. Along it's sides ran two mammoth sized buildings finished in the indigenous local Jurassic white stone shot through with burnt orange. The effect was both commanding and unusual. Located at its centre on a large granite plinth, stood the imposing stone figure of, Louis Pasteur. We continued slowly, until the car swung in front of a six story stone building, of which two floors were contained within the structure of the roof. A young lady, whose studious gaze made me check my shoes and straighten my bow-tie, met us at the front door. She broke into a warm smile, and noticing that Pilgrim had begun reading the inscription of the plaque of Louis Pasteur, she made no hesitation in detailing, in English with a melodic French accent, the proud origins of their patron, and the plinth on which his statue rested.

"The plinth is the same stone as the Statue of Liberty stands on in New York, and was quarried from Damparis, by the chemical giant Solvay, located just outside Dole."

Pilgrim asked to be taken in immediately, ignoring any positive acknowledgements the young lady was obviously used to hearing. My need to exercise good manners was thwarted by the speed at which our hostess responded. Turning on her high heels, she walked with purpose into the main building.

Pilgrim and I, stepped into the flag-stoned foyer of the main entrance, where centuries of use had earned the stone a mirror finish. It was no less grand than the outside, with marble columns reaching up to an ornate stone relief ceiling, detailed in gold-leaf. Despite the warm temperatures outside, the interior was markedly cooler and I felt the need to draw my jacket closer around me. It wasn't just the chill in the air that made me do so, it was also the anxiety of what might lie ahead in regards to the spheres.

"Who are we going to be meeting?" I whispered, not sure how to pronounce his name.

"Dr Bonnin." Pilgrim reminded me.

"Doesn't that mean, 'good hour?'"

"No, Baxter, it doesn't; even though the pronunciation is very similar."

"Ah right, well I can't guarantee my language skills are going to improve whilst we're here."

Pilgrim chose to ignore my attempt at levity. After a few minutes we were escorted up a carved stone stairway and into a large room, whose ceiling was festooned with brightly coloured flags. We didn't have too long to wait, before a middle-aged man with a serious expression entered briskly through the door, his hand out stretched before him like the bowsprit of a ship. He wore a crumpled corduroy grey suit with baggy knees and elbows, that tell of a man who spends most of his time sitting with his elbows on a desk. His relatively dull appearance was in complete contrast to his bright red spectacle frames and blood shot eyes. Despite his hesitant smile, he looked haunted. Pilgrim stepped forward to greet him.

"Dr Bonnin, C'est un plaisir de vous rencontrer et je tiens à vous remercier pour votre temps. Je suis à l'aise pour parler en français mais les compétences linguistiques de mon collègue ne sont pas développées. Je sais que vous parlez couramment l'anglais pourriez-vous nous poursuit en anglais ? "

"Not at all," he replied in stilted English, with a deep voice.

His French accent was very much in evidence, but his enunciation was clipped in such a manner as to allow the listener to understand him completely.

"I, so rarely have the opportunity to speak English, except on the odd occasions we have visitors from English speaking institutes. I cannot say I was expecting a visitor. I am very curious as to why you would like to speak with me?"

"But surely you must have been expecting us, after Professor Cromartie called you?" Pilgrim stated plainly.

It was as much as I could do just to stare at Dr Bonnin and observe his reaction. He nodded slowly,

"Yes, I was expecting you, but not so soon. You understand. Professor Cromartie said nothing other than, two people had asked him about his work and they would probably visit me, although he was not specific about what."

I doubted that very much.

"Dr Bonnin, this is my work colleague, Mr. Baxter, and I am Pilgrim. We work independently and are not associated with any official body." Pilgrim handed him the photographs. "We have access to these, 'black pearls', and have been asked to store them. But first we need to understand their exact nature."

Dr Bonnin's nervous demeanour was immediately eclipsed, by a look of horror. His face crumpled, to one of a man whose fate is imminent. He stood unsteadily clutching the photographs in his hands, which he now allowed to fall to his sides.

"Mon dieu," he whispered, "c'est pas possible."

He staggered over to the window and gazed out. Pilgrim stayed quiet, observing him.

Not knowing what the hell was happening, a ball of lead was forming in the pit of my stomach. Something was terribly wrong. I shot a look over to Pilgrim; the pleading must have been writ large on my face. She held her finger to her lips. The seconds passed, with just the nightmare grimaces exhibited by Dr Bonnin, to allude to those terrible thoughts that were evidently crossing his mind. He carefully placed the photographs on the centre table and ran both hands through his silver hair, like one bereft of hope.

I couldn't move. Time had ended in this room among us three. I wanted to jump up, to say anything, just to relieve this clamp from my chest. I felt the white-hot fingers of exhilarating desperation coiling inside me. Finally, Dr Bonnin turned his ashen face toward us. Those formally anxious eyes had sunken, his face was a mask of desolation. I felt an immeasurable loss, for what I didn't know.

"These 'Perles Noires' where never meant to be. Their existence is an abomination, after Caracas." He collapsed like a beaten man into a chair.

"Dr Bonnin, I need you to listen to me and afterwards I will take whatever action remains open to me. You can help to ensure these," she stabbed the photographs on the table, "do not fulfil their original purpose."

"Then you know what they're capable of?" he uttered desperately. "You have them…you have them all?"

"Yes, I have them all."

"You have all seven?" he continued shakily.

The ball of lead in my stomach fell into my feet. We only had six in the box. Where was the seventh?

"They must be destroyed!" he shouted like a man possessed. "We cannot talk here; meet me later on this afternoon at a quatre heures; when we won't be disturbed, inside Notre Dame, and we will talk." The set determination on his face meant our brief interview was at an end.

At the appointed time we entered Notre Dame church where the heavy pipes of its organ filled that vast space. We made our way unobtrusively through the heavily carved side-door into the Nave. It had already begun to darken outside and the lit chandeliers and large ornate wall-lights gave the impression of a later hour. Looking about us we observed the interior was deserted, apart from the energetic efforts of the practicing organist.

"Where do you think Dr Bonnin is?" I asked with some trepidation.

"I don't know Baxter; but I don't like this."

We had stayed wandering inside the church for some time until Pilgrim made the decision to leave. We didn't voice it, but I knew we were both thinking the same thing; Dr Bonnin was a 'no show' because Dr Bonnin was dead.

Walking away from the church, we took the cobbled walkway with its ancient overhanging buildings, until we came to an unassuming house huddled between two restaurants, that lay next to the river. Unnervingly, the front door was ajar. A flight of narrow stairs leapt up in front and we began to climb.

"This *is* Dr Bonnin's place; right?" I asked quietly.

"Yes, it is." Pilgrim answered seriously.

At the top of the stairs stood an old oak door with the most unusual and large doorknocker, made of the face of a wizened man whose long beard formed the knocker. Using it, produced two metallic booms that echoed inside. Standing there, we strained to hear any noise in response, but nothing came. Pushing against the door, it opened easily and Pilgrim called out.

"Dr Bonnin!"

The silence was deafening. My pulse was racing, but I stood rooted to the spot. Pilgrim moved forward and felt for a light switch. Instantaneously, the room was flooded by light. Stepping forward cautiously; Pilgrim called out again; there was no reply.

"Let's take a look around," she whispered.

I began to move further into the room which doubled as a study and kitchen with small windows opening out to the roofs of the surrounding buildings. I crossed the floor and headed toward a battered wooden door at the far end; whilst Pilgrim shuffled through unopened mail and paperwork that lay on a side table.

Moving into his bedroom; wherein stood a dereliction of unkempt furniture; upon a detailed inspection there was little to remark upon, until I turned toward the bed.

"You'd better come and take a look at this."

Scribbled on the plaster wall by the side of his cot-bed were numerous calculations in different coloured inks, of numerical figures that told of years of mental equations. Some had been crossed out with such vigour the plaster had come away. Pilgrim stepped over and scrutinised it.

"This is interesting." She pointed out three capital letters etched deeply.

"'N.E.G', what's that supposed to mean?" I questioned.

"I don't know. But see how it falls at the end of all this and is underlined not once, but twice. It must be the final result."

I turned around and moved over to a small chest of drawers with a mirror on top. One by one I pulled open the drawers and moved my hands through the old and worn clothes but found nothing. Just as I was about to close the top drawer, I glanced in the mirror and caught sight of a small key taped to the inside.

"Pilgrim, I've found a key!"

Handing it to her, she quickly examined it.

"It's a key to a personal box or something like it. Not a door; it's too small. Take a look under the bed and search around. See if you can find anything it might fit."

We both began to scour the inside of those pathetic rooms, but discovered nothing. As I stood up, from having looked under the cooker, my eyes alighted on a small stack of letters, maybe twenty or thirty in total, all with the same handwriting.

"What do these say? They're all written in French."

Taking them from me, Pilgrim quickly checked the dates and scanned through them.

"They're about nothing really, just general correspondence. Nothing telling, other than; 'hope you are making progress; good luck', and all that."

She handed them back to me. I began to study them.

"No address, or date, but the paper isn't worn, so they must have been written within the last year. This quality paper is unusual, it's obviously expensive, but have you noticed something, it's unusually heavy?"

"You'd expect that with a higher quality writing paper; it carries a greater weight," Pilgrim said dismissively.

I returned them to their original box by the side of the grubby stove.

We left a little wiser and a great deal more cautious, as to the meaning of Dr Bonnin's sudden disappearance and the key.

"One thing is for sure," Pilgrim remarked, "Dr Bonnin lives in near penury. He must be paying for this research himself and it's leaving him destitute."

"He has to be funded, how could he possibly raise the money to carry out his research at the Pasteur Institute otherwise?" I asked.

There was silence between us and then I had an idea.

"He could have done what I did. I saved my money so I could travel and take an extended period of time off. Maybe Dr Bonnin did the same. Saved the money he'd earned so he could spend it on his research, which also implies a break with his original benefactors."

"What did he want to tell us?" Pilgrim mused.

"Do you think hes dead?" I asked gravely.

"I can't see any other reasonable explanation."

"We should have those calculations looked at," I stated firmly.

"We don't need to. We know the Black Pearls are toxic in the extreme and are responsible for the death of thousands in Caracas; we've established that link. Knowing the math behind how they work is incidental to their effect. We have to confirm who was behind the original funding and locate the missing pearl," Pilgrim said hastily.

"What do you mean, *confirm*? Do you know who's behind all this?" I demanded, incredulous to the idea Pilgrim knew who was responsible.

"I can't be sure, no…let's just say it has all the hallmarks, and its a process of elimination. I would prefer not to enter that specific arena of conjecture, unless I have to."

I couldn't think of anything to say. If Pilgrim didn't want to discuss who she thought might be behind the deaths of thousands of innocent people, then we were deeper into these treacherous waters, than I had first realised.

We decided to revisit the institute that evening, to see if Dr Bonnin had returned.

When we arrived, we were informed, Dr Bonnin had left soon after our own departure, and hadn't been seen since. We managed to re-visit his laboratory; under the pretext of leaving a note. Our escort had soon tired of waiting, as Pilgrim deliberately wasted as much time as she could finding a pen and paper. Before she had begun to write, he'd excused himself, saying he would return shortly, to let us out of the building. As soon as he'd closed the door behind him, we both began searching frantically for anything the key might fit. We found nothing.

On our way walking back into Dole, I felt tired, frustrated and down-hearted.

"I say we go back to the church. That's where Dr Bonnin said he would meet us. It's obviously a familiar and safe place to him. We should search it methodically this time," I suggested.

Pilgrim conceded easily, and I realised she was also at a loss to explain Dr Bonnin's disappearance.

Now early evening; we returned and entered Notre Dame. Our footsteps echoed eerily on the stone floor. A handful of die-hard tourists dwindled about admiring the colossal paintings held aloft against the walls. As we waited, while they finished their sightseeing and meandered out, the church was left deserted. The church-bells tolled seven p.m.; when homage would be paid at every dinner table across France. We quickly split up and began searching the interior for anything the key might fit. I began behind the immense and beautifully carved organ, intending to work my way to the front. We had been there approximately half an hour, when we heard an agonised groan. Moving quickly away from our respective areas we looked at one another, listening expectantly. Within a minute, we heard a more stultified moan. Pilgrim and I, tiptoed quickly towards the sound which took us to the altar, but we saw no one. Looking above us and even peeking into the vestry, we couldn't find anyone to account for those painful sounds. At a loss for any evidence, we heard a sudden strangled cry.

"Madame Pilgrim ... down here."

Searching the floor around us, we noticed a large metal grate, moving over we immediately saw the contorted body of Dr Bonnin lying about fifteen feet or more below us. As the ancient cast-iron grating was bolted into the stone surround, there had to be an entrance below us. Before we could leave to look for it, Dr Bonnin spoke up; his feeble voice echoing against the granite walls of his cell.

"You must listen carefully; I don't have very much time. The last letter came today and is fulfilling its purpose. You can't get me out; I have locked myself in. They can't get at me here."

"Who…who can't get at you?" I demanded.

"You must destroy the Black Pearls. I was deceived."

Dr Bonnin gave an incomprehensible and protracted utterance as he clutched his stomach.

"I must be quick. The Black Pearls work on a subatomic level, mapping the DNA of their host. When they discover an anomaly, they replace it with a blank."

"A blank?" I asked, frustrated by my own ignorance.

"Baxter!" Pilgrim admonished me, "continue, Doctor."

"The Black Pearls *were* originally designed to rewrite faulty DNA, but they become sentient in their six-dimensional world. They have self-initialised. They entered the brain of the host on a sub-atomic level and began to measure intelligence. If they discover any inherent flaws either mentally or physically, they terminate the host."

A loud gasp fell from Dr Bonnin's lips as he doubled over, causing him to momentarily spasm. After, his voice became ragged and exhausted, for the last time.

"My notes; they must not have them."

"Who, Doctor?" Pilgrim shouted.

"Le nom de guerre c'est, Gideon des Titans," he whispered, before giving a final exclamation in French. "Sans Dieu rien!"

Doctor Bonnin's dead body slumped forward.

Looking up aghast, I found Pilgrim's eyes fixed upon me. Her pupils had become so dilated; the luminance of her blue irises reminded me of earth rising from behind a black moon.

"The name of war is Gideon of the Titans. Without God, nothing," Pilgrim translated flatly. "We can't talk here Baxter."

"We must call an ambulance; someone!" I shouted dazed by what had just happened and the possible consequences for us.

"It's too late. Besides, we mustn't. We can't risk being associated to any of this. What we need to do, is leave here now, and try to claw back some time. We have to act as if nothing has happened."

I could see the logic of it, but I didn't like it. I had so many questions and no answers. I couldn't begin to discuss what had just occurred and what we'd learnt. I knew we should leave immediately and return to the airport.

We sprung up, heading toward the door from which we had entered. My mind was churning as we walked swiftly past the various chapels of the saints. I suddenly slowed as a thought struck me. It wasn't until I stood in front of the chapel of St Anthony; that I saw on the ornate marble lectern; a thick leather-bound book with a brass fitting and lock.

"Pilgrim, over here."

"What is it?" She was at my side at once.

"I wonder if our key fits a book-lock, and not a box?"

99

"St. Anthony, patron saint of lost things," she said, pointing above to a Latin inscription.

Pulling the key from my pocket, I took a quick look about me before stepping over the knee-high balustrade. The key was a perfect fit and the lock clicked open instantly. Not wishing to be observed, I grabbed the book, tucking it under my arm. We hurriedly left, not looking back, until we were by ourselves, on a wooden bench in Pasteur Park.

There was a decided chill in the air and the large fountain splashing out in front, surrounded by spears of delphiniums and lit from below, did little to draw my attention from the task at hand. The sky had darkened perceptibly, and I felt an ominous presence descend on us, as the gravity of our situation engulfed me.

I had opened the pages at the beginning of the book. They were stuffed with all manner of pieces of paper and notes, each marked with some obscure mathematical lettering or other.

"Here." Pilgrim stabbed the page at the letters N.E.G.

Written underneath was: N. E. G = Neogenesis = énergie'

"*N-E-G;* if you say it phonetically its 'energy'," I said triumphantly before adding a subdued, "what does that mean?"

"We need someone who understands this."

"Professor Cromartie?" I ventured.

"Certainly not," Pilgrim replied firmly, "we have to consider the potentially fatal consequences to anyone we bring into this."

"So, Dr Bonnin has named the Black Pearls, N-E-G."

"He also called them an abomination," Pilgrim uttered.

Seeing part of a headline, I pulled a torn piece of newspaper from the leaves of the book. Printed in bold type; above a photograph showing square-upon-square of tarpaulin, covering lines of bodies; was the header, *'Caracas plague kills thousands in hours.'*

In the book the word 'Caracas' had been ground into the paper with such force, it had ripped through the sheets underneath.

"It's hard to believe Dr Bonnin began as a willing participant to something like this." I observed.

"His specific area of expertise was in Nano molecular biology. Plainly put, he designed and created biological organisms on a sub-atomic level, that meet certain performance criteria. Looking at his notes, it looks as if his research developed into a science for the manipulation of the genome RNA. These are anomalies that exist within DNA itself. But it doesn't fully explain Caracas."

"So, he designed this *organism* to identify faults in DNA, which resulted in it evolving into the N.E.G?" I asked, hoping I had grasped the gist of what she was saying.

"Essentially," she answered with a grim look on her face.

I was looking intensely at some of the diagrams and scribbles, which spoke far more clearly to me than the calculations under them. I pointed to one in particular, which I recognised instantly as the snake shape of a double helix of DNA. Parts of it had been blanked out with lines pointing away from it with the letters N.E.G inserted.

"Baxter, go through the book and tell me what you see." Pilgrim demanded. "I don't want your attempt at a scientific explanation, just what you see."

"Okay." I felt overwhelmed by the request but began to flip through the pages which were all written in French. Therefore, I concentrated on the scribbled pictures and diagrams Dr Bonnin, had made in the margins. "Just by the dates, this research began five years ago. There have been months of concentrated work, and others with little recorded. Every few pages, at the bottom, the word 'Seedertraume' has been written. 'La Poste', is also printed, followed by a check-mark. I would interpret that as, having finished something. It would also explain the letters in his rooms. Someone, in Seedertraume, is following his research."

Pilgrim nodded slowly in agreement.

"Dr Bonnin's work became the catalyst in realising an altogether new science; one that's sentient; driven to identify and destroy. I have a bad feeling about that paper which you tried to draw my attention to. Remember what Dr Bonnin said; *the last letter came today and is fulfilling its purpose*."

"What! I touched all those letters! You mean those letters were contaminated with something?"

"Yes," she answered in a sombre tone. "But not with any virus, or bacteria. It would have to be something that would build up its toxicity in the body, until all that would be needed, was a final dose. My guess is, the reader would hold the letter for a measured length of time, to read its contents. I think we're looking at arsenical poisoning, via dermal absorption. It would also explain the weight of the paper, and the number of uninformative letters."

"I'm not going to die?"

"No, Baxter, you're not going to die…not today."

"You should listen to me more often. I knew there was something odd about that paper."

"Encouraging, of you to notice."

The relief at knowing I was going to live another day, made me feel heady. I began to babble.

"I often write letters as opposed to emailing. Emails are okay for business purposes, but a handwritten letter should be the preferred method of communication, when dealing with personal matters. It shows you have made an effort in its execution, along with your choice of paper and envelope, both of which should match. A decent stamp, nothing too florid, and the recipient will know they are well-thought of."

"Why don't you just tell me what else you see?" Pilgrim hinted subtlety.

"Theres a crude diagram of the cross section of the brain here, and the writing is very erratic, as if he'd written hurriedly."

"Or maybe he was just tired?" Pilgrim interjected.

"Who knows? Oddly, on the last of the pages, he has depicted the N.E.G as a 'Packman'; suggestive of predation?" I queried.

"In my experience, a lot can be gleaned by observation. Building theoretical bridges between these ideas, can suggest something of their reality. We must do the best we can. What we believe we've learnt and some of what is included in this book, can be used to bring us closer to the truth. We can't do anymore today."

"How do you think those people died in Caracas?" I asked, suddenly struck by the weight of knowledge.

"Without pity, or a single mark of violence upon their bodies."

CHAPTER SEVEN

I had thought, that after learning of such a malevolent
weapon, we would have taken off, as if we were about to be
consumed. We should have run from France, as fast as air,
boat, or any other form of transportation could carry us,
anything to put as much distance between ourselves and the
organisation Dr Bonnin had spoken of.

Pilgrim had other plans. She wanted time to think.
She reminded me of the saying, by Rudyard Kipling, *'If you
can keep your head when all about you are losing theirs...'* I
acquiesced to her superior experience in such matters and
agreed, upon her insistence, to go to dinner.

In the early evening, in the centre of Dole, when the
autumnal sun gave up its final warmth through the flecked
indigo clouds, we came quietly, each of us lost in thought, to
the iron studded wooden doors of 'Le Mousquetaire'. We
walked through to a small cobbled courtyard, whose stone
walls stood blanketed in the burnt red and orange flanges of
a mature Maple Vine. A single large ecclesiastic candle stood
fluttering in a glass lantern above the door. Following
Pilgrim, my sombre mood, coupled with the bland exterior,
made me indifferent to my surroundings. Why weren't we
back at the airport, in the jet, on our way home? Anywhere
would have been preferable. Anything to prevent the
situation from deteriorating. But we weren't, and I was
unable to understand why Pilgrim couldn't ponder the
whole situation in the plane.

So, with a marked amount of reticence, I trod warily down the restaurant's shallow stone steps, their worn surface bearing the undulate curve after centuries of use, to be greeted by the most self-effacing pillar of congeniality I have ever met; the proprietor, Monsieur Henri de Long-champ. Despite only minutes before, feeling the weight of the world on my shoulders, I couldn't help but smile in return, and feel genuinely relieved we had found some respite, however fleeting, from our burden of knowledge.

Monsieur de Long-champ had a rotund figure, with a height, I estimated, of not more than five feet and two inches. He was tightly clad in an aged, dark-grey dinner-suit, where worn buttons clung to their last remaining threads. The crisp white shirt burgeoning at his waist was an encouraging testament to an indulgent gourmet. The most striking thing about him, apart from his infectious smile, was the way in which he made a pronounced inclination of his head, at regular intervals, to indicate his affirmation and compliance, of some request or other. It was performed with such regularity, I was able to determine our host not only adorned the crown of his hair with brilliantine, but also, he had been to the barber recently, and his shirt collar was slightly too big for him. Probably deliberate, I surmised, given the head bobbing involved.

"Mademoiselle Pilgrim, how good it is to see you!"

"You've been here before?" I asked her, completely taken aback.

"Yes," she confirmed, with a tight smile.

I waited momentarily for her to explain, but when no explanation was forth coming, I reluctantly followed her as we were led to our table.

The interior was as unremarkable as the exterior, but that is where any sign of mediocrity ended. An aroma of sizzling butter, fresh herbs and fennel, wafted passed my nostrils; my stomach growled in response. A waiter came catapulting out of the kitchen, tray in hand, his head to attention, with two dishes; one a coupé of wild rice with a rosé filet-mignon laid on a crouton, with a generous sprinkling of shaved black truffle, finished lovingly with a nappé of Madeira demi-glace. Yes, I am observant in such matters. The other; a bowl of the fluffiest couscous, with tender lamb and fresh mint. I was right, there could be no mistake, cognac had been used quite liberally in the sauce. Its warm, noisette-bouquet, teased my nostrils. It was at that moment, my mind numbed to our current chaotic predicament, and I was mercifully able, for the first time, to think of something else; dinner.

We were shown to a table, where oddly, the only view was that of a robust Privet-hedge. I was beginning to see a pattern here; the surroundings were quite superfluous to the food. Perfectly starched white-as-snow tablecloths, and waiters with reassuringly clean finger-nails; dispelled any doubts that, this was a first-class restaurant. Looking around at the candle topped tables, I saw each table carried a discreet card with the word, 'Réservé', and before long the restaurant began to fill with the raucous dinner-crowd, bringing their high-expectations to the culinary battlefield. The whole experience of dining at Le Mousquetaire, after our waiter had departed, as if on a mission to the kitchen, was to attain sublime contentment. There was no dining-courtesy overlooked, no crumb un-swept from our table cloth, just the subtle murmurings of a discerning and sated throng, myself included. As I pushed my chair slightly away from the table, Pilgrim smiled at me.

"Not quite what you expected?" she asked, with an underlying tone of curiosity.

"No, not quite, now you come to ask. More importantly; you've been to Dole before."

"I think you've got quite enough to think about at the moment, don't you?"

Her utter dismissal of what I considered an important question, made me suddenly angry.

"Your condescension is staggering!"

She was immediately contrite.

"Baxter, I'm sorry. I didn't mean to say that."

"The point is; you thought it. Let me inform you; if you wish to be *my* business partner, then you'll need to treat me as such. It may be beyond your capability; but I'm going to give you the opportunity to prove me wrong."

"Thank you," she whispered apologetically.

With my anger assuaged, I added.

"I'm sure the last thing on my mind, after the horrifying events of today, was food, but you were right. But, won't someone be looking for us?"

"We'll be out of the country in a couple of hours."

"And easily be associated with the murder of Dr Bonnin."

"Not once they run an autopsy. He did die under suspicious circumstances."

"Quite," I remarked.

Taking the book out from under my jacket, I began to skim through its pages. "What does this say?" I asked, pointing to a rather difficult equation, under which was a scribbled sentence of Dr Bonnin's.

"It refers to a chemical compound, glucose. It looks as if, it is necessary for the Black Pearls to work."

"They have to be swallowed to enter the body. Glucose is also soluble in water. That would explain how they were administered in Caracas; through their water supply."

"It would explain their spread but not their activation."

"Theres glucose in saliva." I pointed out.

"You're right. We know the ones we have are inert unless they come into contact with moisture, with glucose, or are swallowed." Pilgrim said, relieved.

The waiter slid two of the daintiest espresso cups onto the table. The nutty bouquet threaded through the warm air, leaving its unmistakable signature, as the cream froth displayed a fleur de lis. Pilgrim began.

"Yes, I have been to Dole before, on business, and it looks as if my trip many years ago is connected. I was hoping it wasn't, but then, Seedertraume, came up."

"What is Seedertraume?"

"A research facility that I believe has a connection to the organisation thats behind Dr Bonnin's funding."

"Gideon Titan?" I concluded.

"Not exactly, the two names aren't necessarily meant to go together, and it's, *Titans*. We cannot keep the N.E.Gs existence to ourselves. The only option available to us is to share our information with two others that I know

109

can be trusted implicitly, and who can take care of themselves."

Before I could ask her about the Titans, our effusive host descended on us.

"Mademoiselle Pilgrim, what a pleasure it is to see you here. You have been away for too long. You have no right to make Jocelyn so anxious. You know how she worries about such things?"

Pilgrim turned to me and explained,

"Jocelyn, is the Executive Chef, and wife to Henri. She worries my head will be turned by the culinary skills of another. Please send her my compliments, and give her this," she said, turning back to Henri.

Pilgrim pulled out from under the table a thin navy-box with gold-lettering showing the patronage of the Royal House of Innis. Henri immediately began bobbing, as his excitement overwhelmed him.

"Oh, Mademoiselle Pilgrim, she will be so delighted. Let me fetch her."

Before another word could be uttered, he chasséd his generous frame between the tables and chairs toward the kitchen-door, with the mastered accomplishment of a prima ballerina. Within seconds the kitchen door flew open to a slender woman with grey hair wound up in a chignon tucked underneath a chef's hat. Behind her scampered Henri, his right arm outstretched to indicate our table. With a strongly pronounced French accent, Jocelyn greeted us.

"Mon Cherie, where have you been? I said to Henri only last week you were overdue a visit."

After planting affectionate kisses on Pilgrim's cheeks, she turned and studied me with her quick brown eyes; smiling in expectation of our introduction. Pilgrim said solemnly.

"Madame de Long-champ, please allow me to introduce my work colleague, Monsieur Baxter. Mr. Baxter, Madame de Long-champ.

I promptly stood, kissing the back of her pale, perfectly formed slim-hand. She smiled at me, in a manner that made me feel suddenly self-conscious.

"Madame de Long-champ, words cannot express my delight at your gastronomic flair and expertise," My sincerity was not overstated and entirely genuine.

"Please, call me Jocelyn," she offered demurely.

She was enchanting, but I wasn't fooled by her lady-like qualities, to suppose for an instant, she didn't rule the kitchen with a rod of iron, like her own personal fiefdom. I found myself bobbing my head. Now, I knew the source of Henri's habit. With a click of her fingers, a waiter scurried from the shadows with a chair for her. I had been right that the roost was ruled, not by the cock, but by the hen and she had the knives to back it up, no doubt. Pilgrim seemed totally at ease, and began speaking in French to her. The navy-box was opened to the effusion of Jocelyn. Laying, within folds of navy silk, lay a pair of the softest crimson leather-gloves with a cream mink-cuff. The tartan interior of the lid, confirmed the House of Innis; its connection to Scotland. So, that was what she had been doing after she left me outside the Royal College of Surgeons, - shopping. And there was I, imagining all sorts of covert activity. With a sigh, as if sliding into a warm perfumed bath, Jocelyn moved

111

her pale, slight hands into the gloves and marvelled at their fit.

"But they are perfect, Cherie," she purred. Turning to me she explained. "You know, Monsieur Baxter, my hands are very important, not only to myself, but to everyone associated with my restaurant, my guests, my employees, even my bank manager. I must take the utmost care of them. You know, they are insured for a million Euros. Even a cut, can cost everyone dearly, for then how am I to work. It is a curse you know; I am constantly reminded to take the utmost care."

Like any exceptionally, talented artist, she was self-absorbed and blinkered; but nevertheless, she did have a point. Slipping them off, she carefully placed them back into their box and reverently closed the lid. Jocelyn suddenly stuck out her bottom lip, waving her finger like a metronome at Pilgrim, and said seriously.

"You look too thin, Chèrie, you will have dessert, and I will take care of it."

It wasn't a question. With a click of her fingers, she'd risen and darted into the kitchen, as her chair was lifted away. Our waiter was at our elbow within the blink of an eye.

"Un Martini sec, s'il vous plait ; anything for you, Baxter?"

I shook my head. Our welcome interlude was quickly winding-down, as our current predicament came racing-up to my consciousness.

"No, thank you."

Whilst the soothing ether of a pleasant evening still hung in the air around us, I snatched a moment in time to

112

observe my new business partner. My current situation would have been entirely incredulous to me; if I had not lived it. I was beginning to understand Pilgrim's various moods, her very different mental states. To the casual observer, she appeared on the verge of boredom and lethargy; however, I had learnt during our relatively short acquaintance, she had put her conscious mind on the back-burner and was thinking on a clearer, higher level, without the distraction of the common-place. She answered simple questions; but she wasn't there. I didn't want to intrude on those thoughts that might keep us alive, so I kept my questions concerning the Titans for later. She was well into her second cocktail, when she finally looked up with an expression on her face of, affability. She asked, whilst hypnotically stirring her drink with her finger.

"Feeling better?" As she deftly diverted my thoughts from her, to my waistline.

"Yes, the strain, attributable no doubt, to so much responsibility." I admitted.

"What you have to always keep in mind, is that we have knowledge of them, and knowledge is power. Plus, they are human, with all that that entails. You know Baxter, there is a piece of work for us, that will need our complete focus. Moving forward we cannot ignore any subtlety, or dismiss any coincidence. You should understand if you involve yourself in this, any more than you have, you will incur the attention of an organisation, whose leaders are deadly."

"I'm not intimidated by them." I stated strongly, "what's the worst they can do?"

113

"The least would be to kill you," Pilgrim said quietly, before continuing, "I witnessed their retribution many years ago. The innocent party was gradually stripped of everything, until he was forced to take his own life. You must have read at the time, of Sir Geringham, the Cabinet minister?"

"Yes, quite a devious and malicious man. It's his children, I feel sorry for, especially after their mother passed away so soon after him."

"Four months before his suicide, he was hailed by the entire country as the greatest mind of his time. He was a humanitarian and political thinker, of such foresight, in my opinion, to be considered our greatest leader since Churchill. He'd been courting danger since his Loxton days, by campaigning relentlessly for greater transparency in government. Unusually, he rose through the ranks by the grace of the people, not the establishment. He had a touch of 'Robin Hood' about him, which gave him an endearing quality. It was his years of back-to-back battles that made him complacent to danger, that was to be his undoing."

"But he was disgraced, when it was proven he had been accepting back-handers, and all of the money had come from the pensions and charities of the most needy."

"You, the fickle public, believed every morsel of scandal that was served up. What you didn't do is question the validity, source, or motive behind the information."

"I happen to question the authenticity of most of what laughingly passes for the news these days," I answered strongly, in my defence. "What about the evidence given by his long-time friend and confident, former Prime Minister

Lord Elbury? There was no acting there. I've never seen a man of such reserve, quite so angry and upset."

"Precisely, If the allegations had been true, Lord Elbury, a man of integrity, would have happily given him up, despite their long friendship. He doesn't come from a family of sentimentalists. I believe, he was angry because, he was being forced to do something against his better judgement. It's my belief he knew his friend to be innocent and that's why he showed such emotion."

"But if he knew Sir Geringham was innocent, why didn't he stand up for him, rather than publicly denounce him?"

"Because, Baxter, obviously there were greater weights brought to bear."

Pilgrim seemed momentarily lost in her own thoughts, but then continued.

"In short, we need do nothing, to already be marked for some sudden demise."

I was now thoroughly worried, seeing the look of inevitability in her eyes.

"You're exaggerating?" I whispered.

"No, I am not, and you should know that, before making any further decisions to pursue this."

I was not surprised, only disappointed, by the fact I had disguised this information from myself, with all the recent extraneous activity I had allowed to shroud my thoughts. It was obvious, Pilgrim travelled in very different circles from mine. Circles, that meant she had access to the most intimate and sensitive information. The excitement of our adventure had clouded the very real and evident fact, you didn't jump on and off private planes at a moment's notice, without earning the right to do so, and I had the unpleasant feeling the cost of such a life-style was inevitably high. Quietness descended upon us, as I tried to absorb the potential repercussions given by her warning.

"We are the good guys – aren't we?" I asked tentatively.

"That depends on whom you ask, but in the old-fashioned sense of the word, yes we are."

She fell silent. I understood what she was waiting for. She was waiting for me to come to a decision regarding my continuance, which I would not be able to retract, once I rose from the table.

I was resolute; not with bravado or ignorance, as to my current predicament; but with the conviction of any persons right to be free.

"Then you should know, Pilgrim, I do not take lightly to being intimidated by these Titans. Indeed, I take it as my sworn duty to stop those who seek to harm me in any way."

She smiled at me and raised her glass.

"Lets pay a visit to Switzerland."

"No time like the present," I said with more confidence than I was feeling.

Before we could rise, Monsieur de Long-champ swooped down upon us, and very carefully placed a small brown card-board box, no bigger than a credit card wallet, before us.

"Une cadeau, was just delivered for you, Madame Pilgrim," our host announced, lingering no doubt to discover its contents.

Pilgrim and I, looked at one another, and then back to the box. As she reached out to pick it up, I couldn't help but let out an involuntary warning.

"Stop, it could be a bomb."

"I like your new-found cautiousness, but, I don't think so. We were obviously followed; in which case we could have been dealt with far more easily, if this was from an adversary," Pilgrim answered.

Upon removing the outer layer, a small silver box was revealed, bearing a coat of arms, of a fire breathing dragon defending a castle. Engraved underneath it, was the Latin, 'Sans Dieu Rien'.

"It must have been sent by you know who," I whispered, not wishing to be overheard by our host.

"It is Vercingétorix!" Monsieur de Long-champ enthused proudly: "It is the, how you say, the sign of his house."

"Who is Vercingétorix?" I asked.

"He was a great French leader and defender of his people. He refused to kneel before Caesar and Rome."

His curiosity satisfied, he moved to another table of diners.

Opening the lid very gingerly, we were both surprised to see it almost filled to the brim with a white crystalline powder, which shimmered and sparkled in the light of the table-candle.

"What is it, cocaine, heroin?" I asked.

"Neither."

Pilgrim placed the box on the table between us, as we both studied it, puzzled by the contents.

"There must be something else," Pilgrim pondered aloud.

I reached for the cardboard lid; to my surprise, wedged inside, was a note, hastily scribbled in French. Pilgrim translated.

Mademoiselle Pilgrim

The inevitable has occurred, and I cannot say I am remorseful. I deeply regret my naivety, but contained within this box is the means to my redemption – the antidote to the Black Pearls. You are the only one, who can save my eternal soul. Be cautious when moving the contents of the box, as the rarest pearl, the only one in existence, is contained in it. All my research on it, has been destroyed by my own hand. It works in the same fashion as the N.E.G, with the ability to neutralise it. I ask only one thing, if it is within your power to pursue it; that you restore my family name.

San Dieu Rien   Bonnin

With the gentlest of movements, Pilgrim rocked the box in her hand causing the white powder to fall away, as an incandescent red pearl erupted to the surface.

We both held our breath. I was bewitched by the asterism projected from that perfectly luminous orb. The fact this remarkable and unique structure could potentially be at the nucleus of our specie's survival was beyond my level of comprehension at that point. My mind balked at the idea. This pearl's importance in our immediate future, could

118

hardly be more critical. And yet, despite the enormity of what we were involved with, it was the small and mundane matters that flooded my mind, and therein lay my mental salvation.

I'd decided, if this was to be my last meal, then I was certainly in the right place. I made a mental note that I would think of it in my final moments.

Closing the lid of the box, Pilgrim stood abruptly.

"We need to get going," she said, "but first, I'm going to contact an old friend of mine. You'll excuse me, Baxter. I'll pick you up outside shortly."

With that cryptic dismissal, she left.

When we arrived in Geneva Switzerland, less than four hours later, the sky was dark and brooding. I had previously spent a small amount of time in Switzerland with my ex-employer, Mr. Stenmore, Chairman of London's unique Crisid bank. As usual, when Mr. Stenmore was forced to leave London, he had been on the trail of some antique automaton and a Swiss one at that. For a remarkably quick witted man, his isolation from the rest of the world was baffling. With all the money and prestige to visit some of the more interesting places and people on the planet; he preferred to work, with the same religious fervour reserved for Benedictine monks, within those cold stone walls of Crisid bank. He had always been a courteous employer; just the minimum that good manners demanded. Not friendly, hospitable, or particularly caring. Perhaps that was why he had such an affinity with mechanical objects. Thinking back on Mrs. Cotterill's words, I wondered if there might be more to my present situation than met my eye. The coincidental probability of her knowing of Mr. Stenmore and me; although not unlikely, given the conservative number of competent valets and small circle of people inhabiting that upper echelon; caused me momentary consternation. Still, I waited to see if anything, either by person, location or reference, came up, to push my curiosity over the edge to abject concern.

Now over twelve hundred feet above sea level, the air was cold enough to exhibit plumes from our warm breathes. Their autumn was decidedly chilly. Time had stopped somewhere along our journey, and I had neither the strength nor inclination to find out what ungodly hour it was. Pilgrim had stated, upon observing me earlier during our brief flight.

"Over the next few days you're going to feel time, either standing still, or rushing past. You should know this is not time, as there is no such thing. What you will experience, is your personal ability to absorb events, some of which you will, and others, depending on their content, you may never truly suffer. I'm sharing this truth with you, so you can recognise it for what it is…when the time comes. You've heard of people who are in a car crash, saying the crash seemed to happen in slow motion. Or, they say it happened so quickly, they can only remember snippets, even though they were conscious throughout. All I'm saying is, be accepting of yourself. We are moving into uncharted territory, and I'm not sure what to expect. My ability to move forward through difficult events is greater than yours. With time and experience, you will be able to …"

"Be able to…what, be happier after a car crash?" I had uttered with resignation.

"Something like that."

After that brief pep-talk, I suppose knowing the correct time had no bearing on the matter at hand.

The starlit night gave the voluminous clouds a silvery halo in contrast to their black centres. Following my gaze, Pilgrim looked up.

"Looks like snow," she said, with the faintest foreboding in her voice.

As before, we were met by a car, which this time circled out to us on the iced tarmac. Sleep deprivation, or a sense of my own impending mortality, was beginning to take its toll, and I felt slightly disorientated, causing me to say.

"I'm concerned about Mrs. Cotterill."

Pilgrim didn't utter a word, but I knew she'd heard me. Her steely nerve moved me forward.

Our car took us to a substantial house overlooking Lake Geneva. By the time we'd arrived outside a large house, the snow had begun to fall in large soft flakes that settled and began to cast its white shroud on everything it touched.

We didn't knock or ring at the pillared entrance, as the gates whispered open automatically. We walked through and began to follow a gravel drive to the front of a large austere looking mansion, where neither light, nor any person could be seen. We had barely started, when we were met suddenly by two large black dogs, that quietly and with purpose ran their noses obtrusively from our lower torso to our shoes. Apparently satisfied, they escorted us to the entrance. Occasionally, they'd looked back at us, in a manner that made me feel decidedly vulnerable. At the large ornate door the dogs fell back.

We were met by Mr. Grey; as Pilgrim addressed him. 'Grey by name and grey by nature', I'd thought. With his steel-grey hair swept back and neatly cut, his sombre dove-grey eyes, and a melancholy disposition, I couldn't imagine how this person figured into the whole scheme of things. Pilgrim's raised chin was enough to convince me, our journey to his front-door was necessary.

"This had better be good," he grumbled dismissively, turning and holding a lantern high, as he walked down the unlit hallway.

Pilgrim answered curtly.

"I tell you what; you don't waste my time, and I won't waste yours." There was no mistaking the bite in her words, even though they were barely whispered.

The whole atmosphere felt as tight as wax. I thought my best step forward was to keep silent and observe. We followed, Mr. Grey, into a large room laid bare to the walls, apart from four chairs and four large candles throwing their light up from the floor. I flippantly thought, apparently someone had forgotten to pay the electricity bill. I followed suit and sat down. Who was the fourth chair for?

"Who's joining us?" Pilgrim asked impatiently.

"I have extended an invitation to our mutual acquaintance; as there is no point in us being covert about this."

Seeing the anger flare in her eyes, he added.

"Your safety is assured."

"But yours is not," she replied menacingly.

"I would rather incur your wrath," he stated firmly.

My personal feeling on the matter, was that he greatly overestimated Pilgrim's leniency. This man obviously didn't know her as well as me. Even given our short time together, I had witnessed her ability to become totally detached and without feeling. Who knows what one is capable of inflicting on a loved one, or friend, let alone a person she evidently had little time for, during such states? No, I saw them as combative adversaries, and certainly not friends.

"Our *acquaintances* are close-by?" Pilgrim enquired.

"Please don't waste my time with rhetorical questions. I heard you were more…insightful than that," he finished, with a smug look on his face.

Immediately, Pilgrim's face became blank, and her eyes began eerily to illuminate. I sat rooted to the spot, frozen, as I heard a gasp from Mr Grey, as if he were choking. Something had been disturbed in Pilgrim, and was now emerging from its slumber. Its evidence was clear, not only in her eyes, but also by the thickened atmosphere in the room. Seeing a brief look of panic in his eyes, she said.

"You know, Mr. Grey, it strikes me that your superiors don't think a lot of you. Indeed, they must consider you expendable. Otherwise, why would they have placed you in this precarious situation?"

Doubt was borne on his face, but either to his credit, or his folly, and I plumed for the latter, he gasped.

"What is it you want to know?"

"Seedertraume; is it worth our time?"

"Yes, but not at this juncture."

123

I couldn't look at Pilgrim, nor did I want to. My whole body felt completely unwell. I had difficulty in suppressing an overwhelming feeling of nausea. I noticed the adverse effect it was having on Mr Grey. His mouth was open, and he was taking quick light breathes, and frequently licking his lips, as if he had spent too much time under a blistering sun.

"Whats at Seedertraume?" I managed to ask.

"Mr. Grey, would you care to enlighten my colleague?" Pilgrim asked, her voice inducing a calm compliance.

There had been some inner struggle before, Mr. Grey began to relay information, he was evidently struggling to withhold.

"Seedertraume is located on the Swiss south east shore of the Rhine. It is the Titans' pre-eminent research facility. It spans fifteen square kilometres, and includes an autonomous water and energy supply, with its own underground factories and workforce."

Pilgrim leaned forward, her concentration focused on Mr. Grey; who was now perspiring heavily.

"You are keeping something from me Mr. Grey, please tell me what it is?"

"They are preparing for you," he grunted, before collapsing onto the floor, unconscious.

Without warning, Pilgrim rose, and moved toward the door.

"Baxter," she whispered.

I automatically answered her summons. I was stunned and shocked by what had just occurred. As I followed her back down the path, I became conscious the dogs were not following us. I looked back at the house to see them strangely lain down, cowering. Turning back to look at Pilgrim, I witnessed for the first time a glimpse of her true nature.

She had continued down the path but must have felt me instinctively stop behind her. She turned slowly toward me, and in doing so, time slowed, her hair rose, swirling and lifting from her shoulders in slow motion. Her eyes were iridescent erasing her other features by their brightness. Her mouth parted, as if about to speak, but no words came, just a deafening roar entered my head. I felt on the verge of collapse. In self-preservation I gave a strangled cry.

"Pilgrim," before I gave a final yelp, "Neath!"

I watched in horror, as she fought to regain her composure. Feeling her mental grip on me subside, I took a deep inhalation, as her eyes resumed their natural hue. Staring at her in shock, she held her finger to her lips.

"Shh."

There was such a devastating look of sadness on her face, I immediately felt sorry for her. Whatever had just happened, she didn't seem to have any control over it. I blurted out, in fear.

"What the bloody hell just happened."

Her anxious expression changed to one of resignation.

"I'm sorry Baxter. I never meant to harm you."

"You…you almost killed me."

"You're alive. That in it's self tells me I was right about you."

"Right about me?" I bellowed.

"Yes, that part of me trusts you, and that's why you're alive. You have the capacity to absorb my, *events*. I'm just hoping you're also able to now move beyond them. I need you."

I can't explain it, but I walked slowly toward her, in acceptance.

It wasn't until we were back in the car, and Pilgrim had spoken curtly to the driver, that we pulled away into the night. We had been driving for approximately half an hour, when the car-phone rang. Answering it, the driver listened. Shortly after he'd hung-up, he spoke over his shoulder, to inform us a visitor had arrived at the Palais du Lac, our hotel and destination, and would be waiting for us. At this point, I did want to know what the time was. I felt it must be very early in the morning, as every bone and muscle in my body was begging for a reprieve from the relentless stress. Finally my nerve broke.

"With the greatest respect would you mind telling me what the hell is next?" I hissed.

Pilgrim seemed to be elsewhere, and it was a couple of moments before she answered.

"I'm not normally so unobservant, and for that I apologise."

"Unobservant, I don't follow?"

"Mr. Grey was decoyed to slow us down," she paused, before continuing, "he belongs to that small set of privileged people who try to do the right thing, but are easily swayed by power and money. He is neither foe, nor ally. We're now up against a syndicate of people, who's existence

126

never enters the public domain, and therefore, will never reach the public consciousness; the *Titans*. And I need to…"

Here is where Pilgrim hesitated in her summation.

That was the third time I had witnessed the physical change in her eye colour. Her blue eyes became shadowed, and when they cleared, they seemed to have taken on a bright hue, a bordering luminescence that formed a halo around her black pupil. It was a worrying and mesmerizing occurrence; as I listened and learnt about the Titans.

I recall, after asking her if that was the 'car crash' she had analogised about, if she had any control over these ominous changes. She described her experiences of them matter of factly. She described it as, an ability to access a level of her conscious mind that could open out, and reveal to her, people and events, as if she were a witness, and she'd added, if she chose, she could also become a part of their reality. It wasn't as if I could have said anything at the time; my mind had moved from exhaustion to numbness. She stated.

"I don't understand it myself. As far as I know, I've never seen these people or places before. What I do know, is that its triggered when I'm angry…its definitely not pretty if my life is threatened."

She'd shocked me to my core, making me fear not only for my own life, but also for my soul. I retreated to my thoughts.

I'd observed her. Her eyes wide open, staring ahead. She was seeing something other than her surroundings. She had continued in describing the Titans. They were comprised of the intellectual elite of the elite. Their secret governance of our world could be traced back through

127

millennia. Pilgrim gave me their condensed history, as she currently knew it.

"A Trust, as it was once described; never has a title been so debased. They are the twelve greatest minds of their time, each with eleven disciples with an estimated average IQ well in excess of the brightest known. Each one of the Titan leaders is harnessed and systematically replaced after mortal loss. They've used their accumulated wealth and power, from centuries of industry, to create a new race with exceptional mental capabilities, for what I now believe, has the sole purpose of eradicating our current one, their ultimate goal. A persons physicality is of no interest to them. All they covet, is higher cerebral functioning. This pernicious unitary, of each natural resource on the planet, exert their influence to meet their own ends with anonymity and impunity."

She had turned to me, and continued with contempt laced through her words.

"Unlimited privilege breeds insatiable ambition; mortality should be our deliverance, but these people do not recognise their end. They prepare for it, by grooming their successor. The Titan's name, as they are known by today, was given to them upon their murder of Caesar; his primary assassins numbered twelve. In truth their history is far earlier and more, bloody. Cleopatra and Socrates, for example, were both rumoured to have held the title during their lifetime. I've conjectured each Titan operates and governs not by country, but by those factions that ultimately hold the greatest influence over humanity; natural resources. Their control permeates through everything; through political leadership, global economics, scientific research and the governance of the basic elements that go to sustain life for us on this earth. There can't be much remaining to shock God."

"My minor intellect thanks you for believing there is a God. I'd hate to think our future lay in their hands."

"There is an omnipresent consciousness, Baxter, and if we've learnt anything, it's that our future lies in our own hands. I believe we are all of that special matter, and when we learn to think and act collectively, we will evolve as a species. But for the moment…"

Her depth of sadness, so profound, sudden and unexpected, plunged me into despair. If Pilgrim was despondent, there was reason for us all to tremble.

"If the majority of us are hard -working and law-abiding people, who know the difference between right and wrong, well then, it gives us a greater advantage against these people," I stated.

"You're optimistic, keeping in mind, even if we were to show to the world the true ambitions of the Titans, nobody would believe it, especially given their manipulation of the world's media?"

"There is safety in numbers," I stated.

"Not if you're a Caracas slum dweller," she pointed out, "Their involvement in this matter has taken me off-guard. I hadn't thought to come across their interests so soon after…the last time."

"You're certain it is the Titans?"

"Yes, I'm certain."

As tired and worn, as she must have been; I admired her ability to think more clearly than me.

"These people; you believe they were connected with Dr Bonnin?" I asked, exhausted.

"The Titans can act autonomously. That is one of their strengths. I believe in Dr Bonnin's case, only one Titan was involved directly. Dr Bonnin's point of contact would be merely a disciple, of a collective of eleven people who serve that Titan. The disciples are extremely competent and not to be underestimated. Its my understanding they wouldn't recognise their leader if they were introduced. How far this secrecy trickles down the chain of command I have no idea, but I wouldn't be surprised if they didn't know another member of their group. There's nothing so trite as a special ring, or handshake to identify them, none that I'm aware of anyway."

"How much worse can it be, than the distinct possibility of an untimely death?"

"It's less of a possibility and more of a certainty. Killing a person is simpler than you think, especially for a supposedly sane person who manipulates the law to suit their own personal rule book, and whose forbearers wrote it. On the other hand, if one needed to extract information, the process becomes infinitely more intricate and the methods more creative. There are people, well respected and highly acclaimed, who willing sign up, performing some of the most monstrous and diabolical acts perpetrated this side of hell. Fortunately, it's a niche market."

I didn't know if she was trying to be funny, but the blood in my veins felt like ice. Whoever these people were I would meet them head on. I couldn't do less, and my heightened sense of self-preservation and the sudden rush of adrenalin, only allowed for the single thought of defeating the Titans. Pilgrim read my inexorable purpose accurately,

"The object of the game Baxter is to get to the end, first and alive."

"I fully intend to."

The question that had been burning at the forefront of my brain since she began this shocking oratory was, how did she know so much about them? There was obviously some history between them and I had to know what it was.

"I think now, is as good a time as any to tell me how you know so much about them."

"Because of what I am – they've shown an interest."

I waited.

"There was a time, when they approached me to join them. I refused."

"You'll forgive me, if this sounds rude; but you can't even pay your car-tax on time."

Pilgrim laughed quietly, adding, "They didn't want me for my stunning intellect."

"I see."

We both fell silent, as the images of Pilgrim strapped to a gurney leapt into my mind. I said with all seriousness.

"I'm not sure what help I'll be to you if it ever comes down to that. What I do know is I'll do everything I can to prevent it."

Little did I know that those words were to be prophetic.

Pilgrims spirits seemed to immediately rally, as she stated.

131

"Then I congratulate you. You are the man for the job. By the way, I've had to call in reinforcements. I've told them about the N.E.G."

"Who is *them*?"

"'H', to be precise. He'll decide the best person for us to liaise with. The less you know about intermediaries the less you can give up."

When we arrived in the late evening at the hotel there was only a skeleton staff on duty. We walked through the sumptuous, dimmed lobby to the reception desk and were greeted by a young woman in her early twenties, with her hair tied back, and a dark skirt suit that appeared slightly too large for her slim frame. She seemed relieved to see us, and I immediately thought of our guest.

"If you would like to accompany me to the salon, Madame Pilgrim and Monsieur Baxter, your visitor has been waiting for your arrival," she finished, drained by her best attempt at a clipped English accent and correct grammar, which her native Swiss-tongue could articulate at such an early hour.

We stepped down into the elegant reception salon where, to my stunned surprise, the Deputy Prime Minister of England, Mr. Nigel Chandler, sat waiting. He rose from his chair to greet us, dressed in a dark suit with a pristine white cuff-linked shirt with some insinuation to a nautical theme, he smoked a Metropolitan cigar. As the aroma of the finest tobacco wafted past, I was helplessly transported to the front-door of Nat Sherman in New York. I must be tired; I hadn't smoked in a very long time, still that cigar smelled mighty fine.

Judging by the remainder of his cigar he must have been waiting for some time. He was well into middle-age with wiry hair, greying at the temples, and cut admonishingly short. His face, although clean shaven, was set grim and serious behind gold-rimmed bifocals. Sitting back down, he gave a strained smile to Pilgrim. His involvement didn't take any stretch of the imagination, but why here?

"You've heard?" Pilgrim stated quietly.

"Bad news travels fast. 'H' contacted me four hours ago, he brought me up to speed on this N.E.G business," he replied solemnly. Turning to me he said, "I don't believe we've met before." Lifting his chin, he observed my face through the bottom part of his glasses, as he continued, "you must hold a unique set of credentials Mr. Baxter. I'm not aware of a single occasion when Ms Pilgrim, has sought assistance."

Knowing, Chandler would have been made familiar with my unremarkable history to date, along with a list of my colourful ex-employers; I could see he was intrigued. No one had ever found me intriguing before, I was quietly pleased.

Pilgrim offered the smallest of smiles, saying assuredly,

"Mr. Baxter has proven to be invaluable to me during the arduous hours of the last few days and has kindly agreed to help me."

My heart soared at her commendation, that is until a sobering thought crossed my mind; would I be alive, to be congratulated.

Chandler arched an eyebrow in my direction. His curiosity satisfied, he called over the night-porter.

"I believe a night-cap is in order; Ms. Pilgrim?" Chandler asked.

"Taittinger Champagne Rosé," she requested.

I politely declined; on the grounds I was already mentally drained. I certainly didn't want anything in addition to cloud my judgement. As seemed to be my present role, I sat quietly and tried to absorb everything that passed between them. Chandler began.

"You realise my presence here must be kept entirely between ourselves. At no time, either now or in the future, can you divulge anything that is stated or implied by me.

Before he could finish, Pilgrim had held up a hand to halt his earnest speech. She clarified.

"You may rest assured your trust is not misplaced. This situation is a serious one. You yourself must acknowledge, if you harboured any doubts as to my abilities, we wouldn't be having this conversation," she finished quietly, never taking her eyes from his. Folding her hands on her lap and leaning back into her chair, and seeing he had relaxed somewhat, she said. "You understand the risk you've incurred simply by being here?"

"Naturally, is the Prime Minister implicated in any way?" he asked quietly.

"I have no reason to believe the Prime Minister has any knowledge of the N.E.G, and I very much doubt he knows more than was inferred, in order to ascertain his ignorance on the matter. Therefore, any involvement by him is entirely unnecessary," she stated succinctly.

"Then we'll keep this between ourselves?" he said seriously, continuing, "very well than, tell me what you've discovered."

It was at that moment the porter returned with our drinks and a whisper from Pilgrim was the prompt to send him scurrying off, I hoped, for some sandwiches. After a long sip and an expectant look from Chandler, Pilgrim gave the smallest smile and began one of the most frightening speeches it has ever been my misfortune to hear.

"From what we've learnt so far, the N.E.G measures intelligence on a sub-atomic level within the brain. We know this is one of its functions. Another is to kill, by *switching-off* those that don't make the grade. The N.E.G, which becomes active when it comes into contact with glucose, is distributed through water. It was trialled in Caracas, with devastating results."

The atmosphere had suddenly become leaden and tasteless. The gravity of Pilgrim's words rang heavily for mere mortals, until its resonance made me numb. She continued.

"I've given considerable thought, giving those I know are behind it, to who the N.E.G is aimed at. Although, I have to say, even for me it's a reach. But I can't ignore the conclusion I've come to, and that's why you're here."

"I know you're not given to hysteria, or exaggeration…so, lets have it," he breathed.

"If I were to say the *Titans* are behind this, would their name have any meaning to you?"

The ashen pallor that diffused across Chandler's face was confirmation he'd heard of them. Leaning forward, he took a large swig of his brandy.

"As a young man in government, rising through the ranks, I heard a rumour of them, too far-fetched to be taken seriously. When I became Deputy Prime Minister, a brief conversation with a person I respect and trust, made me reconsider. But with no tangible proof over the years, I'd dismissed the story."

"They exist," she stated matter-of-factly.

"You're certain?" The tone of his voice sounded as if his worst fears where being confirmed, "and you know they're behind the N.E.G?"

"Without question; as you've heard, they have unlimited wealth and power, and the single mindedness needed to create the N.E.G," she finished coldly.

There was a look of disbelief on Chandler's face, as if he didn't want to face the truth. I couldn't blame him; knowledge of this magnitude, would make his professional position virtually intolerable.

"I'm not entirely convinced. Whats their motive?" he asked, clearly struggling with the idea such an organisation could be influencing vast global economies anonymously.

"This business in Caracas with the N.E.G was only the precursor to something that can only be described as a war."

Chandler pursed his lips and said.

"Still not convinced. Nothing's been proven. You have tangible evidence they were responsible for Caracas…and why a war…what kind of war?"

"We have the N.E.G and it will prove their role in Caracas."

He was obviously stunned, as Pilgrim continued.

"Now you're going to need to use your logic, accept the Titans exist, and imagine their world. A world without borders, races, or separate economies; that is the world they inhabit and operate within. This *war,* which is upon us, has been millennia in the making. It is arguably the first real *holy-war* because it will be against every living person. There has never been a time like this in humanity's history that our species has faced annihilation on such an unprecedented scale. The great plagues, the Black Death for example, which killed twenty-five million people, and which I now believe the Titans were responsible for; was a necessary step to attain their goal and for what is about to come."

Chandler swallowed hard and kept his nerve. I had to give him some respect for that.

"Notwithstanding your unique insight on this matter; I need you to base the information you give me, only on what can be substantiated," Chandler said.

"I understand why you'd think that necessary. However, I would ask you to consider this, not as a leap of imagination, but as a rational and feasible plan of theirs."

Chandler sat back in his chair staring contemplatively at her. Pilgrim continued.

"I believe the N.E.G will be deployed, en-mass in the UK."

Time held its breath. Chandler's voice faltered as he said.

"Why us?"

"Its pure mathematics. We know the Titans covert mental agility, to what end, I've yet to discover. The indisputable first law that applies to every living thing on the planet is survival and we're masters at it. We're all familiar with those times in history when nations have turned on one another and human collateral has been high. We've always assumed war is about gaining, or retaking territory, and clearly for the leaders of the time it was. I'm asking you now to consider that behind these conflicts there was an alternative motive, orchestrated by a more malevolent strategist. Overall, each war equates to one person in three being killed; that's an historical fact. If we're to examine this extrapolation, this thinning of the combative herd it's; resulted in a more mentally adept and resilient gene-pool. It's survival of the fittest, both physically and mentally. As Great Britain tops the historical list for engaging in wars, we're the obvious target. It stands to reason we've inherited and evolved, as a nation, a very unique strain of genome."

Chandler was about to raise an objection before, Pilgrim cut him off.

"Think in terms of centuries. I'm not saying we're war-mongers…although, it is an obvious and necessary means to maintain and self-perpetuate our mental distillation…my point is, we're on the threshold of a new consciousness, which I believe has been honed deliberately. Think about the historical steps. You can't get past the fact, not just in war but with any perceived threat to our way of life, we act against it collectively, as a united people, without centralised direction. When we go in, we *don't* go in *just* to conquer, but more interestingly to *assimilate*. It's the behavioural intelligence behind the survival and dominance of a superorganism."

"Without wishing to ruin my chances for re-election, how do you explain the idiots?"

"You're not thinking collectively, Deputy Prime Minister. Some of those *idiots* put you in power…how stupid are they looking now?" Pilgrim said.

My own mortality was pinioning my ability to comprehend the viability of a centuries old plan that might achieve its goal in my life-time. As I struggled with such an unbelievable concept it suddenly crossed my mind, I was going to be the N.E.Gs first victim.

Chandler thought aloud.

"The N.E.G exists; its use is to streamline this gnome…for what purpose?"

"As the Americans would say, this is not the Titans first rodeo."

"Meaning?" Chandler asked.

"They've had plenty of practice. What their ultimate objective is…I can't be sure…biocybernetics…who can say. They'll separate the wheat from the chaff, enter stage left, the N.E.G."

Chandler, smiled, but didn't laugh. I thought that was telling. There was a pause before he stated.

"The age of mass-domination is past. There isn't a civilised nation on Earth that needs to achieve that goal."

'We're not discussing the machinations of civilisation. You're referring to physical domination; I am not. This isn't about the most mentally educated. This is about the Titans elevating the brain-power of a few.

"Mental domination…its preposterous, and serves no viable purpose."

"It does if you're a Titan."

Silence, momentarily engulfed us. Chandler sat up, grinding his cigar into the ashtray. He began steadily.

"Correct me if get this wrong. You're saying the Titans, have spent centuries refining a genome that's inherent within a small population, to what…take over the world?" he stated incredulously.

"Now, that is preposterous," Pilgrim said, adding, "it's not to take over the world. That's the kind of secular thinking of a mortal."

"For what reason than?"

"Truthfully, I don't know. I can postulate, but that's all. The N.E.G performs a very specific function and we've established a match for its use."

"*You've*, established a match," Chandler corrected

"You can't ignore the facts. We've evolved as a people. The acquisition of money, or territory is not what drives us now. We're the proverbial guinea-pig. Our particular genome is about to be measured, and for those found wanting, they'll die."

"Impossible, you can't have people dropping dead in their thousands, or millions."

"As we're not in the age of the Black-plague, when ignorance and fear would have cancelled out reasoning; its far more likely those found wanting, will be rendered sterile, wiping-out their genetic line."

There was a pause before Chandler burst out laughing and shook his head, saying.

"Please forgive me. Whilst, against my better judgement, I find your argument somewhat plausible, I cannot take it seriously."

I'd been listening intently and was willing to follow Pilgrims logic. I spoke up.

"It might go some way to explaining, why, we shipped-out thousands-upon-thousands to the penal colonies in America and Australia,"

"You can't justify a theory based on approximately two percent of the population." Chandler pointed out to me.

"True, but it wasn't a decision based on economics. The cost of transportation alone exceeded any which could have been spent for reform. Makes you wonder where the money came from at the time and who was behind the idea."

"It may smack of a *cleansing,* in your vocabulary, but any country has to have law abiding citizens in order to prosper."

I quickly added.

"An ex-employer of mine once pointed out that, the individual GNP per capita of both the United States and Australia, far exceed that of the UK. For a bunch of *undesirables*, I'd say they're doing pretty well. There had to be an alternate reason."

"Lets say for the sake of argument, the UK gnome has been groomed, cleansed, however you want to put it…to achieve a Titan goal; it still doesn't explain, why?"

141

"If I knew the answer to that, I'd tell you. I'm not expecting you to do anything other than pay attention. If, you become aware of a sudden drop in birth-rates that cannot be attributable you're to contact me immediately. Whether you believe it or not, we're at war."

"What are you proposing?" Chandler asked, clearly exhausted by the conversation.

Baxter and I will work this from our end. As you might imagine the Titans have an interest in me and I'm going to exploit that and hopefully run them to ground."

I mentally took note of two things; firstly, she didn't mention the antidote, and secondly, she didn't mention the seventh pearl.

"Any credence I give to this will be instantly dismissed by the Cabinet. I'll be lucky if they don't have me sectioned on the spot." Chandler stated wearily.

"As far as I can predict the N.E.G will leave behind, in one generation, only those carrying the genome strain in its purest form. This leads me to believe, the Titans are looking for something in particular. The Titans represent a real threat against the human-race at this particular time in our evolution and they must be stopped."

The Deputy Prime Minister had aged before our eyes.

"I'll take whatever precautions I can. If what you say is proven true, the Titans have underestimated our response to such a threat. Our war will be for the self- preservation of diversity, with deadly consequences for the aggressor."

I quickly quashed the thought that Chandler could belong to the Titans. I trusted Pilgrim's choice.

He paused, "there's something else you should know." He wavered in speaking and the hesitation in his words and manner made my gut harden.

"It concerns your housekeeper, Mrs. Cotterill. She has been found dead."

"How?"

The question fell from Pilgrim's lips like the dull thud of a heavy stone.

"Her death is being treated as murder. Given our discussion in all likelihood the Titans were trying to trace your whereabouts. I'm afraid there is no mistake. Your name was carved into her back."

"Then it has begun," she uttered ominously.

CHAPTER EIGHT

Our return to England was swift and grave. Words were inadequate. With nothing but the incessant hum of the jet engines, I did a lot of thinking. I recalled, directly after our meeting, watching Pilgrim stand up and shake the Deputy Prime Minister's hand, promising he would hear from her. I remembered following her out of the hotel-lobby and toward the car; what happened after that, was just shapes and muffled sounds. My bravado at the restaurant, an age before, had vanished and the cold reality of my situation was staring me in the face. I understood because of my involvement, my fate now rested solely with me. I would find those directly responsible for the unspeakable murder of Mrs. Cotterill. As if listening into my thoughts, Pilgrim finally broke the silence.

"I guess you were thrown in the deep end, Baxter. I've had blood on my hands before, but none I so bitterly regret as Mrs. Cotterill. She was an innocent and to bring her into this matter tells me several things of importance about our immediate adversary."

"Like what, that they're unhinged, psychotic lunatics," I gasped, angered by the senseless violence that had been inflicted on Mrs. Cotterill.

"What intrigues me is why the Titans should fear me."

"Have you met yourself; you're scary."

"We make an interesting combo. That side of me…the scary side…doesn't normally discriminate when it comes out, I think it likes you."

"Lucky me," I said unconvincingly.

"Yes, I have abilities, but I also bleed like everyone else. If I'm such a threat, why haven't they killed me?"

"Have they tried?"

"They tried strapping me to a gurney once…that didn't work-out too well…for them."

"Its obvious, they're after your DNA."

"That's what I thought, at first, but there wasn't a needle or knife in sight."

"They were learning about you."

"So, they've established I've got a temper."

"Yeah…you may want to do something about that."

"My question still stands; it means they know something about me, that I don't know about myself. Whatever it is, Baxter, I swear to you I don't know."

"They know you have some rare gifts, things I've not come across in real life…until now."

"I've never exhibited my abilities to anyone…who'd remember. You're the first person to witness those changes and not be effected by them."

"I was effected, believe me."

"There are only two people alive who know I can see things, but they just think I'm some sort of medium. The rest…," she finished exasperated.

"The rest; what about Mr. Grey?" I asked confused.

145

"Mr. Grey will wake up and not be able to explain what happened. He won't be able to remember my influence on him, they never do," she stated matter-of-factly.

I didn't ask what she kept hidden, partly because I didn't especially want to know. My mind was bursting at the seams, trying to collate all the information I'd had to absorb over the last few days, and because one look at her made me shut-up. She was thinking and that was definitely worth every millisecond of my silence.

Just before we touched-down she laid her hand across the sleeve of my jacket. I'd been so lost in thought I almost jumped.

Pilgrim had become quiet but when she spoke her words wafted toward me, calming my mind.

"Baxter, we're going to L'améthyste, where we'll freshen-up. There should be a parcel waiting there for you. I've taken rooms for us, until we can find alternative accommodation. I can't live back at Bow Lane."

"But what if they come after us at L'améthyste?"

My mind was racing. How could we possibly protect ourselves, given we didn't even know who to look out for?

"They'll come. I've requested a particular room which is designed to meet our needs. Only one door, in and out."

I was aghast and frightened at the same time. Events had moved forward and were well beyond my control. I welcomed the calm Pilgrim was applying, and allowed it to descend upon me, like an enveloping shroud, its cool fingers smoothing my brow with the lightest touch of her voice, willing my heart to beat slower. I allowed my breathing to return to normal, for me to sit back into my seat and to my great relief, feel less anxious. I looked across to Pilgrim who was looking right back at me, the slightest of smiles on her face.

"We're not going to have to kill these people, are we?" I asked with some hesitation.

I needed to know how bad our situation was going to become. I had to mentally prepare myself, perhaps for a fight to the death. Just the words in my head seemed absolutely ludicrous.

"Only in self- defence."

This time when we entered L'améthyste, we headed straight for the front desk, where Pilgrim was handed a small, thick envelope. We were then escorted by an efficient bell-boy to the door of an inconspicuous elevator tucked discreetly away behind reception and bearing the L'améthyste coat-of-arms. This was not the elevator I'd seen used by members. Looking at the elevator buttons, I noticed they didn't rise above our current floor, but descended to three different floors below. I felt strangely uncomfortable as the bell-boy looked everywhere else, except at the two of us. Suddenly, the elevator-door slid open and we were asked to step in, unaccompanied. With a swish, the door slid closed and we began our descent. One floor, two floors, and finally at the third and last we came to a soft halt. The door opened into a wide corridor completely lined in stainless-steel. Stepping out, the feeling under-foot was not one of a solid floor. I followed Pilgrim to a large stainless-steel door at its end. As we approached, the door opened, closing noiselessly behind us. Lighting recessed in the walls, flashed to life, drenching the interior in cold, white light. The entire space was devoid of a single thing, but felt dangerous and oppressive. With no heating, our warm breath showed within its interior. The room was approximately fifty feet long by fifty feet wide and about twenty feet in height. It was the most extraordinary place I had ever entered. The walls, floor and ceiling were made of stainless steel. A thin central grid ran down the floor's centre and I looked-up at water sprinklers dotted above. In the far corner, I noticed a stainless-steel door of a size and purpose unknown to me. It was situated at waist height, about four feet in width and no more than two feet in height and ran flush to the wall.

"Here, take this, it's from the Major." Pilgrim tore off the end of the large envelope, tipping a gun out into my hand.

It was the perfect weight and size. After just a few lessons, I felt competent to handle the basics. I clicked out the cartridge to check it was full, jacking it back into place. I placed it in my jacket pocket. I wanted to be of some real help to her.

"Okay, what is this place?" I asked, feeling its chill finally creep through my clothing and place its icy grip on my skin.

"It's the point of no return, for either us, or our would-be assailants. It's called the Cold Room. It's used by certain members when they need complete privacy."

"How can this be private? We're waiting for our killers, aren't we?"

"I've been down here before. We're approximately one hundred feet under L'améthyste, in a suspended room where no one can hear us, or anything else for that matter.

This is how its going to play-out. I guarantee we won't be here longer than a few hours, at which time you will be wiser but not necessarily happier. In any event, we won't be kept waiting, or incur the curiosity, legal ramifications, or housekeeping, if we were to use somewhere else. You understand?"

"I understand, but there's no cover, nothing to hide behind."

"It comes down to nerve, and expertise," she stated.

"What about the lights, maybe we could turn them off and surprise them?" My voice sounded empty and wooden, as if all hope was beginning to evaporate.

Pilgrim gave a light laugh, but there was underlying tone of seriousness. I clung onto it like a mental life-raft.

"They know we're here and they know we're expecting them. If they enter this room, they accept their fate. How many come down, and who they are, will tell me a lot about the person directly behind this."

"Are you sure they'll know where we are. I mean we may have been watched coming into L'améthyste, but how many people would know about this place?"

"If they don't know, they'll be informed, and they'll come because they don't know any better. And if I don't come out of L'améthyste shortly, it will only lead to one thing; they'll come in. These people, Baxter, are not just common-grade killers, they've been deliberately moulded for the task."

"You make them sound inhuman."

"They're human, but predisposed to violence on a scale you don't want to know about. Don't presume they're thugs; they're driven to this sort of work, the fact they're paid is just a bonus."

I felt unsteady on my feet. There was a moment when reality and time began to fray apart until an almighty whack struck me across my face. My hands flew out at Pilgrim, grabbing handfuls of her lapels. She had slapped me - hard. My impulsive reaction only made her smile. I was unnerved more by her response, then what lay in-wait from our would-be assailants. I allowed my grip to relax and let my hands fall to my sides. A question fell involuntarily from my cold lips, before I could register it.

"What are you?" I whispered. I saw a momentary flicker of sadness in her eyes.

"Don't you think it's a bit late in the day to be asking that question?" She stuffed her hands into her pockets. "Follow me, we'll walk. It'll keep us warm and we'll talk while we wait."

We walked steadily around, me following behind her. I must admit, I made a point of putting some space between us. I'm not a coward, but I'm also not stupid.

"I'm the same as you, Baxter, designed for the purpose and the longer we stay together the more you'll learn of me, and I of you."

"What kind of bullshit is that?"

"Alright, try this on. We're a couple of people, that unusual things happen to; in the process of getting to know one another," she said in a dismissive manner.

"Works for me."

I was feeling a little more courageous. Pilgrim's slap had had the desired effect, as I felt the adrenalin course through my body.

"When we leave here, they won't use brute force again; it will be much subtler," she said.

I clung onto the words; *when we leave here.*

It'd felt like hours before we heard the deliberate footsteps of one person in the hallway outside the door. It opened to reveal a slim-built man, just above being called short, in his late forties. The gun in his hand was pointed directly at me. I watched, frozen, as he squeezed the trigger. In the same instant my eyes turned to Pilgrim, a look of peace on her face, as a penetrating blow struck me.

When I regained consciousness, I doubled up from the agony in my side. Looking across, I stared into the dead eyes of the man who had held the gun. Pulling my palm back from the excruciating pain, I saw to my shock, no blood, but a clean palm.

"Sorry, about that, Baxter, I had to push you out of the way. If I hadn't, you'd be dead."

Taking the wrists of the dead man Pilgrim began to drag the body over to the small door in the wall. "Do you think you could help me? He's actually heavier than he looks." She threw me a nervous smile.

There was something innately vulnerable and endearing about her at that moment, which was shocking to my psyche. She was, I believed, embarrassed; never mind she'd obviously killed the man, and was dragging his corpse across the floor.

151

"Is he dead?" I wanted to confirm.

"Quite dead."

"But there's no blood. How did he die?"

I was momentarily distracted by this puzzle. He'd had a gun. Surely Pilgrim had used a gun. Gun versus gun, but then I'd never seen her with a gun. I couldn't comprehend what had just happened.

"I stopped his heart," she stated without any emotion. Opening the stainless-steel door in the wall, she pulled out a gurney, whose wheeled legs sprung out underneath.

"There was no need for violence. I'm not a monster. Now, help me lift him onto this thing."

I couldn't think, only act. Straddled over him, I sat him upright, circling my arms around his chest from behind. Pilgrim took his ankles. Bracing ourselves, we lifted him onto the gurney. Tucking his jacket in-off the side-rails, I walked back for his missing shoe, resting it on his chest. Pilgrim pushed the gurney back in and closed the door, wrenching the handle up to lock it.

"Well, now that's taken care of; I think a well-earned drink is in order."

My mind had become oblivious to both my surroundings and the events which had just taken place. I couldn't have asked a question, even if I'd wanted to.

I followed her to the outer-door and we walked through silently. As it closed, I heard the blast of a furnace start-up and the sprinklers came on.

As if we had simply been visiting another floor, we returned to the reception lobby via the lift. Without a raised eyebrow, or knowing look, the courteous man at reception smiled, handing Pilgrim a note.

"Your apartment is now ready and at your disposal, Miss Pilgrim, Mr Baxter."

With the slightest inclination of his head, he dismissed himself to attend to another member. We moved across the lobby to the main-lift and waited for it to descend.

"I'm going to take you up on that drink," I exhaled.

Entering the lift, Pilgrim pressed a blue button on the panel, denoting the floor. The lift ascended, and we exited, where we were given a cursory nod from security. Walking down the grand-corridor, we came to a double-door, where Pilgrim opened them and passed through. I desperately needed that drink and to discuss what had just happened. I had so many questions; I couldn't prevent them from tumbling over one another, until my mind finally gave in.

Our apartment was named the, L.T.Ollinger suite.

"Who is L.T.Ollinger?" I asked.

"L.T.Ollinger was the man responsible for discovering the planet, 'Hibis', the only known, habitable planet, in our distant solar-system."

Pilgrim's matter of fact delivery of this monumental piece of information, made me falter.

"I wasn't aware such a planet exists."

"It's not generally known. No point in broadcasting it; as we've no way of getting there … alive."

"Right." I dismissed that piece of information from my thoughts. Right now there was no room for it.

Our apartment consisted of two separate bedrooms set on opposite sides of a large and sumptuous living-room. Each had an en-suite bathroom and walk-in closet. The opulence of our new living-quarters was entirely lost on me. I may as well have sat on a plank of wood rather than the finely upholstered antique chairs. My eyes did not admire the original masterpieces gracing the walls. My only reaction was to be startled, when there was a discreet tap at the outer-door. I opened it gingerly to a well-built man in his early fifties wearing a butler's uniform. He took one look at me, and ventured in a timber voice:

"May I bring you a large whisky, Mr. Baxter?"

"You may bring me the bottle and leave it on the side," I replied firmly.

Curiously, he stepped past me toward our bar, when he turned quietly on his heel, came back, and removed my hand to close the door, saying.

"Allow me."

"May I have your name?" I asked.

"Horatio Dark Dashwood, Sir."

I admit there was a momentary pause, before I answered.

"Perfect."

I slumped down in the nearest chair and sat numbly.

Dashwood poured, Pilgrim and I drank, and after I don't know how many, we began to talk.

"We must be vigilant, alert, we can't afford to relax until I tell you," she said in earnest.

"The Titans can bite me!" I replied in anger.

I felt trapped and unable to see past their menace. When I thought of their domination of my physical and mental state, I wanted to go back to the time, before I had noticed Pilgrim, and she had noticed me. My regret, must've been writ large on my face.

"I'm going to be honest with you, Baxter, and tell you that from this day forward I will never lie to you, your life is worth that at least. I did bring you into all of this and I did orchestrate the means to accomplish it … for purely selfish reasons. I *need* someone of your calibre. However, if you want to leave now, I can still manage for you to live a peaceful life. But you must decide before we move any further forward. They won't have known you were in the, Cold-Room."

This conversation, only a few days before, would have been unthinkable. Knowing how bad things had become, I surprised myself that I would never want to be anywhere else, but working alongside her. I had found my true niche in life. I would rather live a moment of complete physical and mental exhilaration, than a lifetime of mediocrity, and I would rather die defending my right to do so. Being honest with myself, I realised I had made my decision the moment I'd set eyes on her. It wasn't a physical thing; it was spiritual. I wasn't blinded by her, but there was knowledge, understanding, and something other worldly conveyed in the way she looked at me that day, that burnished life into my soul.

"Even I think that's naïve," I stated.

"You're probably right," she conceded.

"We need to get a handle on these people. I think I know someone who might be able to help." I said assuredly.

155

"Anything, that can give us an edge, could mean the difference between life and death," she stated.

CHAPTER NINE

The following evening when Pilgrim returned to L'améthyste, she appeared worn and concerned.

"Where have you been?" I asked mirroring her worry.

It was past eight pm and food was definitely on my mind; despite all the chaos surrounding us. I had dressed for dinner, and was left fumbling with a particularly uncooperative cufflink. Our fastidious butler entered carrying a tray with our aperitif, two Kier Royals, in Champagne cups. Pilgrim raised a disapproving eyebrow to me. I, in return, raised my own eyebrow in rebuke to hers.

"It seems to me, to be the best time to toast our precious lives," I answered squarely.

She lifted her glass from the tray, took a large sip, and purred in satisfaction.

"To your very good health, Baxter."

"I'll drink to that." I took a sip and nodded in satisfaction.

"You're absolutely right. I've forgotten how to appreciate these moments in life, when I should acknowledge I'm alive. It's the work. I love what I do, but I've immersed myself to the point, I don't know where my work ends and my life begins. You'll help me with that, won't you?" she asked genuinely.

"I believe I already am." I raised my glass to her. Despite us only knowing one another for a few short days, those days felt like years, and good ones at that.

After a sumptuous dinner, we returned to our apartment for coffee and a digestive. After some minutes of silence, Pilgrim said.

"I visited a friend of mine today, a doctor in psychology. Our next step is to locate the missing Black Pearl which, will in turn, I believe, give us the person directly responsible for their commission. From the profile hes given me, there are only three people in the running. The Right Honourable, Anthony Glassmere, now Minister for Foreign Affairs and friend to the nouveau riche; namely the Chinese and Russians. Mrs. Bettina Zia-Tanner, matriarch to the family which owns Tanner Pharmaceuticals; and Mr. Benjamin Short, eighty-three-year-old, self-made billionaire, and staunch supporter of all things military. Each of them has heavily supported research into molecular biology."

"I can't believe anyone who rejoices in the name of Benjamin can be responsible for such cruelty and violence; more likely that Zia-Tanner woman," I offered.

"How curious of you, Baxter. What on earth would lead you to believe such a thing?"

Pilgrim was almost laughing, but not quite. Recognising the underlying seriousness of her tone, I answered honestly.

"Well, think about it. Benjamin, is a cuddly sort of name. No one that grows up, being called by his mother, Benjamin, Benji or Benny, could ever really turn into a homicidal maniac. No, my money is on that Zia-Tanner woman."

"How supremely naive of you, and you believe this, because?" Pilgrim's eyes were upon me in a most searching manner, and I felt a momentary danger.

"Simple. The name Bettina is pretentious."

"To you, maybe."

Ignoring her lack of enthusiasm for my preposterous argument, I continued unabated.

"This means her parents were also. This in turn suggests shes had a life-long struggle, to achieve more than anyone else in her immediate circle. Shes probably your garden variety megalomaniac."

To my surprise Pilgrim didn't say anything; she just looked at me with curiosity. I continued, momentarily buoyed there might actually be an element of truth in what I was hypothesising.

"I know this because she has married and kept her last name, and her husband's name." Even to my ears it didn't sound plausible, so I finished confidently. "Who in their right mind would want to be called Bettina Zia-Tanner? You see my reasoning?" I asked with slightly less confidence than I was feeling.

"Not really, but it's true; Baroness Zia-Tanner, to use her full title, isn't known for her generous spirit. They each fit the profile, even Benji," she finished. "We need to establish, if any of them have visited New York in the last six months, and more importantly, which of them visited your banker?"

"He is not *my* banker. You know for a smart woman…," I trailed off.

"The people I've mentioned would certainly have someone else to run their errands for them," she pondered.

"Not necessarily. These types of people are a suspicious bunch, especially those of their immediate circle. A faithful old retainer knows them too well, a new employee hasn't had long enough to prove their competence, and a private-hire would keep records, and records can be traced. No, this would require a personal visit," I corrected.

Suddenly rising from her chair, Pilgrim looked down at me.

"Baxter, I need you to check an item in the Vault for me, package 2841." "Here, write it on your palm."

Before I could get to my feet she was writing the numbers across the palm of my hand.

"What, now?" I asked.

"Yes, now," she answered firmly.

The warmth of the apartment, the gourmet dinner and brandy I had consumed with much alacrity, anchored me to my chair.

"I don't suppose this can wait until tomorrow?"

Seeing the stony expression on her face made me immediately leap to my feet and go in search of my coat, hat and gloves.

Fortunately, it had stopped raining when I found myself walking briskly toward the Tube station. My protestation that the London Underground would be closed for the night was met with a look of incredulity at my lack of foresight. I gave an involuntary 'humph' at the memory.

Reaching the north-bridge straddling the train tracks, I walked over to the other side and took a sharp right where an ancient waist-high, wooden-gate covered in lichen, creaked wearily upon opening. Looking down into the pitch-black the only objects I could make out from an almost moonless night were the silver threads of the tracks below. The stone stairs leading down to them were shallow and treacherous. Pilgrim had forbidden any torch or light to be used, in case it aroused curiosity from an on-looker or passer-by.

Having made it to the bottom I breathed a sigh of relief I hadn't fallen and broken my neck in the process. Staring into the tunnel I stepped forward gingerly, hearing the exaggerated crunch of the blackened, angular ballast resound off the walls. Carefully picking my way further in, my eyes gradually become accustomed to the dark, and I was able to detect the inset of the wall, where the outer door to the underground lay. Pilgrim had told me not to expect a key-hole in the door, but to feel on the right for a small button the size and form of an iron door stud. Annoyingly, there were several and after pressing a few, one gave in. A round opening the size of an orange silently appeared at face level. Feeling rather foolish and apprehensive at the same time, I spoke into the hole saying, 'open.' To my relief the door popped inwards and I hurriedly stepped through into the warmth and familiar smell of diesel fumes and rubber. The door automatically closed behind me with the barest whisper. A sense of being trapped with no retreat possible permeated my consciousness and it was only the steely look of disapproval from Pilgrim which flashed before my mind's eye that made me keep my nerve. A single dirty lamp and saucer, the same as I had seen in the Vault, provided the only source of light and struggled to glow dull amber. I found myself at the top of a wrought-iron spiral staircase, cemented into the walls by large iron rods. As I had stepped onto it coming through the door, the only way off, was to walk down. Looking apprehensively through the iron filigree of the steps that descended at least fifty feet, I wanted to get this errand over with as soon as possible. Upon reaching the bottom there could be no chance of becoming lost, as a long and badly lit corridor stretched out into the gloom. I hurriedly reached its end. I told myself, quite firmly, one of the first things I was going to do was to change the lighting into something much more efficient and definitely brighter. Once at its end a similar iron door to the one in the train-tunnel presented itself; again, I followed the instructions given by Pilgrim. This method of opening doors seemed quite extraordinary to me at the time. Of course, now I know them to be a necessary and important part of the security for the Vault. As Pilgrim pointed out after my return, locks can be picked; retinal and laser finger prints can be overridden, copied, or at worst, removed from their owners. However, the breath of a person is laden with their own unique DNA markers, which are specifically variable within the parameters of the host as well as the information being provided at a particular temperature and rate of expulsion. To her it was all academic but I appreciated her indulging me.

Once in the Vault I followed Pilgrim's directions to the letter and quickly located package 2841. It was wrapped in the obligatory brown paper the shape of it suggested a shoe box. Checking the number across my palm which was now smudged with perspiration, I picked it up. I had not been prepared for its weight, which must have been about five pounds or more. Taking great care with it, I returned the way I had come and found myself relieved and out of breath as I stepped up to the entrance doors of L'améthyste.

Upstairs, as my hand reached out for our apartment door handle, it was opened by our most congenial butler. Helping me to remove my coat he suggested a hot toddy, 'purely to keep those nasty winter bugs at bay,' he'd diplomatically added. I thought, if anything ever was to happen to Pilgrim and me, at that moment, I would miss him the most. The idea of taking him with us to our next residence was extinguished as quickly as the thought was conceived, by the memory of poor Mrs. Cotterill.

"What is it?" I enquired, warming my cold hands by wrapping them around my hot toddy.

"Why don't you open it and find out?" she offered. "But be careful, Baxter."

"Careful, careful of what?" Her warning instantly put me on my guard.

"I can't be sure at this time but I do need to satisfy myself on one point. Why don't you open it and I'll observe," she said, sitting back in her chair and scrutinising the parcel on the table between us.

"You think it's safe for me?" I asked tentatively, but feeling justified in asking the question given the chain of events leading up to this moment.

"For goodness sake, Baxter, It's hardly likely to contain anything living is it." She sounded exasperated by my procrastination.

"How do you know? It could be some deadly bacteria or airborne virus designed to be released at the moment I open it. I presume you've heard the name Howard Carter and the curse of Tutankhamen." I knew I was allowing my imagination to run away with itself, but I couldn't help it. I wanted to remain cool and in control but at this early stage in my employment I just couldn't be. Then with a sigh of relief I suddenly recalled how Pilgrim must have examined it, before she had agreed to store it. "You already know what it is, so why are we looking at it again?" I asked.

"Because, I might have missed something." She sounded disappointed and impatient at herself.

Without another word spoken I undid the brown paper, and opening the cardboard lid of the outer box, I allowed my jaw to drop open. I can't remember what I said after, but it wouldn't have been anything intelligible. That explained the weight; a magnificent gold box encrusted with precious jewels, as the light caught them, it threw shimmering colour across the walls. I lifted it carefully out and moving the paper to the side sat it on the glass table-top. Its resplendence was mirrored on all four sides with cabochon opals and Peruzzi cut diamonds. I had never seen anything like it before in my life and I had seen some very nice jewellery in my previous positions.

"It's magnificent," I breathed in awe.

Noticing Dashwood was unobtrusively picking up my coat from the back of the chair, I looked at him.

"What do you think, Dashwood?"

"It's a minimalist's nightmare, Mr Baxter, Sir." Dashwood retreated back to his work in the next room.

Pilgrim looked at it, silent and brooding.

"Who does it belong to?" I asked.

"In truth it belongs to the people of Russia. It does not belong to one of our suspects; but the Right

Honourable Antony Glassmere was asked to *store* it, so he made contact."

"By whom?" I asked warily.

"Nadejda Alexandrovich, Great grand-daughter to Tsar Ivan Alexandrovich, and the last legitimate heir to the new throne of Russia."

"New throne of Russia?"

"Yes, well, we'll see, won't we. The box was created for the first Tsar of Russia and it is absolutely priceless. It disappeared shortly after his death and resurfaced approximately one-hundred and fifty years after. Its current owner can't afford to have its existence confirmed, let alone admit to owning such an object."

"But why not?"

"In the changeable Russian political climate, she can't afford to be associated with it. Especially given her ambitions."

"Don't tell me, I don't want to know."

"There is a baseness to the psychology of our species to possess those things that are gratuitous to our existence, which defies justification."

"Oh, this from the woman who owns a Jaguar. Excuse me, *owned* a Jaguar."

"I'm not exempt to those kinds of frailties."

"That's because in general we're not robots. People are complicated creatures. With all our traits good and bad, we're pretty much where we expect to be. The good thing is, we hope to be better. Besides, you're the keeper of some of the world's most precious items, are you not?"

"Yes, I am. But they are not *my* possessions."

"That's a minor technicality. Nine tenths and all that."

"My business is not about possessions, its about secrets."

As that was the truth of the matter I fell quiet. She continued.

"I think I may have been blinded, but now I'm beginning to wonder." A recognisable look of pondering eclipsed her face. "Open it and take a look inside. I want you to close your eyes and run your fingers along its interior. You're feeling for any anomalies in the finish."

I did as she instructed but felt nothing other than the smooth surface of gold against my fingertips.

"Nothing," I stated flatly. "Why don't you have a go?"

"I already have. I didn't find anything after my inspection. Maybe one of the stones? I didn't believe it necessary to examine it to that degree when it was deposited."

Again, I ran my fingers exploratively across the stones and their ornate settings attempting to move them. To my surprise, one of them gave a little. It was a large ruby set as the eye in a gold dragon. After I pressed down its head, a click sounded on its underside, releasing a hidden compartment within the interior wall of the box."

We both looked at each other surprised.

"What's in it?" Pilgrim asked excitedly.

"A photograph of three men." I turned the photograph to read the back. "Taken in nineteen-twelve.

Their names are listed, along with the date. Tsar Petra Dimitri Alexandrovich, Sultan Rabia Banu and Mr Algernon Pennyweather. In parenthesis it says, 'seismic engineer'."

"That's a bit of a strange line-up," Pilgrim remarked. "There must be some connection … but I don't see it. It can't be as simple as an old photo of friends, otherwise why hide it?"

"Somebody Tsar, and Sultan whats-his-name; those two seem to go together; the odd one out is, Pennyweather."

"I'm not looking for the odd one out. I'm looking for the connection."

"There is a connection between the Tsar and the *now* owner of the box. Perhaps there's a connection between Benjamin, or Zia-Tanner and these people?" I proposed hopefully.

"Not that I'm aware of," she finished despondently.

"Who is this Pennyweather anyway?" I asked. "A seismic engineer might specialise in subterranean buildings. So where does he fit into all this?"

"I don't know, Baxter. But I'm sure we're going to find out."

The next day just before lunch found us both deep in thought. Just then Pilgrim arose.

"I have to previous engagement. I'll see you later."

"Another pair of gloves?"

"No, an appointment with someone special."

My look of surprise did not go unnoticed.

167

"I can be distracted occasionally," she smiled.

"Shouldn't I know the name of this mysterious man?" I knew enough about her to know it was definitely a man. I was observing something in Pilgrim I had never witnessed before. This man meant something to her on an emotional level. "For security, let alone anything else," I added in response to the query on her face.

"Hes above suspicion. MI6."

"In my experience even more reason to take care."

"In your experience?" she laughed.

"You're not the only one who has interesting friends," I answered truthfully.

"*Friends*, or just past employers?"

"Both actually now you ask. I could rustle up ..." I stopped; this wasn't a subject where a boastful comment was appropriate. There'd never been an instance when I had been compelled to call in a favour from my small circle of border-line friends. Although, I knew with certainty I had only to ask. Years spent forging trust had resulted in deep alliances that had withstood the vagaries of time. My friends came from all walks of life. We all had one thing in common; we were loners; and it would be a cold day in hell when one of us might be forced to ask for help.

"Me?" Pilgrim offered charitably after a pause, interpreting my silence incorrectly. She inhaled deeply, "it's, H, if you must know. Drinks aboard the Cutty Sark."

I was beginning to learn more and more about H; and his name seemed immaterial at this point.

"Pilgrim, I have a former work colleague. I'd like to run the Titan name past him, see if he knows anything. He has a sterling reputation for complete trust and discretion; any objections?"

"As the Titans already know we're onto them, I don't see why not. And as to your friend; wherever his loyalties lie, any information, however erroneous, we can pick the bones out of. We don't have the luxury of tip-toeing around this one. We need to discover as much as we can, in as short a period of time as possible – that will be our edge. Large organisations are sluggish in their response, and when they're as complex as the Titans, we must exploit such weaknesses to our advantage," she answered, heading toward the door.

"Don't forget to duck," I called out after her.

If Pilgrim was going to be busy over the next few hours that suited me. I'd been waiting for just such a gap in our time to locate a very important old comrade in arms, Mr. Worthington, otherwise known as the 'Sage'. He had a well-earned reputation both in society and in private-service, for arranging matters that required absolute discretion and delicacy. His word was in violet, and I hadn't once heard a hint of scandal surrounding him. His family had been in service to the same line for five generations, and his extended family worked for many of the high chancellors of Europe. If anyone could shed any light on the Titans, it would be him. His connections ran like arteries through the aristocracy. He was currently in London, overseeing the opening of Charlington Hall for the season. Finally, after a brief phone call, we agreed to meet the following afternoon.

Leaving L'améthyste at around three o'clock the next day I took a taxi. Pilgrim was nowhere to be seen.

"The Blue Bowler, please," I instructed.

We'd decided to meet at a favourite watering-hole for those in private-service. Ideally situated on Kensington High Street just west of Hyde Park, it afforded the privacy and elegant surroundings so many of us had become accustomed to in our professional lives.

As I entered through its distinctive revolving-door, I immediately caught sight of Mr. Worthington sat in a comfy chair next to a roaring fire, looking as dapper as ever. Seeing me enter, he stood up and shook my hand.

"Mr. Baxter."

"Mr. Worthington. Thank you for seeing me at such short notice and for signing me in."

Since my departure from my professional life as a valet, my membership to the Blue Bowler had automatically been rescinded.

"Not at all, I was intrigued by your call. Please won't you take a seat? I hear you're now moving in quite exalted circles."

Sitting down, we ordered drinks and sat back. Mr. Worthington, as one might expect, was impeccably attired in his Saville Row butler's uniform. Despite his advanced years, his thick dark hair was trimmed and coiffed to perfection with the thinnest horizontal sideburns accentuating his high cheek bones. Perfect teeth, and the signature sparkling lunular of a 'Harvey' manicure; so named after Harvey Banks, the diamond industrialist, who began his fortune digging with his bare hands; completed the picture. All in all, Mr. Worthington was ahead of his time in gentleman's fashion and taste.

"I've been working closely with a lady, Miss. Neath A Pilgrim," I began.

"Miss. Pilgrim is a member of L'améthyste. She has enviable connections, which is to be expected given the nature of her business. Her past is not without blemish, Mr. Baxter," he added seriously.

"Who's isn't?"

"Quite, you're a gentleman for whom explanations are of secondary importance…when it comes to your heart."

"Mr. Worthington, whatever you think you know, or have heard, its wrong. I am Pilgrim's business partner and nothing else."

"Of course you are. Please forgive an old man's romanticism."

Mr. Worthington's deliberately inaccurate dismissal only served to underline his true thoughts on the matter.

"Yes, Pilgrim is a member of L'améthyste," I answered.

"I had high hopes for you, Mr. Baxter." He paused, "I suppose that Phelps business didn't help."

"I'm my own master now Mr. Worthington."

"Are you indeed?" Mr. Worthington didn't sound convinced.

"I've come to ask you for a favour. Something has come up and I might need a, JFC."

"And what indiscretion do you foresee that would necessitate a 'get-out-of-jail-free-card'?"

"It's difficult to explain."

"Explanations are best left to the defence council. As you're no longer a member of staff who may be forced to perjure themselves for their Principle, this must be something Miss. Pilgrim is mixed-up in."

"We're in it together."

"I fail to see why I should help; now you're no longer one of us."

"You might make an exception when I tell you the Titans are involved."

Mr Worthington visibly blanched.

"And you came here, to meet with me, knowing this?" He dropped his head. "How could you." When he looked up, his affable countenance had changed to one of steely determination. "You neglected to inform Miss. Pilgrim you were meeting with me."

"I did…but, I didn't…"

"Mention my name," he finished.

"I didn't think it was important."

"If, I tell you everything I know about the Titans; I'd like something in return."

"Which is?"

"A note; written and signed by a boy who'd been compromised, and couldn't have predicted the ramifications, if it became public knowledge today."

The book, Pilgrim inherited from her father during his decades spent as bursar at Loxton, with all its promissory notes from errant students, loomed large in my mind.

"Any note that may, or may not exist, doesn't belong to me."

"It doesn't belong to Miss. Pilgrim either."

"Even if I had it in the palm of my hand, I wouldn't give it up."

"Why, because that sort of leverage is tantamount to blackmail?" His countenance now changed to one of serious contemplation.

"You hold a unique position Mr. Baxter. One that I can't begin to imagine how you secured." He breathed a sigh.

"The Titans are as covert as it is possible to be. They make the M.I.s look like a bunch of town-criers. Most of what I've heard over the years can't be proven. They hold unlimited wealth and power that makes my particular billionaire look like a tramp. The only reference that I would put any store in comes down from my Great, Great-grandfather. At the time he was under-butler to his father. That would have been around about the late seventeen hundreds. He was in a young New York at the time with the fifth Earl. There was to be a meeting between a number of higher echelon people."

"A meeting, what sort of meeting?"

"A group of twelve men and women. Which was noted at the time, as being odd. Ladies weren't involved in business, at that level. It had something to do with the founding of the New York Stock Exchange."

"So they were Titans?"

"That can only be conjectured. The only name to come out of it was remembered only because it was such a mouthful. Are you ready for this?" he questioned seriously.

"Yes," I said tentatively.

"Imperator Gideon Valdic Abdemon."

There was a pause between us as I mentally gathered up this name and tried to think of the next pertinent question.

"That's not easy to forget," I remarked.

"Yes, once heard – never forgotten – as my father said."

Mr. Worthington looked at me solemnly.

"I should impress upon you, Mr. Baxter, if you continue to pursue this matter you will fall beyond any influence I have to assist you."

"No one appreciates how precarious my position is, more than me. Is there anything else you can tell me?"

"Only this Imperator fellow was known to frequent a certain place. It's quite an historical landmark with a certain fraternity and one you're already familiar with. That's why I gave you that warning."

He paused long enough to make me feel uncomfortable.

"Well, what is it?" The hair on the back of my neck was bristling against my shirt collar.

"Crisid Bank."

"You mean Mr. Stenmore?" I asked perplexed.

"I do not mean Mr. Stenmore, although there are levels of interest there. I mean Crisid Bank. Now I should be getting back. We won't talk again, Mr. Baxter. May I wish you a long and happy life."

Mr. Worthington stood with his hand outstretched, which was my cue to leave. I left the relative gloom of the Blue Bowler, and stepped out into the cold wind and rain of mid-day, descended the steps and entered a beleaguered taxi waiting for me outside.

"Crisid Bank please."

"Never `erd of it."

"Sorry, corner of Pall Mall and Waterloo Place."

"Right you are, Guvnor."

Without further ado we lurched into traffic and within a few short minutes had pulled up to the address I knew well from my previous employer's business card: Mr. Stenmore, Chairman, Crisid Bank, Pall Mall London. What the connection was, if any, between Mr. Stenmore personally and the Titans I couldn't imagine. What I did know was Mr. Stenmore would be at his desk at this time and not in the least interested in seeing me. Still, it was the only lead I had.

With the taxi gone and the inhabitants of that great metropolis milling past, I began to look around for the bank. I leaned over the pedestrian guard-rail and peered into the dark below. I had overheard Mr. Stenmore say the bank stood below the pavement, and had remained in the same location for hundreds of years. And there it was approximately twenty-feet below. I was just able to make out its Greek ionic columns in the gloom. An old cobbled path ran from its entrance and disappeared under what was now the main Waterloo road. With no visible access down, I was at a loss to know how anyone could reach it; and yet

Mr. Stenmore did, five days a week! After some minutes I deduced the entry point must be from the opposite side of the road. Upon arriving on the other side I espied an ornate black wrought-iron gate some eight to ten feet in height; it was locked and guarded. Beyond it ran a very ancient iron-railing alongside a cobbled path leading to a large, black door. There was also a very unusual door knocker which I couldn't make out at such a distance. My lingering presence prompted a uniformed man to step forward from behind the gate to ask if I needed assistance. My hesitation caused him to ask if I had an appointment.

"No, I apologise. I'm looking for the entrance to Crisid Bank."

"This is the entrance to Crisid Bank, Sir, but I can't let you in without an appointment."

"Yes, I'd like to make an appointment, please."

"I'm afraid that will not be possible. Appointments are by invitation only, Sir."

He had just been about to retreat back into his weather-proof alcove when a black saloon, slid up to the pavement. Its nimble chauffeur opened the rear-door to an emerging tanned, slim leg, belonging to a middle-aged lady with a disdainful glance. Around her neck swung a lengthy gold chain with a black seal at its end. She was admitted through the gate which locked automatically behind her, and escorted through the black-door leading into the bank. Her car melted back into traffic.

I had stepped back, so as not to be observed. What I couldn't have known at the time was that I was being watched from inside the bank.

Deep in thought about what my next move should be, the gate was reopened by the guard and he beckoned me over.

"I apologise Sir, for being so remiss in my duties, Mr. Stenmore asks that you visit with him."

"Thank you."

I did enter through the gate and subsequently came to the entrance door, and yes, my alarm-bells were ringing. Especially, as I was certain Mr. Stenmore was as likely to have extended an invitation to me, as ride a bicycle backwards; the whole thing was unbelievable. So, why did I go so willingly? For no other reason than I couldn't have done anything else. Given the circumstances and with my new commitment to embrace life, I interpreted this decision as such.

As I approached, the door-knocker came into full view. It was of such an unusual design and subject matter I had to marvel at it. It depicted two lionesses rampant either side of a quadrilateral containing a small star with six points. Over this lay a circle with two curved lines coming from its rim with a further six small stars. The doorman fell back and a young lady with a serious frown, which sat at odds with her beauty, escorted me through to a large salon, where I was asked to sit and wait. I felt at this point it was highly unlikely Mr. Stenmore even knew I was in the building. A sense of foreboding had thrown its heavy cloak about my shoulders, causing them to round under the imminent weight of my risky situation. A quiet tap at the door and the young lady returned. She gave no smile, but bore a small tray on which sat tea for one.

"Earl Grey, Mr. Baxter."

"Thank you."

She promptly left, leaving me to sit alone in the austere room, for all its fine upholstery and furnishings. If they thought I was going to drink the tea they were very much mistaken. I might be in the lion's den but that didn't mean I should stick my head in its mouth. I told myself to observe, watch, listen and ask questions. Before long I heard steps coming toward the room. I sat to attention to await my visitor. To my horror and shock, the impeccably dressed man who now stood in the doorway, with a thinly veiled look of satisfaction on his face, was Mr. Phelps. I imagined him still incarcerated at her majesty's pleasure. My resolve was as granite and my nerve one-hundred fold what it had been moments before. I stood silently as my left arm involuntarily squeezed my shoulder-holster and the gun it sheathed. I would not make the same mistake twice.

Mr. Phelps had not changed but for a graduating grey moving away from his temples. His face had become slightly craggier, if indeed that were possible. To look at us, no one would imagine we were of the same age. His face had succumbed to the canyons and ravines cleaved by the psychotic mind of a man who had never been a boy.

Sitting down, he pulled out a cigarette case and offered me one. I shook my head in response and remained standing.

"What do you want?" I ground out.

"Surely, that should be my question." The memory of the deep timber of his voice made me straighten my spine. His perfectly clipped Etonian enunciation sat awkwardly, as he was neither a gentleman, or well-bred.

"I'm not surprised to see you here. Although I'm disappointed Mr. Stenmore is a part of this?"

"Won't you sit down, Mr. Baxter? I promise I'll not detain you for long."

"Crisid Bank and the Titans what a corrupt collaboration."

"You know you really ought to keep their name from your lips, or you'll discover, too late, why they're the most powerful legion in history," he stated carefully, malice lacing his words.

"And you at liberty. It's a farce. Still, they've got you nicely leashed, haven't they, Mr. Phelps."

"Your goading is amateurish, and I have not allowed you in here to exchange pleasantries."

"You're a henchman, nothing more, nothing less, although I concede, a very practiced and imaginative one I'm sure. I don't believe for a moment you invited me in; you're just the lackey."

"I can smell your fear Mr. Baxter and ordinarily such a heady scent as yours would cause me to take my time for such a prize. However, you know you mustn't distract me, even though I've asked for us not to be disturbed." He gave a coitish giggle that caused my resolve to falter slightly.

"Your Achilles-heel is showing, Mr. Phelps. Maybe you can drag yourself back to the matter-at-hand."

In one swift movement I pulled out my revolver and pointed it at him.

"Now perhaps you can get to the point," I added sternly.

"Well, I am disappointed but if you insist," he added, churlishly.

179

Suddenly, all pretence to whoever his previous personality was vanished, to be replaced with the stone mask, of the man I remembered, who had butchered his wife, her lover and almost his children – if it hadn't been for me.

Within an instant and without my having time to think Mr. Phelps leapt toward me. In one fluid movement he'd snaked his arm across mine causing my revolver to clatter to the floor, as he pushed the heel of his right hand under my chin and thrust me back against the wall. Every fibre of my being became electrified at the memory of him and I responded with equal violence; but he wouldn't balk.

With his forearm now pressing violently against my throat, and his face next to mine the blackness of his soul was clearly visible in his eyes. With my free hand and twisting my body to gain some leverage, I gouged at his eyes. I felt my nails dig and furrow from his forehead across the bridge of his nose and upper cheek. As he grunted and gave a little, I was able to gasp a breath. Instinctively, I disentangled my arms and ducked whilst using the wall behind me as ballast, I slammed his upper-body with an almighty shove. He broke away momentarily but just as quickly hurtled back at me. I bent, taking the full force of his body against my side. Grabbing his waist I rugby tackled him to the floor. He fell into the furniture as I rolled off onto the floor, snatching up the gun and raising it just in time. Stopped in his tracks and panting only slightly he straightened his tie and picked up the chair, placing it back. Sitting down he pressed his palm against his forehead and observed the smudge of blood. Pulling a white handkerchief from his top pocket he shook it out and dabbed lightly at what was now an angry gash. My fingernails were packed with his skin, yet my arm was steady and rigid holding the gun.

"You ought to be careful, Mr. Baxter, if that thing goes off, I won't be held responsible for my actions," he said quietly and deliberately.

"If you move out of that chair I'll shoot you. Not to kill you, just so you'll need crutches for the rest of your life," I stated with conviction.

For the first time I saw a fleeting glance of doubt cross his face.

"You made a mistake by inviting me in here." I saw the truth of my words confirmed by his implacable expression.

"You will tell me the Titan behind the Black Pearls?" I demanded.

Mr. Phelps gave out a derisive laugh.

"Is that what you've called them? How quaint. If you're referring to the 'Drepáni', than you're wasting my time. Do you know how far down the food chain I am? You cannot possibly hope to influence the Titans in any way. We are fleeting, Mr. Baxter, they are eternal," he said, with something approaching honesty in his voice. He paused, before adding. "Its true you don't bring out the best in me. You quite surprised me all those years ago. I didn't think you had it in you, and today...well, let us just say I had to be sure it wasn't a fluke. Your instinct for self-preservation is remarkable. You'd be surprised by the complicity of some to hasten their own death."

"You might not realise this, Mr. Phelps, but you have very little time remaining before you'll be joining them."

"Bravado as well; you don't disappoint."

The curl to his lip made my skin crawl. He was leisurely smoking his cigarette as if we were passing the time of day.

"My question still stands and you will answer it, or I will ensure you are perceived as a liability," I avowed with confidence.

"When my time comes, Mr. Baxter, it will be entirely of my own volition. There can be no amount of coercion you can apply that will compel me to divulge such a piece of information, and as I don't know the answer to your question, I perceive our little fracas at 'nul points'. You can leave with your life, which is more than I planned for you when you entered."

We were at a stalemate. I knew another physical clash would result in silence from him, or my possible demise. If certain death held no influence over him, then I was at a complete loss to know what to do. Even a man like him must cherish something. At my hesitation, Mr. Phelps ground out his cigarette.

"Don't embarrass yourself."

He rose and walked from the room.

I fell heavily into a chair, hunched over and breathed deeply. No thought entered my mind. My body began to shake after the sudden exertion and I twisted and gripped my hands together in an effort to abate the response. I was suddenly aware of another in the room. The woman who had escorted me in, looked at me with an impassionate stare.

"After you've composed yourself, I will escort you to Mr. Stenmore's office."

I hadn't even thought this a strange summons. I needed answers. Going back to Pilgrim with details of a fight, in no way moved us forward. Standing up, I allowed my legs to steady and proceeded to follow her through the high ceiled passages until we reached a stone-carved stairway heading nowhere but up.

Reaching a large oak door she hesitated and I instinctively checked my collar, the front of my jacket and my shoes. I was a mess.

Moving forward she opened the door inviting me in to a large reception room; the antechamber to Mr. Stenmore's office. I was taken aback by the plain furniture and décor of so important a bank.

Gesturing for me to take a seat, which I readily accepted, she gave an almost imperceptible tap to an inner-door of that sanctum and stepped inside closing it behind her. It seemed a protracted length of time before she reappeared saying.

"Mr Stenmore will see you now."

I stood up and entered his office. At the sight of me, the look of consternation on his face was immediate.

"Miss. Stone; some tea and something for…" he brusquely waved his hand at my face.

Miss. Stone quietly left the room, closing the door behind her. Stone by name, Stone by nature, I thought. The afternoon day-light had been snuffed-out by rain from an iron sky. Only a single desk-lamp threw a yellow glow, barely illuminating the room and giving it a haunted feel.

In my years of service as Mr. Stenmore's valet, I had never cared to imagine his office. Now that I was here, I wouldn't have made an accurate picture of it before, but its sterility made perfect sense.

Mr. Stenmore was sat behind a desk of epic proportions, his office was very much in the Quaker style, as was Miss. Stones. Rows of shelves lined the walls with all manner of highly polished leather bound books, all of which seemed to relate to financial matters. The desk stood upon a square of carpet which had long since given up its pile and the long curtains drawn back at the large casement-window behind him, hung sun-bleached and worn. I found this minimalist frugality surprising. His bachelor house, which I had thought conservative, now looked comparatively sumptuous.

Mr. Stenmore leaned back in his leather chair, scrutinising my dishevelled appearance.

I immediately recognised his working suit, Mortimer, of Saville Row, as one of a dozen three-piece suits. All of them were identical, and heralded to those familiar with his routines, reliability, trust and continuity. His grey silk-cravat with his favourite gold pin, glinted at me.

"Mr. Baxter, I suggest you sit down before you fall down." The laconic lilt of his voice served to remind me he didn't suffer fools gladly.

I hastily took the seat opposite. His perfectly groomed silver hair and moustache had whitened, but his face showed no signs of aging from the intervening years. A razer-sharp mind behind his piercing eyes quickly appraised my condition.

"Mr. Baxter…" he began quietly, stating my name in such a way as to secure my attention. "Perhaps you will be kind enough to explain your presence here and the reason you are quite so, 'déshabillé'?"

There was the slightest tone of concern in his voice that at once released my tension. How much did Mr. Stenmore know? He had to be involved, but I couldn't believe it. Not, unimaginative, pedantic Mr. Stenmore? How else could Mr. Phelp's presence be accounted for here at Crisid, other than Mr. Stenmore's involvement of the Titans? The idea made my blood slow, as I felt it drain from my face. It suddenly struck me I had actually walked into his office of my own free will.

At that moment there was a slight tap at the door and Miss. Stone entered. Carefully placing a tea tray on a side-table, she began to pour out two cups. She handed me a gauze swab, motioning toward my lip. Leaning forward, I heaped two spoons of sugar in my tea. Miss. Stone turned and left, closing the door behind her. Upon taking a tentative sip, I recoiled from the pain that shot through my lip. I dabbed it gently, wincing as I saw a blotch of crimson blood there. I looked up to observe the slightest lift to Mr. Stenmore's brow.

"I was unaware you take sugar in your tea?" Mr. Stenmore noted inquisitively.

I was stunned he knew such a fact. These were treacherous waters I had voluntarily waded into and I reminded myself although I had once been Mr. Stenmore's valet, there was a great deal I didn't know about him.

"I don't normally…but…"

"No doubt it will bolster your nerves? You'll make every effort not to bleed on my carpet." Mr. Stenmore stated without reprimand. "As we're acquainted perhaps you'd care to explain your presence here at the bank and your haphazard appearance."

"I was invited into the bank by Mr. Phelps."

"Were you indeed?" he said dryly.

"Yes, I was."

"Continue."

"I wasn't expecting Mr. Phelps. I was invited in and shown to a downstairs room. Mr. Phelps entered and we had an altercation."

Mr. Stenmore paused. "Your account matches what I've been told. Why should you and Mr. Phelps have engaged in such behaviour?"

"Mr. Phelps and I had some unfinished business. It was not my intention for this to happen."

"What brings you to Crisid, Mr. Baxter? I'm not able to satisfactorily understand why you're here and your motive for entering my bank in the first instance. It seems to me our business was concluded years ago."

I was surprised Mr. Stenmore might think I was here because of our previous association.

"I'm not here to see you Mr. Stenmore." Now was the moment to exercise all caution if anything was to be gleaned from this unlikely conversation. "I'm here because I was lead to believe Crisid might be able to provide some answers."

"You have questions concerning Crisid? That seems unlikely…and yet, here you are," he pondered. "These questions must be pressing to have a man of your sobriety entertain such measures. Being, lead to believe something, suggests you are not in your right state of mind. What are these answers you seek?"

As I was no good at lying I felt an edited version of the truth was my best bet.

"In my current line of work, which requires my upmost discretion, I have been compelled to research a group of people going by the name of the Titans." I studied his countenance for any indication their name was familiar to him. He revealed nothing. I continued. "They're known to me as, intellectually elite, powerful, moneyed beyond all comparison and extremely dangerous."

I fell silent. What did he know?

Instead of the response I'd expected, he leant over and carefully lifted his teacup to his lips, sipped and placed it back on its saucer.

"If we had not shared a minor and intimate history, I would have you removed from here. However, your years in tenure as my valet gave no indication of mental fragility and I find myself with no other recourse than to allow you to elaborate. You will tell me in a factual manner all that you know of these Titans, in relation to Crisid."

"If you would indulge me, I would like to ask a few questions of my own."

"Proceed."

"Crisid bank handles the bank accounts of the seriously affluent," I stated.

"Crisid, has not seen a single paper-note, nor coin of the realm, for over one-hundred and fifty years."

"Excuse my ignorance, but I thought…that is to say, Crisid is a bank, isn't it?"

"Not what constitutes a *bank* in your experience. Crisid manages trillions of net worth on a regular basis. Members constitute economies, countries, and in rare instances individuals. Deposits are made in raw commodities and bullion. Then there are precious stones, predominately diamonds, unless they are of significant historical importance or value. A significant proportion of these are by way of shares and deeds. If anyone is foolish enough to break into the bank they will be disappointed, as nothing of tangible value is kept here. Our most valuable commodity is financial information, which is not stored collectively, apart from, up here." Mr. Stenmore tapped the side of his head, reminding me uncannily of Pilgrim.

"The Titans work in a similar fashion, Mr. Stenmore. Their influence is derived from their wealth. It is said they own and manage two thirds of the planets natural resources."

I paused to allow Mr. Stenmore to absorb the implications of Crisid being involved. If he found truth in the statement, the Titans would most certainly have financial dealings with Crisid.

"What evidence do you have they even exist?" he asked.

"I don't. They're understandably covert. Although I can't imagine a bank more suited for their purpose than Crisid." My observation hung in the air between us.

"Your deduction is a plausible one, particularly given my historical banking experiences. One must remain vigilant against corruptive subtleties. However, I fail to see where your concern lies. Anyone can read a national paper and know there are those with the resources to influence currency."

"I'm not here because of the price of Cox's Orange Pippins, Mr Stenmore. The Titans are an ancient society, these people have spent generations manipulating our planet to meet their own ends."

Even, to me it sounded farfetched. I quietened, and dabbed at my lip, as the blood leeched down my chin. Mr. Stenmore was also quietly thinking and I was momentarily relieved all this had occurred at his bank. Just the fact Crisid might be linked to the Titans meant I had his attention.

"What role do you believe Mr. Phelps plays in all of this?" Mr. Stenmore asked seriously.

"How much do you know about Mr. Phelps?" I countered.

"Mr. Phelps works as an intermediary between some of our members and Crisid."

It was entirely feasible Mr. Stenmore was unaware of my connection to Phelps through the murder of his wife. Realising I knew so little of Mr. Stenmore's background, I kept the information to myself.

"Really, would you care to tell me who those members are?" I asked.

"No, I would not."

"Perhaps the lady that arrived in the black limousine?"

"Hardly."

"Is Mr. Phelps employed by Crisid?"

"No, he is not."

"I didn't think so. I can't imagine you'd allow a man like that to represent the bank."

"Your obvious history of him, gives you an alternate perspective to mine."

"Yes, my *perspective* is considerably different to yours."

I will be speaking to him after our interview. Until now, I had always found him to be excellent in his position."

"I don't doubt it?" I uttered, with derision.

"You mentioned these Titans are dangerous - how so?"

I momentarily gauged Mr. Stenmore's capacity to entertain the incredible. I believed, despite my assumptions of his character from the past, he would evaluate what I told him, collate the facts and form an opinion that I hoped wouldn't be a million miles away from my own.

"It's said the Titans covert those who exhibit remarkable mental intellect. Their interest is more than an obsession. Theres a lot of information I've learned about them recently that I'm still struggling to believe. There is evidence to prove their intentions for creating..." I stopped. I was stumped by how to convey the fantastic.

"Yes?" he prompted.

"I'm just going to come right out and say it. The Titans are after those that are at the high end of the scale in smarts. Its been suggested, rather than wasting time searching for those random few, they'd create them." I stopped for the laughter, I'd felt sure to hear from Mr.

Stenmore, but he remained serious. So, I continued. "This is an ancient society, with unlimited wealth and power. Why hang-out for eternity, with what they believe are a bunch of half-wits. They've spent generations, supposedly working toward refining genetics, building their own people, if you want to look at it that way, and manipulating the rest to suit their own needs. People designed for a specific purpose – that's pretty much it."

Mr. Stenmore's eyebrows lifted. "Allow me to conclude your unbelievable hypothesis for you." He began in a grave tone. "These people, who secretly govern our lives, would ultimately prefer to live just with their own kind. Therefore, they've created and developed a genetic pool to achieve this. You perceive their danger in terms of human collateral damage?"

"I can see I've said too much," I added deflated.

"Why stop there Mr. Baxter. If the Titans have been working on this utopian society for so long, it stands to reason they've already created genetically modified human-beings to meet particular tasks integral to their ultimate goals. What do you think?"

The intensity of Mr. Stenmore's stare caused by heart to race and I felt the 'fight or flight' reflex throb in my veins as he continued.

"My own mental architecture has not made it possible for me to assimilate into the society of today. Does that make me a product of the Titans? No, It just makes me intelligent enough to know where I am best suited and to what. I am as sentient as I can possibly hope to be within the confines of my own DNA. I live without time. I do not recognise the passing of the days, months or years. I experience no repetition, as the slightest anomaly, I observe. We are each of us unique, but I share the same flaws of every other person. I covet, which is surely the most prevalent of all vices. You would like me to consider that our race is being systemically altered and that those traits that define us will be eradicated, and yet it is those very traits that have achieved our supremacy on this planet. Where would we be without them? Where would your fictitious Titans be without them. Whilst I find your story momentarily intriguing, I am unable to sustain any interest in the subject. You *were* an excellent valet Mr. Baxter, and it grieves me to discover you've allowed yourself to be taken advantage of in this manner. You gave no mention of the work you are now in, or with whom?"

I hadn't anticipated his skilled analysis to be quite as effective as it was. I felt alone both mentally and physically.

"I'm a partner in a storage business." I uttered quietly.

"Storage? I had imagined you had become some sort of investigator. An unexpected line of work given your professional background. How you've managed to conjure these Titans from your current line of work is something I have no wish to spend any additional time on."

"I find the work fulfilling."

"Do You? Then given your current physical and mental state this storage business must be quite unique, to have secured your allegiance."

Mr. Stenmore smile suddenly became fixed as he visibly paled. He asked quietly. "Who is this partner of yours?"

"There is only one."

Mr Stenmore stood abruptly, moving to the window he looked out and whispered. "And her name is Pilgrim."

I was aghast.

"How could you possibly know that?" I demanded.

Mr. Stenmore turned, his face bearing a grim expression, as if cleaved from granite. What could Pilgrim possibly mean to him? Within a moment, the look that had frightened and startled me was eclipsed by a fluttering across his face of incredulity and fear.

"Pattern equals prediction, Mr. Baxter," he added quietly. "I have an innate ability to recognise its serpentine signature in all things. Its presence cannot be disguised from my mind. I am its master and slave. Your story begins to assume some weight."

I was at a loss for words.

"Mr. Baxter I believe it will be in both our interests for you to leave my office and never return." He held up his hand preventing my protestation. "You have unwittingly shared with me information of a sensitivity that can hardly be exaggerated and I with you. What its effect will be, I cannot foresee. 'A little knowledge...'. Your colleague's name has never been mentioned, but passed across my desk many years ago, and will again I'm sure. I'm beginning to see a pattern Mr. Baxter, and I do not like what I see."

Mr. Stenmore's eyes held a look of panic, as the strength of this foreign emotion began to swiftly overcome his reserve. I could see the agility of his mind was gaining momentum pushing him to the verge of irrationality. As he gripped his desk his voice become harried.

"I cannot entertain this line of reasoning Mr. Baxter, as its sum is inconceivable!"

Mr. Stenmore's reality was unravelling before my very eyes.

"How free are we to follow our own path in life, or has that path been predetermined for us?" He continued with a strangled cry. "Our lives are short, I don't know how I could continue if I were to discover I was alive simply for the purpose of fulfilling someone else's goal." He looked at me beseechingly, and then angrily stated. "I won't have it – I won't have it I tell you! My dreams are my own… aren't they?"

Suddenly, Mr. Stenmore grabbed fists of my already torn jacket and was man- handling me towards the door, just as it was opened by Miss Stone. He shoved me through it slamming his door behind him, I stared vacantly at Miss. Stone and ran from his office with Mr. Stenmore's words, 'predictability and pattern', ringing in my ears.

I found myself walking halfway down Pall Mall, before I had the sense to hail a taxi.

"L'améthyste," I croaked.

As soon as I sat back in the taxi every muscle, tendon and bone in my body cried out for attention, in particular my throat. As I gingerly felt my neck, I realised my shirt and collar had been ripped in the scuffle with Phelps. Several buttons where either missing or hanging by a thread and my underarm seam was gaping open. I flinched as I applied a little pressure to my larynx.

Entering L'améthyste, my appearance caused the doorman to become overly solicitous and attempt to help me. I thanked him and made my way wearily upstairs. As I neared our apartment Dashwood opened the door. His congenial air and greeting evaporated into one of shock and concern.

"Mr. Baxter, Sir. Whatever has happened?"

"Mr. Worthington is as salubrious as ever and my appearance is not as a result of our meeting. I think a large brandy, Dashwood," I croaked feebly.

"Yes, of course."

I collapsed in the nearest chair and waited for the welcoming ministrations of my butler. He returned with such haste he was clinging to the stem of the goblet to prevent it shooting off the tray.

"Miss Pilgrim is in her rooms, Mr. Baxter. Should I summon her?"

"No, thank-you, Dashwood."

"Very good sir."

Dashwood disappeared and I felt sure Mr. Worthington was his next point of contact. My appearance couldn't be all that bad. Rising to my feet, I hobbled over to the mirror. Oh, crap! The face staring back at me, told of a bare-knuckle fight, not a scuffle. My hair was all awry, I had sustained a nasty rip to my bottom lip that was now caked in dry blood, and a blue-black bruise was very much in evidence around my neck. A small exclamation behind me caused me to turn and look into the anxious face of Pilgrim.

"Baxter! What happened!"

Twenty minutes passed before I finished relaying the details of what had occurred at Crisid Bank and Dashwood had finished applying initial first-aid.

"I've heard of Mr. Phelps. You must have hidden talents, to have left there alive," Pilgrim remarked. Her face was set in stone and her glacial eyes flickered over me with concern.

I took another swig of brandy wincing as the alcohol seeped into my cut-lip. Dashwood appeared at my side.

"I'll finish taking care of your lip, Sir, once you've sufficiently imbibed," he said authoritatively.

I continued to talk whilst swigging my brandy which Dashwood topped-up.

"He's a nasty piece of work. Now we know there's a connection between Crisid Bank and the Titans. Phelps didn't deny it. Plus the Titans call the Black Pearls 'Drepáni."

"Drepáni – how appropriate," she said.

"If only we knew the Titan behind them." I couldn't hide my frustration.

"We might not know his real name, but we know Dr Bonnin called him Gideon, which cannot be coincidence. They must assume the full name of the Titan they take over from. Plus we now know his Titan name is Cronus."

"Cronus?" I repeated.

"Yes, hes the Titan who wields the scythe, or as it's called in Greek, the drepáni."

"But that takes us no closer to identifying him. He could be anyone."

"On the contrary, he must have similar habits or traits as Cronus. It might help us to narrow our search. I wonder if the other Titans know what he's up to," she contemplated.

"Of course they must. They're in collusion with him even if they don't know the exact details. What do you know about Cronus?" I asked feeling quite better, now the effects of two large brandies were beginning to smooth out my fettered brow.

"Cronus is the Titan of time and ages. He has a bloody history involving castrating his father and ruling over humankind."

"I think we've identified our man, and what's more, hes mortal."

"Where would a god of time and ages hang out?" she wondered aloud.

"As he can't really influence time and ages, I'm guessing hes somewhere he believes he can. We can attribute the Black Pearls to him, perhaps hes a scientist?"

"Grubbing around in a laboratory? No, it doesn't fit the profile. We know he commissions scientific work. Therefore, it would need to be isolated, secure, and if I know anything about the self-absorbed he must enjoy an unparalleled level of comfort and facilities," she said thoughtfully. "I'm thinking an island, and I think I know a man who might be able to help us identify which one."

She picked up her phone and made a call which was answered almost immediately.

At this point, I was thinking H, was turning out to be quite useful. I listened as Pilgrim asked.

"Hi, I'm looking for an island. Remote, privately owned, no indigenous population, no visitors or tourists, with a pharmaceutical supply-chain; any ideas?" she mused, biting her bottom lip.

It was a few minutes before I watched Pilgrim nod her head and hang-up.

"Tidy yourself up, Baxter, have your neck looked at and let Dashwood sort out your lip."

"Am I correct in saying you've exploited the resources of H, yet again."

"Yes, and what of it?" she asked defensively. "It could be that his compliance may be due to a mutual interest. He has one idea for the island but I'll fill you in later. More importantly he stated, neither the Right Honourable Antony Glassmere nor Mr. Benjamin Short has been anywhere near New York within the last six months."

There had been a perceptible pause from Pilgrim which I took as my cue to say, with inadequately suppressed gloating.

"And Mrs. Bettina Zia-Tanner?"

The look on her face said it all.

"Aha!" I said triumphantly.

Quickly groaning as the pain from my cut-lip seared through me. Pressing my palm against my lip, I asked, "so what do we do next?" I knew it had to be some sort of covert surveillance of the pretentious Mrs. Zia-Tanner.

"We're to be the guests of Mrs. Zia-Tanner at Dracon Hall, the family's country seat."

"Are you sure about this?" I asked, after a deep breath. I felt a great deal of apprehension, given the fact we would effectively be alone with this viperous and calculating harridan and on her turf. I had no qualms about wrestling a man, but a woman? Then the memory of our time in the

Cold Room blinked on in my consciousness and my fear was immediately quashed.

"Yes, I'm sure about this and you would do well to be cautious of this woman, because she's no lady. She has potentially sanctioned the murder of hundreds of innocent people including the death and torture of Mrs. Cotterill."

Those final words made my heart turn to flint. If, Zia-Tanner, was responsible, her billions wouldn't protect her.

"Then I need to be sure," I stated with conviction. Knowing I would not be able to find my way back from the consequences, if there was any doubt left in my mind. Her entire involvement would be exposed.

"Oh, and that island sits off the horn of Africa in the Arabian sea," she added for good measure.

"Great, at least we'll get some fresh air," I commented sarcastically. I watched, surprised, as Pilgrim ducked quickly into her rooms, until I felt the shadow of someone at my shoulder. Looking up I saw Dashwood with a look of grim determination on his face carrying a tray with various medical supplies. I instinctively gulped down the remaining dregs of brandy from my glass and manned-up.

The following evening, for dinner, we found ourselves at a little Vietnamese restaurant reassuringly packed with Vietnamese people. My lip was throbbing incessantly and despite the meds I had taken I felt something with a minimum of ninety percent proof would take care of it, so I could enjoy the evening. Pilgrim looked stunning, as she always did in public. All other times she looked like a commando bag-lady with khaki trousers or jeans and a spaghetti strapped t-shirt over which she invariably threw a loose top. Tonight her hair was pinned up and she wore a dark green trouser suit subtly accented with diamante. Her eyes looked vibrant and alert, her make-up was minimal and finished with a soft nutmeg lip colour. If we were celebrating anything, it was surviving thus far.

Thinking back on those moments of us entering the restaurant and being honest with myself, I had felt her on her guard. Sure, at the time I myself felt somewhat wary, especially given the fact we had made our presence felt to the most covert and dangerous organisation in the world? After our trip to Switzerland and the unwanted visitor in the Cold Room; our following assignation was not entirely unpredictable.

If any conscious fear had risen to the surface at the beginning of the evening, I couldn't recall it. As far as I could remember, I anticipated a rather good meal ahead amid fresh surroundings.

Upon our arrival at that modest and rustic restaurant, we had been shown to a table on the right that was positioned against the wall. I was somewhat perturbed there were only a dozen tables which to me immediately translated into the restaurant not being entirely successful, despite being occupied. The tables were lined up, four along the two opposite sides of the room and four round tables to running down the centre. The diners momentarily hushed as we entered before the room returned to its original volume.

Through the dense steam that came belching out, every time the kitchen door swung open to a runaway waiter, a glimpse of flame and the rhythmic clank of a metal spatulas placated my culinary nerves. It was like a hot-house and I felt as if I had been transplanted into the Vietnamese jungle. A large, robust tropical plant sat to the right of the entrance, straining to gather any light and moisture. It had created its own microclimate, as the condensation from its leaves was clearly visible on the glass window it was pressed up against. At the opposite end stood a burgundy Formica desk with a large photographic print on the wall behind, which I could only deduce was a nod to a Vietnamese native landscape. Behind the desk standing to attention and ready to perform any bidding, stood the daintiest Vietnamese woman with long, black hair flowing past her shoulders. Each time I looked at her, she gave me a bright grin and raised her eyebrows in question.

"Please stop looking at her, Baxter; you're going to wear her out." Pilgrim observed with a bored tone to her voice.

In contrast, a young reluctant waitress strolled over to our table with a small pad, chewing gum with the distinct demeanour of a teenager asked to help out in the family business on a busy night, when she'd already made plans to meet her friends.

"Ready to order? Today's special is…"

When Pilgrim began to speak in fluent Vietnamese and placed what sounded like a huge food order, there was a miraculous change in our waitress, resulting in her straightening her back, nodding attentively and then shouting at two young boys leaning against the wall behind the cash-register. They bolted to our table with a number of condiments, fresh herbs and ice cold, cloudy drinks that turned out to be sweet coconut.

"That's handy," I mused, as I fussed over the positioning of my chopsticks.

"I like to think so," she added lightly with the faint curl of a smile.

Fragrant dishes with the most sublime tastes were ferried to our table with satisfying regularity, until I finally gave up. As the only non-Vietnamese people there I felt we had achieved quite a coup in finding this mini culinary-oasis which I fully intended to keep to myself. Therefore, I was a little put out when two new faces turned up that where distinctly non-Vietnamese. Instead of accepting the table that was being offered, for some unknown reason they approached ours. Before I had time to register their menacing intent, Pilgrim, shouted.

"Baxter!"

If she hadn't alerted me my senses would not have leapt into action quite so soon. Staring at what I believed to be a revolver being lifted, gave me a second or two, as I shoved our table with such force away from us, it crashed into their legs. As, dishes and plates clanked and smashed on the floor, we charged into the only open path available to us, the kitchen. Without time to think and amid the shouts of anger from the chefs, I began pulling any and all shelving down into the oncoming path of our pursuers. I saw Pilgrim already at the open back door. At that precise moment the first of the two men swung the gun toward Pilgrim, she snatched up a cleaver and hurled it at him, burying it deep into his shoulder. With two random shots fired, he fell back and hit the floor. His partner leapt over his body and continued shooting at Pilgrim as she ducked and weaved around the remaining shelving. Suddenly, he grabbed me by the throat using me as a shield. I struggled violently, as his grip increased I could feel his fingertips tearing at my flesh trying to force me to yield, but I couldn't think of anything other than freeing myself and trying to protect Pilgrim. I saw the device in his outstretched hand was in fact a dart gun. It was then, as I was beginning to lose consciousness I felt the air familiarly still. From behind my now closing eyelids, as I began to lose consciousness, those in the kitchen began to drop like empty clothes to the floor. The grip of my assailant weakened and I broke free coughing and spluttering, trying to catch my breath. The shooter momentarily looked at the various bodies strewn about the floor, confused. There was a feeling of something ominous lying invisibly about us. To my amazement and horror the remaining shootist pointed in my direction and squeezed the trigger. I witnessed, in slow motion his guns almost imperceptible wavering from the pressure exerted by his fingers as they tightened around the grip as a single dart shot from the chamber, missing me by inches. I was no longer scared, just unbelievably angry. Kill angry, maim and torture angry! Pilgrim, stood absolutely still with a look of quiet concentration on her face. At no time did she look at me.

The man gave a self-conscious laugh and spoke with a eastern European accent as he addressed Pilgrim. "You very quick like a cat. You crazy, I will shoot your friend. Is not my fault you not stand still? You moving all over. It is better you calm down. Is all over, I don't need my fun now, just put you under."

The ominous look on Pilgrim's face was one I now associate with death. When that mask rises up from the depths, it is time to let go of all your earthly concerns. Whatever it is, or wherever it comes from, I still have no idea – but I understand its presence equates to ultimate destruction. It is a weapon of such epic influence and energy and yet she can apply it with such precision. On those rare occasions when there is no alternative and no quarter being given I don't know whether to be grateful, or if I should run and seek solace in death. In truth, I don't believe I'd make it in time. It's a phenomenon I rarely witness. It is Pilgrim, and I accept that. When I catch glimpses of it from time to time before its fully emerged, it's a terrible and beautifully hypnotic thing to witness. Its presence becomes immediately felt in everything, in the air, in your body, in solids that seem to quiver in your periphery – its permeation fluctuates through all matter, coins in your pocket become soft to the touch and you feel as if you have expanded past your body shape. Then time ceases to exist and that's the moment I want it to be over. I don't want to see, feel, witness, cry, fear; because when it is manifest I experience all of those emotions. It doesn't come to save or salvage anyone or anything; there is no human trait in evidence like mercy or regret. I've never spoken to her of it – what would be the point?

I thought I knew what was going to happen next but I shouldn't have been surprised when I watched Pilgrim gently exhale and relax. Seemingly without prompting, the man's arm fell to his side and his gun clattered to the floor. There was some inner struggle that played out in the fear in his eyes which was quietened by Pilgrim's influence. She was staring blankly, her eyes a myriad of blues, when he fell to the floor, lifeless.

"Sorry about that, Baxter. I really thought it was just going to be dinner."

"No problem, if I could just get to a hospital?" I struggled to say.

She had turned toward me with concern.

"Don't try to talk."

I spent enough time at the local hospital's A & E for them to examine the damage to my neck. It was very badly bruised and several tendons had been stretched. With a prescription for some heavy painkillers and a warning to rest, my immediate treatment was completed. As we were leaving I whispered.

"I'm going to buy a company vehicle. Catching taxis is damn inconvenient. Also I'm taking some time off to recuperate."

"Of course. Your name is registered with the bank, buy anything you want. A few days and the swelling will have gone down and you won't look as if you're wearing a purple and blue scarf."

I spent a few days, not necessarily comfortably, but planning any stratagem I could to ensure we got out of this alive. I also shopped for an appropriate vehicle. Pilgrim had been correct in her summation of our predicament; it wasn't hopeless. I was spurred on by the fact I had now come up against three attempts on my life and had lived. My determination now to expose Cronus and his ambitions lay at the forefront of my mind. But first we had to visit the lair of Bettina Zia-Tanner. I had not been surprised just doubly on my guard, knowing our invitation was still open.

CHAPTER TEN

A few days later, in the late afternoon, we arrived at Dracon House, country seat of the Zia-Tanner dynasty. As our chauffeured car turned left onto a wide cobbled drive we headed west into the shallow light of a beaten-copper sun. Despite the warmth of the car's interior my fingers felt cold and numb. I wanted to rub them but the task ahead overshadowed any other thought. We soon arrived at a pair of ornate iron gates. The family crest of a gold serpent coiled about a red staff, stood in high relief, setting a sombre tone for all that passed under it. I thought it quite apt, and immediately recognised it by the description given by Dr Bonnin. Not once did I notice Pilgrim's eyes on anything other than the scenery in front of her. Nor did I take it upon myself to speak. Instead I thought about how I might best help, if our situation turned hostile and we were forced to defend ourselves.

We had already passed through the gates and were continuing up the drive when the sight of Dracon House began to reveal its grandeur in momentary flashes, as we passed along an avenue of Beach trees. Once we reached its end, the house presented itself in full gothic splendour with its pointed stained windows and flying buttresses. Our car moved silently under the ribbed vaulted entrance. Stepping out we were met by the butler. He seemed such an amiable and pleasant person; I wondered what he knew about the true nature of his employer. Passing through a wide corridor, its walls covered in rich tapestries and dotted with modern sculptures, my eyes fell upon a large portrait of Bettina Zia-Tanner, as its plaque attested.

"Pilgrim – it's her; the woman I saw get out of the car and go into Crisid." I whispered.

Pilgrim's eyes fell briefly upon the painting as we followed the butler.

We finally entered a high-ceilinged room where we were announced and cast adrift.

At its end was a desk situated in front of two large French windows that opened out onto a vast lawn. Sat behind the desk, occupied by some task was Mrs. Bettina Zia-Tanner. Instead of looking up at us, she continued to write slowly and deliberately, finally folding her correspondence and placing it neatly in an envelope before carefully sealing it with wax and adding the stamp from the black seal attached to the gold chain around her neck. As we approached she raised her head. Her piercing, ice-blue eyes made me shudder, as they were the first distinctive feature against her white translucent skin. Despite her obviously advanced years, she was as perfectly preserved as money could allow. She gave no smile, just the slightest derisive curl to her bright red and remarkably thin lips.

"Now, you have my full attention. Not something that's normally sought out, or advisable for that matter. What do you want?" She smoothed an invisible hair to her perfectly coiffured white chignon.

"I would have thought that was obvious even to the meanest intelligence," I said, quickly glancing around me for any sign of Mr. Phelps.

Instead of answering me, or acknowledging my existence, she looked directly at Pilgrim.

Pilgrim subtly turned away from her and to my puzzlement began to examine the paintings and various works of art in the room.

"You have a very fine collection here at Dracon House, it must be worth millions."

Pilgrim picked up a small jade sculpture from its plinth and turned it in her hand.

"It's so seldom pieces like this come on to the market, maybe only once in a lifetime, if that. I should know. I placed this item in an international charity auction eight years ago, to recover a debt and send a message. As I recall it was purchased by the Hammond-Schnikel museum. I had specifically stated no private collectors could bid for it. So how then does it happen to be in your possession?" A look of studied annoyance fell across, Zia-Tanner's aquiline features, but she remained silent. "Even given your considerable influence, you should not have been able to acquire it. Which means you have very influential friends who in turn can become very powerful enemies?"

A flicker of apprehension in Zia-Tanners eyes was enough to spur Pilgrim on. "So they've become powerful enemies, or so you've just realised. That's a bitter irony isn't it? To be lead to believe you're of intrinsic value by the reward of such trinkets, only to discover you've become expendable."

"Your point?" she grated through perfect teeth.

"A woman of your intellect and experience has already considered your position." Pilgrim lifted her eyes to the sealed envelope on the desk. "However, I believe we can reach a compromise, if not amicably, then with less serious consequences."

"Name your price," she uttered coldly.

I stood ready, an observer to this battle of nerves.

"I'm afraid this predicament you find yourself in will not be easy to extricate yourself from. Answer my question and earn your liberty."

Mrs. Zia-Tanner rose gracefully to her feet. Her striking looks and regal poise left me with no doubt why people felt subservient to her. With both hands on her desk she observed Pilgrim with a keen determination. There was rigidity to her form which stated this was a formidable woman who was not prepared to lose and would fight with everything in her arsenal. For the first time since we entered her domain, I felt unsure of our safety.

Pilgrim showed no sign her confidence was undermined, exactly the opposite. She moved toward the desk.

"Where is Cronus?" Pilgrim's manner was serious and grave.

A crackled burst of laughter, as if the punch-line to a long joke had finally been delivered, rang hollow against the walls of the room, but I could see from the fear in Zia-Tanner's eyes, Pilgrim had dealt her a fatal blow.

Zia-Tanner's surprisingly swift movement from behind the desk to the French-doors took both of us by surprise, but she stopped and turned to us.

"I believe we should move out into the garden, there is less likelihood of us being overheard."

We both followed her out, Pilgrim watching her like a hawk and I watching Pilgrim. I felt the climax to our journey was about to happen and the danger surrounding us palpable.

At the end of a well-groomed lawn sprang-up the grassland and wild flowers. Instead of stopping at its border, Zia-Tanner continued to walk slowly through it, allowing her fingers to trail through its soft tips. Before I could follow, Pilgrim held out her hand and grabbing my coat sleeve prevented me from continuing. Sensing we were no longer directly behind her, Zia-Tanner turned. The anxiety and anger that had clouded her features had vanished, and was replaced with something akin to relief; she gave a slight smile.

"I've always enjoyed this part of the garden. It's the chaos amongst the order; they've been the virtuosos of my life. I've built an empire single-handedly, by being a servant to structure, perseverance and sheer bloody-mindedness, but I crave chaos. Chaos, is what makes us feel alive and create things only dreamt of." She held us still with her self-summation, as she absently ran her hand down her gold chain to the seal. Looking at Pilgrim, she asked. "Do you believe we are created in God's image?" Pilgrim didn't answer. "I believe we are and it follows we must also have something of its mentality, surely that's only logical. I'm not saying we are anywhere near to approaching that level, but we strive to, don't we? Perhaps we're trying too hard for perfection? Do you ever wonder why you are the way you are?" She looked kindly on Pilgrim, and I instantly knew something was terribly wrong. I couldn't think clearly, only feel an oppressive sense of danger.

"You asked me about Gideon; once Imperator and now elevated to Cronus, a Titan." She allowed the weight of his name to linger in the air between us. "Such conscious commitment is rare and the kind coveted by creative man. Cronus is expecting you. Order and chaos, what is its product, Neath?" Without saying another word, in one swift movement she lifted the seventh Black Pearl to her lips and swallowed.

"No," Pilgrim whispered.

Before our eyes Zia-Tanner turned away from us. A spasm threw her head back as she gasped and stumbled forward, crumpling into the long grass, dead.

Neither of us moved. Seconds seemed like minutes. I finally began to move forward, but was stopped again by Pilgrim.

"Don't touch her. Don't go anywhere near her. We can't be sure the N.E.G. won't pass through her skin. We need a plastic sheet and something to move her onto it."

Realising the danger we were in from coming into contact with the N. E.G, I staggered two paces back.

"She should have survived that, shouldn't she? I mean, she's smart enough to survive it. What the hell happened? We can't leave her here," I stated frustrated.

"The N.E.G obviously didn't think so. I guess it has its own plans," she stated seriously.

"Maybe it wants to get rid of all the smart people now?" I thought out loud.

Pilgrim looked at me, her eyebrows arched in disbelief, as she took out her phone and dialled.

"I'm going to need some major containment. Have you got me? Good." She finished carefully with, "don't be long."

I marked the anxiety in her voice. Questions, they were a good way to think about something other than your potential demise.

"How can Cronus be Gideon? They must pass the names down. What do you think she meant with all that cryptic stuff at the end?" I asked, confused by Zia-Tanners implication that Pilgrim had something to do with the Titans. As the potential answer registered in my consciousness, I turned to find Pilgrim's eyes fixed upon me. What I saw reflected there, was nothing, no feeling, no recognition, just a dark and forbidding void. In that instant I felt as if I was staring into eternity, for that is the only way I can describe it. The next thing Pilgrim whispered to me, as quietly as a child in church, swallowed-up my sanity.

"I'm not sure what I am, Baxter. You'll help me with that, won't you?" she asked sweetly.

CHAPTER ELEVEN

Our handing over the body of Mrs. Bettina Zia-Tanner happened with such measured efficiency I can barely recall how we came to be sitting in the rear of the car, returning the way in which we had arrived. I had fallen silent trying to assimilate the information available to me while reconciling myself with my gut-instinct that we were on the side of good, Pilgrim had saved my life, more than once therefore, she didn't want to kill me. At that point I'd grab onto any mental life-raft I could. I chose to ignore any doubts that bubbled to the surface of my consciousness, concerning her motives.

"Pilgrim, Zia Tanner said Cronus was expecting you."

"He'll just have to damn well wait!"

Her anger was oppressive within the confines of the car and I stared out the window, hoping it would dissipate soon.

Our next port-of-call was New York, where a certain banker was continuing his lot in life. I'd thought that I would be excited to tramp around some of my old haunts, or bump into the few friends I'd made, maybe regale them with tales of adventure, but I accepted what I had shared with Pilgrim could never constitute light conversation.

Pilgrim had stated she wanted to reassess his level of involvement and therefore, with considerably less effort than I had made, she secured the position of PA to Gerald Albion Whitingstore III, otherwise known as G.W, my former employer. Nightly, she returned to our hotel, never once mentioning what a complete ignoramus he was; I had to admire her for that alone. Within two days, Pilgrim had been able to ascertain exactly what he was up to, and somewhat predictably, it wasn't much. Basically it was the acquisition of as much money as he could figuratively lay his hands on. Tanner Pharmaceutical's forty million investment of other people's money had already paid its dividends, both to its board of directors, who couldn't have been happier with the demise of their CEO and, Pilgrim believed, to the Titans, who had successfully tested their new piece of technology. During the short time it had taken to confirm his ignorance as to the real reason his business was being used, there it came as no surprise when he was found dead one morning on his bathroom-floor. The coroner entered a verdict of coronary heart failure, a not uncommon occurrence for men of his age and lifestyle. Pilgrim later informed me she'd discovered his bath towel had been sprayed with a highly-potent analgesic. After coming out of the shower and drying himself; the combination of the moisture on his body, open pores and increased body temperature, had been the ideal osmotic conditions for it to react quickly and with deadly efficiency. When Pilgrim had thrown herself on the sofa of our suite at the hotel and told me of my former employer's demise, it hadn't taken more than a couple of seconds for her to swing her legs off the sofa and ask me point blank what, if anything, I wanted to know about her. She had moved to the drinks-bar where she furiously dug her glass through the ice-bucket and began to pour a large gin and tonic, dropping the merest slither of lime on the top. She handed it to me and fixed herself another.

"I would interpret that as Cronus tying up loose ends!" I said.

"Mm, I think you're right."

It was true that I'd wondered if she'd had any part in G.Ws death, using the same method as the man in the Cold Room. With her somewhat predatory nature, the idea was perfectly feasible, but I thought unlikely, as she hadn't mentioned she was responsible. As odd as our situation was, I believed she would have told me had she been involved. I asked the first question that popped into my head.

"Tell me what happened when I blacked out in the Cold Room." I had sat down on a large Chesterfield chair and extended my legs onto the ottoman.

She returned to her chair, lying perfectly relaxed, she moved her finger around the rim of her glass in a hypnotic fashion.

"I don't know exactly. I can tell you how I feel and what things look like and the result of my actions. I've never had any witnesses to what actually happens – well, that is until you." She paused and turned toward me with a strained smile. "Well, no one that survived, long-term."

"Okay, that might present a few problems." The danger signs pointing to a short but eventful life loomed large. "But let's not get off track. Tell me everything that happened." I needed to hear exactly what I might be up against and yes, my life depended on it.

So we began the most unusual and nerve-rending conversation. I hoped to live to tell the tale, but as I asked more questions my fear dissolved into curiosity.

"Before the man reached us, I saw him enter L'améthyste and come down in the lift, therefore, I was more prepared than you for his arrival. I didn't know he was carrying a gun and I wasn't sure what to expect. But I felt his purpose and it was resolute and deadly."

"But we knew that whoever was coming, it would be dangerous, I mean physically critical." I wondered, exactly what she'd been expecting.

"I was prepared for the worst, but I couldn't be sure. People are complicated creatures, remember?" She took a large sip of her cocktail and continued. "He came through the door and something in my psyche changed. Time began to slow very rapidly, so when he pulled the gun, and I saw you hadn't moved, I had time push you out the way. I didn't feel the movement of time, but I was drawn to the heat of his heart-muscle thumping wildly, I curled around it and stopped it beating."

Pilgrim was drinking deeply, to stop herself from feeling, I guessed. I couldn't be sure, but I think if she hadn't she might have shed a tear, just the one, and not for the dead man.

I remember at this juncture that I didn't think our conversation odd. With everything that had occurred up to this point, the whole scenario sounded perfectly acceptable.

"When this change occurs, I've seen it change you physically; do you feel any after-effects."

"Other than exhaustion, if its been intense, no." She paused. "What kind of changes?"

As I didn't feel capable of dispassionately relaying what I'd witnessed, I deflected her question by asking.

"Have you ever been hurt?" I had to know whether she was mortal. I didn't want to be out there hoping that as bad as our situation might become, I could rely on her to win the day.

She laughed, relieving some of the tension in the room. "Of course, I've been hurt." She sat quietly for a long moment. "Once, quite badly."

She was looking at me thoughtfully, we both knew what the other was thinking; this work could well be the death of me, and she might, one day, not be able to save me, or herself.

"I told you, I don't know what I am, and it's true, I don't. I react in a certain way when my life is threatened, but that's only a small part of it. I don't have an on/off switch and most of the time nothing happens. I have a way of feeling and knowing information about wherever I find myself and with whom, and when I need to, I can influence people and see other things," she finished contemplatively.

"Like what?"

"Other dimensions," she stated without emotion.

"That will be handy." I quipped before I could stop myself.

"I think that should be all for the moment, don't you?" she said dryly.

I hadn't meant to sound flippant. Pilgrim saw my ability to keep it together was beginning to fray. She remained perfectly still and had changed from listening, to watching me. I can't remember specifics after that. The last thing I recall consciously, was feeling quite peculiar. I heard myself say.

"Yes, I've reached saturation point."

I remember trying to stagger to my feet, and feeling more than a little disorientated. The small amount of alcohol I'd drunk couldn't account for my confused condition. As I lurched forward, I put my hands out to grab on to something, but my movements had become leaden and slow. I was falling toward the floor when time slowed to the point I was left a few inches above the carpet. My brain felt too big for my skull. It didn't hurt, it wasn't painful in any way, but it felt as if it had traversed the boundary of my cranium and was widening and becoming flatter. My points of reference disappeared and I was seeing through the walls, ceiling and floors. I thought I recognised the outline of a vase as the contents of it shimmered. Then as soon as this strange phenomenon had occurred, it vanished, and I hit the carpet with a muffled thud.

"Sorry about that," Pilgrim said regretfully. "That's never happened before. It must be a combination of trusting you and a softened psychological knee jerk reaction to protect myself. I'm really sorry, Baxter. It's the first time I've reacted that way."

"Did you just do that to me?" I was having difficulty gathering my thoughts. As I got up from all fours and fell back into my chair.

"Yes, I felt the same mental state move over me, but this time it didn't consume me. I'll tell you what I saw; time slowed as you were falling and just before the point of impact you moved from three to four dimensions. What's very interesting though is I saw what you saw, and that doesn't normally happen." She said puzzled.

"And what did I see?" A wave of nausea was about to overtake me and it took all my will power to suppress it.

"It was like looking through your eyes. You saw through matter, the walls, floors, you could also see the outline of matter, like the vase when you focused directly on it. Satisfied?"

"Don't do that again; I almost threw-up."

"I'll try not to. You survived and that's a plus, right?"

She sounded so unsure of herself, I couldn't be sure if it was an act, or what had really happened. Had she drugged me? But how did she know what I'd seen? It was too much information for my brain to absorb and I gave in.

"I'm off to bed. Let's talk later." I wandered like a beaten man to my bedroom and fell almost unconscious and fully clothed onto the bed.

When I awoke, it was dark. Squinting for the blue luminous dial of the alarm clock I noted it was 03:18 am. As I moved to get up a stabbing pain shot through my head. Holding my forehead in my hand I moved toward the bedroom-door. The outer living-room was in darkness with no sign of Pilgrim.

Whatever had happened to me I believed Pilgrim was telling the truth and the implications were frightening. I returned to my room exhausted. With no signs of life, there was no need for me to be up and around so I staggered thankfully back to my bed.

Quite contrary to my imaginings, our breakfast that morning began as a very light-hearted one. We revisited the events of the previous day and talked in general about what it could all mean. I learnt something about myself that morning. I am a survivor, Mr. Phelps had been correct. I could have left those two incredible weeks behind me, shut it away somewhere, until its memory had faded. Instead, I chose to embrace it and even though I didn't consciously think of it at the time, I decided to follow it to whatever conclusion it might reach. However, even with Pilgrim's insights gathered over her lifetime, we were left with, 'ifs, maybes, and worst case scenarios', leaving little room for comfort. We finished our breakfast with as much gusto as two people who had been starved of food and shelter. Our final agreement, which came after a great deal of discussion, disbelief and protraction on my part, was to go after Cronus immediately. Pilgrim sounded self-assured in her reasoning; he should be made accountable. If, he was everything I'd heard, it meant he would not take any infringement to his operations lightly.

"You have to keep in mind, Baxter, these people are a product of centuries of selection. They covet all that is at the pinnacle of mental ability."

"So what do *very* smart people really want?"

"Considerations such as race, gender, religion, age, all these things have ceased to have any relevance for them. But given the implications of a negative gene-pool, I'd say they're in the process of creating their own."

"What about cloning?"

"You're forgetting that's simple physicality; we're talking about brain-power here."

Pilgrim always looked strained during these conversations, as if just the knowledge of the Titans existence was enough to exhaust her. She sat cross-legged in that enormous chair resting her hand in her chin in a contemplative mood. Those bright eyes that saw everything were momentarily obscured by doubt as she lit a cigarette and inhaled.

"We know there are one hundred and forty-four of them with only twelve of them as Titans," she said.

"That doesn't sound like a lot to me," I stated honestly.

"Keep in mind, we have countries on our planet that are run ostensibly by one person and most of the time they're not very bright."

"Where did Zia-Tanner fit into all of this?"

"She took the last pearl because it was the only option left to her. She might have believed it would open her mind." Pilgrim lifted a questioning but doubtful eyebrow. "In answer to your original question, I think the Titans are looking to become the founder members of a new race."

I stared at her in disbelief, asking. "And what happens to the old one?"

"They'll be phased-out. The current gene-pool will be run dry within two generations once the N.E.G hits water. By that time they will have everything in place. "

"We've got the N.E.G."

"They have the ability to replicate it."

"We have the antidote."

"We can't be sure it will work. I can't risk the future of our next generation to a *maybe*."

The words she was using and their meaning blunted against my mind. The conceivable fallout from a wrong decision on our part was too much for me to accept. Pilgrim continued.

"There's a revolution taking place within our own species."

"Stop…stop!" I begged. "Pilgrim, I'm drowning, this can't be left up to me, or not even me, it can't come down to someone like me. You, yes, I understand that, I'd buy that, but me, no."

"You think I can handle this…by myself?"

"Eh, yes. You say, *our* species this, *our* human-race that, when you're clearly not a part of it. Yes, I think your alien-butt can handle it!"

"I'm human Baxter, flesh and blood, one-hundred percent home-grown. I'm just a fast-tracked version of the rest of you."

"I don't believe it."

"Okay."

Pilgrim fell silent for a moment and then continued.

"I get that its hard to accept, but think about it. The advances in medicine and technology have been fast forwarded in the last one-hundred years compared to any other time. Look around you, Baxter; in your life-time alone technology has surpassed your understanding. Do you even know how your mobile phone works? It would be the same as if you showed anyone your phone, fifty or a hundred years ago; I'm not an inconceivable concept. I don't believe I've made a mistake in bringing you in to all this. I don't know why you and not someone else." She was clearly moved in her sentiment. "Whatever happens to us, Baxter, I'll never regret my decision."

"No, but I might." I said with definite reservations. It seemed my protestation that I wasn't up for the job, had fallen on deaf ears. Even though I still believed I wasn't capable of stopping the Titans, neither did I believe that anyone else was, except Pilgrim.

The gravity of our situation enveloped us both. The one thing I clutched onto in the mire of our current predicament was the self-awareness I had experienced in an altered state that Pilgrim had induced in me. As far as my logic was concerned, I believed Pilgrim was the only person who could bring down the Titans.

"Now to Cronus," she stated decisively.

CHAPTER TWELVE

I awoke with stiffness in my aching limbs and a dull pain travelling from my right shoulder blade through to the muscle in front.

The clatter and hum of our current transport; an ancient diesel train on its way through northern Somalia; moved centre-stage in my conscious mind. The wooden-slat seating we had been forced to occupy in third-class had mercifully been worn smooth from decades of passenger use. Still, as I attempted to stretch an arm, a look of admonishment came from the woman sitting to my right. Packed tight as we were, there was no room to manoeuvre, other than to rise and walk about, and so I did. Stepping over ancient suitcases stuffed to breaking point and the legs of still sleeping passengers, I edged my way gingerly to the carriage-door and out into the train's corridor where an overflow of men had decided to doss down; they were obviously seasoned travellers on this particular railway. The open upper sliding windows pushing the hot arid air into the corridor came as a blessed relief from the overpowering odour of stale bodies, to say nothing of the rancid tobacco and coffee breath leaching past sixteenth-century dental-work rising up off sleepers prone on the industrial linoleum floor.

Thankfully, the perfume of various potent aromatic dishes bubbling merrily away on handmade stoves wafted from carriage compartments to give my nostrils some respite. I was now roaming along the second-class corridor peering into these confined areas, where industrious cooks camped out, attesting to the length of time some of my fellow passengers were expecting to travel. I was looking for Pilgrim. She had settled across from me in the early hours but was now nowhere to be seen. We hadn't taken any luggage, Pilgrim had stated everything we would need could be acquired on route. Plus it removed the temptation to rob us. There was nothing for me to do but to continue my search along the train.

After yesterday's breakfast, Pilgrim had left me to make some enquiries. I had been only too pleased for her to leave. In my limited experience a day with Pilgrim was a life-time with anyone else and frankly my nerves were wracked to shreds. I needed to relax and not think about anything other than me. I know it sounds selfish and actually it is, but it was the only way in which I could function. On our last morning at L'améthyste, Dashwood had run my bath, using a bottle of something claiming to hold earth's essences. I took the brunt of the heat and steam which instantly turned my skin bright red and made my nose run. I stayed in the bath until my fingers wrinkled.

It wasn't until the late afternoon when Pilgrim came through our apartment door, obviously in a hurry and quite breathless.

"Quick, grab your coat, you won't need anything else, we need to leave in forty-five minutes."

"In forty-five minutes? I don't understand. That means we've got plenty of time. Where are we going?" I called after her, still sitting in my chair, the TV remote-control in hand, as she stormed into her room. Less than a minute after, I heard the toilet flush and she appeared at her bedroom-door, tugging on a black hooded tunic.

"Forty-five minutes to get to the airport and leave the country; we need to make the Aden Express train."

"The Eden Express train sounds rather nice."
I quickly rose and fetched my coat from my room.

"It's not Eden, its Aden, as in the Gulf of Aden, between Somalia and Yemen, in the Arabian Sea. We're going to Korando, on the northern-most tip of Somalia, the horn of Africa; the train stops at Korando and from there we go by sea around the Cape. Let's not keep Cronus waiting any longer."

"No time like the present." I mumbled, knowing whatever lay ahead would be momentous in every sense of the word.

It had taken three planes, several bribes and a taxi driver, I swore was a young girl with a fake moustache, before we only just climbed onto the train from Luwanga, in time to travel the four hundred miles to Korando. Along the way, Pilgrim had explained how she'd been researching Zia-Tanner's movements and history. The 'Zia' in her name had originally come from an Arabic line of extremely wealthy merchants located in northern Somalia and could potentially be traced even further back."

"But Zia-Tanner's family are old European money, one of the oldest and wealthiest, everyone knows that. Apart from that, she was white."

"It helped that generations of her ancestors settled north of the equator. If the earth were to move one degree from the sun within a few generations we would all have a paler pigmentation and if we moved one degree toward it we would all develop a darker skin tone. Our skin colours and features evolve to survive within our environment, nothing more. I doubt that Zia-Tanner knew of the connection herself."

"Unbelievable."

"Not really. Remember the Titans' only discrimination is IQ. Where do you suppose *my* gene pool originates?" she asked.

"I'd prefer not to think of that right now; besides you maybe a freak of nature."

"I'd rather be a freak than a monster."

I ignored the hint of concern in her voice.

"Are you sure we're going to find Cronus out there?"

"Yes," she replied.

"You don't believe Zia-Tanner's motive was to use the Black Pearls for the pharmaceutical industry to, you know, get a leg up on the competition?"

"We're way beyond that at this point. We're going to have to broaden our minds on this one, that's too simplistic. Firstly Tanner Pharmaceuticals is the wealthiest in their industry, their financial foothold in the world's economy is assured. So this is not about money. What possibly could a wealthy, well established and respected woman be doing with a weapon as deadly as that? The two don't fit together."

"Her company might have used them and then been able to provide a cure, at a huge profit." I was racking my brain for any reason that would stand up to scrutiny.

"The profitability of a company is built on the living, not on the dead."

"Not if you're in the funeral business," I suggested under my breath.

I knew she had heard me but had chosen to ignore my sarcasm.

"What are we going to do when we find Cronus?" I asked.

There was the slightest of pauses before she answered.

"We're going to either expose him, and someone else will kill him, or we kill him ourselves."

So there we were, with nothing other than our courage and determination to meet Cronus; who was awaiting our imminent arrival. I fully understood this part of my time was going to be short, eventful and over. I wasn't sad or regretful. I had experienced a zest for life with Pilgrim; my nerve would be tested at my end and I hoped I would not be found wanting.

"I'm sure you've thought about the fact they want your DNA to experiment on, either with or without your permission."

"I would have thought that obvious after the Vietnamese restaurant. Besides, I've thought of most things which all result in the same inescapable conclusion, Cronus must die."

The weight of the duty before us felt heavy, rendering both of us silent for most of our journey.

Having made my way back to our third-class carriage, I eventually found Pilgrim. I picked my way over to my seat, which had since been taken over by various livestock in cages. Keeping a smile on my face, I handed them one by one to the owner who shrieked at me in a language I didn't recognise. I tore off a piece of paper from a nearby crate and laid it on the soiled slates. At that moment I received a swift kick to my shin. I crumpled down and was about to complain in the strongest terms to the woman in the burka opposite; when she looked at me and hissed, "Baxter!"

"Pilgrim, I've been looking for you everywhere, where have you been?"

"Right here, I watched you take off down the carriage. I thought you were going in search of food, did you find any? I'm starving."

"You're lucky I recognised you in that get-up. What have you done to your eyes and skin?" I was beginning to realise the extent of her disguise. The area around her eyes, visible through the burka head-dress, was tinted brown and she was obviously wearing brown contacts. On her feet were her steel capped black boots, which I recognised immediately as *de rigueur* for her off-road expeditions.

"I suppose this disguise is necessary?"

"Yes, and until we're alone I recommend we don't communicate in English, and as you don't have any other language skills it will mean silence between us."

Her reprimand brought home the seriousness of our situation. I reminded myself we were not there for any other reason than to meet our objective and who was to say we were not being followed, or watched, even now? These unbidden thoughts occupied my mind until Pilgrim nudged me from my contemplation.

"Be a good man, Baxter, and find me some food, would you?"

I had forgotten she was hungry.

"And how am I meant to do that when there is no refreshment trolley or buffet car to speak of?" I, too, was feeling the pangs of hunger and must have sounded desperate. Men tend to sound desperate when they're hungry.

"You have only ever travelled first-class, haven't you?" she remarked with amusement.

"My travel experiences may not be as bohemian as yours, but I'm quick to learn. What do you want and tell me how to get it?"

"You saw the food-cabins in second class?"

"Yes," I answered, wondering if they would know where I could purchase some food.

"Find one you like the look of and buy a plate of whatever they have. Be extremely courteous, thank them and count out the money, and I don't want anything tough to digest."

I kept quiet about thinking those people were cooking just for themselves. The ingenuity and commercial attitude of the indigenous people was commendable, and a welcome relief.

I headed back down the aisle and into the corridor, my nostrils set on full alert for the most pleasant culinary bouquet. What I had failed to observe when I had first entered the corridor; having been preoccupied with the various dormant bodies scattering the floor; were those few waiting inside the cabins fervently holding tin plates and bowls; into which steaming meat and vegetables were being ladled. The sixth cabin I passed had the longest line, and therefore in my humble estimation must be the best. I stood at the end of the queue, coins in hand, hoping they might have a couple of extra plates or bowls I could borrow, or buy. I had barely been stood there for thirty seconds when a shout went up from the front which rumbled down the line toward me, and I was ushered to the front. Passing those in front, I nodded my head and threw the word 'Salaam' about me. Some smiled and nodded back, some just stared, whilst others chose to ignore me. When I reached the front, I found an elderly man who looked as if he'd been fashioned out of pipe-cleaners. He was stood shouting down the line, relaying the food-orders, whilst taking the money. He stood above a group of three women waving a fist of notes which he frequently drew between his thumb and forefinger. Clad in their burkas, chattering away, they seemed oblivious to his presence. They continued stirring, ladling and lifting the lids from large aluminium pots. To my relief the man spoke in English with a heavy Arabic accent.

"What would you like, Sir?"

"What do you have?" I asked. I had no idea of what was on offer.

"We have lamb, cockerel, and goat, with couscous and vegetables. The finest, fresh today."

His sales pitch complete he grinned at me and my face shrunk back from the two teeth remaining in his head. I fixed a smile on my face and politely said.

231

"I would like one lamb and one cockerel please, both with couscous and vegetables, thank you."

A reinforced tin-foil bowl, more likely to hold a steak and kidney pudding, was plucked up and filled before another word was spoken. He expertly relieved me of all the money I had in my hand, piled me high with tin-foil bowls and continued shouting down the line. As I made my way back, I felt the heat from the food begin to permeate through my outer-clothing and hoped I would reach Pilgrim before I had to put the whole lot down for fear of being scalded. Getting back with not too much difficulty, Pilgrim was obviously delighted to see me as she fussed around me picking-off foil-pots and plastic forks. Within minutes we were replete, and I confessed to Pilgrim I had seldom tasted a better meal. She pointed out somewhat wryly, that was often the case when one was hungry.

Our journey across northern Somalia was thankfully uneventful. I don't know what I expected, but I hoped our travel experience wouldn't include us being maimed, robbed, or killed. I'm sure if I had voiced my concerns to Pilgrim she would have replied that I was being dramatic, and exhibiting the sort of unwarranted paranoia that she despised. I had observed that Pilgrim rarely watched, or listened, to any news media. Surprisingly that didn't diminish her in-depth knowledge of current affairs.

The scenery passing our window was truly stunning and like nothing else I had ever seen in my travels. The train ran parallel to the Arabian sea, which lived up to its reputation as being one of the most breath-taking sights in the world with its carillon blue waters folding to cobalt under the pale lemon sun of the late afternoon. And just as you became accustomed to the landscape, the colourfully painted fishing boats with their characteristic crescent sails; could be seen working off-shore. If it had been at any other time, I would have spent it enjoying the scenery. As it was, my mind was continually being brought back to the fact that this was serious work and I should remain vigilant. The closer we neared our destination, the more passengers disembarked, until we were alone in our creaking carriage, and Pilgrim could remove her head cover, revealing a panda face. Her wearing of the burka seemed entirely necessary, given the austerity with which the inhabitants of this part of the world practised their faith. The remainder of our solitary journey passed between us with bouts of discussion and sombre intervals, each of us mentally trying to prepare for whatever lay ahead.

I realised our arrival was imminent when Pilgrim replaced the burka head-dress.

It was night when we arrived. Our train creaked and groaned during the final few miles which it took at a snail's pace, until we finally ground to a shrill stop at what could be best described as an encampment. There were several rudimentary huts with five large tents, each the size of a marquee to the eastern side. In front of these, I observed men hunkered down tinkering with their fires whose glowing orange embers flecked toward the night sky.

As there was no station to speak of, let alone a platform, disembarkation involved standing on the lowest available step and jumping the three feet down into the sand. I landed like a stone and stood up to my shins in sand that was still warm despite the cool of the evening. Pilgrim swung down gracefully using the handle to the side. Looking right and left and finally under the train to observe the opposite side of the track, she stood up.

"Let's wait until these people have moved on," she said.

Four Arab men, each carrying large rolled bundles, were warmly met by their friends escorting camels. Deftly mounting and securing their packages, they headed west into the desert with only a crepuscule moon to accompany them.

Under Pilgrim's instruction, I trod a few steps in front of her before noticing a man in traditional garb with an intimidating girth heading our way. As he reached us he held out his hand.

"Mr. Baxter?" He spoke with a distinct and deep Arabic accent.

"Yes." I was completely taken aback but managed a reasonably confident response.

"I am Hakim Kareem. I am pleased to meet you."

He shook my hand vigorously and revealed the best set of gleaming white teeth I had seen in a long time; well, definitely since I had entered the train. Stepping past me, he greeted Pilgrim in what I thought must be a the traditional manner, bowing his head and touching his fingers to heart, lips and forehead.

"Salaam."

"Atcham Salaam," Pilgrim said softly and bowed her head.

"Your timing is fortuitous." He pointed to the sombre yellow light from the moon. "Allah be praised."

With the pleasantries observed, he asked us to follow him. We walked a short while through the sand, which began to make my thighs ache. Turning toward the sea, and striding

234

down the sand-bank, I was glad we weren't trying to climb up it. Despite not having been physically active during our journey, I realised I was exhausted. Within a few minutes we stood by the Arabian Sea. The soft ebb-and-flow could be seen but barely heard, as it whispered up the sandy shore-line and lapped gently against the side of a moored fishing boat. There were no other sounds apart from Hakim softly greeting the skipper and introducing me, and secondly, Pilgrim. The fishing boat was relatively comfortable and to my surprise seemed larger once aboard then it did from the outside. It was fitted with large worn planks from side to side and I sat down quickly as Hakim and the skipper pushed us quietly and effortlessly out onto the water, before jumping in. Taking up the oars, they began to row us out to sea. Before long we turned and began to cut silently through the water as we ran parallel to the shore, with just the rhythmic creak, thud and splash, as the oars were lifted, swung and dropped back into the water. Pilgrim remained silent. Within minutes the small settlement was far behind us. Straining to see the shoreline, I realised there were no other signs of life along this part of the coastline which looked completely uninhabited. With not a tree or shrub to take a mental note of, we continued without talking, under the canopy of a million twinkling stars.

We had been on the water for almost an hour when a murmur passed between Hakim and the skipper and our boat turned and headed for shore. Although I couldn't see anything untoward my heart was hammering in my chest and my adrenalin surged in anticipation. We stepped out into a foot or so of sea water that despite its surprising chill came as a welcome jolt for me to reclaim my senses. I followed Pilgrim's lead and kept silent. To my surprise Hakim and the skipper pushed the boat back on the water and hopped in. Turning to Pilgrim, who was already walking away from me, I whispered as loudly as I could.

"Where are they going? They're not leaving us, are they?

"They need to move off shore, otherwise they could easily be spotted." She had stopped and was looking back at me. I hurriedly caught up.

"Okay, what are we looking for?"

"I already told you, I don't know."

"But you must have some idea?"

"Well if I'm right, and having done a small amount of investigating before we left England, I believe there might be a facility here."

"A facility?" My bowels didn't like the sound of that. My worst nightmare was to wind-up strapped to a rusting table in some old 'facility' run by a madman. I was blessedly thankful Pilgrim could not read my thoughts.

"Yes, something covert. I'm imagining it's not above ground."

"Ah, Mr. Pennyweather?" I concluded.

"The money and connections are there, so it's a distinct possibility isn't it?" she said breathlessly, as she began to take the strain of hiking through sand.

"If it's anywhere, it'll be here. This has got to be the eastern-most tip," I said.

"Precisely."

We continued to trudge for almost an hour in an unchanging landscape. The lack of sand-flies and anything that might bite us came as a huge relief. Eventually, as my ankles were about to give up, we saw the curve of the headland. Walking another ten minutes, we came to its apex where the sea folded against the rocks. Then we saw it. Set back about some thirty feet and sunk deep into the bedrock stood a large circular structure, about the same size and shape of a defensive pill-box. Similar in construction to those used in the Second World War to defend the shoreline, but without the holes for weapons.

"This must be it," Pilgrim assured.

"It has to be. There's nothing else around here for miles, unless it's sunk into the sea."

Made from sand coloured stone, it would have been almost invisible from above or out at sea. Simple and ingenious. Moving closer to it, I began to fear we might be moving into a trap, or worse, be blown up by unseen landmines. I didn't voice my fears, but disturbingly, Pilgrim, read my thoughts.

"Too much television, Baxter. This isn't quite what I was expecting," she sounded disappointed.

"What *were* you expecting?"

Instead of answering my question she walked confidently toward it and began to examine the outside, running her hands across its surface.

"There must be some kind of opening. It's obviously man made, therefore it has to have a function."

Try as we might we couldn't find any fissure, man-made opening, sign, or symbol on the outer surface to reveal its purpose or contents. Finally we both stood back and looked up. Then, looking at one another we both said in unison,

"What about the top?"

The structure stood at least fifteen feet above our heads. Looking about us for anything that might be able to help us, there was nothing but sand and rocks. After having racked our brains for any other way of reaching the top, we looked at one another blankly.

"How about you standing on my shoulders?" I proposed. I certainly didn't want to have come all this way only to discover we should have brought a ladder.

"No, it's too high." she answered quietly, obviously trying to think of a solution.

"Okay, rocks and sand. We'll build a ramp! If we create a sand-bank against it, we can climb up." I thought I had the solution.

"It won't work. The sand won't be dense enough, the incline would be too steep, we'd just sink right through, it couldn't hold our weight."

"Stop thinking of why this won't work, and think of how it can work."

After a few seconds a thought did enter my mind. I recalled a television program I had watched about the ancient Egyptians moving extremely heavy blocks of stone up the side of the pyramids. I persisted in defending my solution.

"We can do it, if we create a sand platform some distance away that widens out and comes in and finishes a few feet from the top. Let's try it and make the sand wet so it clumps together with the rocks. We can use my shirt and run sand through the fabric to make it hold water for longer."

Pilgrim began by collecting armfuls of rocks and dumping them at my feet as I scraped and pushed large quantities of sand with my hands and feet.

Some hours after the crescent moon had arced across the night sky and after several failed attempts Pilgrim laid her burka tunic on the ground and placing both feet in the arm holes, she knotted the sides together to create what can best be described as one large shoe cover.

"Good thinking," I congratulated her.

"It's the camels. They distribute their weight across the sand, to stop them from sinking, by splaying their toes."

Pointing down to her encased feet she had already begun to place a foot to one side and bring the other upwards and across, causing the fabric inbetween to strain over the sand, and more importantly she wasn't sinking. For the first time a glimmer of hope ignited within me. Taking it very slowly and carefully she inched her way to the top of the sand bank and placing both hands on the top of the structure hoisted herself up. She stayed on all fours and began to scour the top.

"You're going to need to hurry; it's almost daylight." I stated.

The soft purple and gold accents of whisper thin clouds were beginning to emerge from the dark, underscored by the first rays of dawn.

"There seems to be some sort of circular indentation here. No larger than a dinner plate and only about an inch deep."

Suddenly and without warning a profound hum and violent vibration shook the sand ramp from the wall, toppling Pilgrim unceremoniously beside me. The fall had winded her and I helped her to her feet, ready to run as fast as I could away from the place. Instead she stood up whilst the heavy vibration jolted through our bodies and we both watched agog as a tubular shape emerged from the centre of the structure. It finished at approximately twenty feet in the air when the humming and vibration was replaced by a series of bursts of white light darting miles across the sea.

"I don't believe it. It's a signal-light," she whispered in awe.

"What's its saying?"

"How the hell would I know?"

As we silently watched, the messaging stopped. Suddenly, far away in the distance over the water, flashed a single piecing blue light. If we had not been staring directly at it, we would have missed it. After the bursts of light flashed their reply our surroundings where once again plunged into darkness. As I tried to focus on anything around me, a halo of light remained within my sight obscuring my vision. Pilgrim was obviously experiencing the same problem when the vibration and hum struck up again and the tubular shaft sunk down into the structure.

"So the island is occupied. We need to get over there as soon as possible." Pilgrim stated, with more urgency than I felt comfortable with.

Before I could say anything else she had begun to head back the way we had come. She was striding across the sand with such purpose I had to struggle to keep up with her.

"Pilgrim…Pilgrim!" I called after her. In the end I had to pick up the pace until I was beside her, panting and puffing. "Where are we going?"

"Back with Hakim. I need to ask him some questions."

That same morning, we found ourselves in Hakim's tent on the banks of the Arabian Sea with the waft of freshly caught grilled snapper soon to be eaten for breakfast, passing tantalisingly through the tent. Hakim's cook was excellent. I had watched how he had scaled and gutted the fish, and then taken them to the water's edge to wash them. He had neatly, and with the precision of a culinary expert, taken handfuls of olives from leather pouches, removed the stones, and tossed them into the moss green oil. After, he laid them on a hot skillet over a wood-burning fire that caused them to rumble and hiss as the fragrant aroma of fennel coaxed my nostrils. Pilgrim was dressed not in the tattered burka from the night before, but in khaki trousers and a camouflage top. Her long hair was drawn back, her coloured contacts and panda make up gone, she looked fresh faced and ready for anything. I decided my own apparel to be inadequate.

"Hey, where did you get those?" I asked.

"Hakim has some for you too. He's a very resourceful man and is an excellent trader who anticipated what we might need."

She turned back to speak to Hakim. Whilst they were deep in conversation, our breakfast was served and my clothes laid out for me in a secluded area in the tent. After bathing in my shorts and vest by taking a dip in the sea, I returned to the tent to dry off and don my new clothes. After inspection it was plain to see the clothes were new to me, but not new in their own right. As I sat down next to Pilgrim, I said.

"Take a look at this. These have been worn before. Look there's a hole here." And to reinforce the point, I waggled my finger through to the front.

"It's been made by a bullet, Baxter," she stated dryly, picking up her conversation with Hakim.

The sobering point that the previous owner of these fatigues was in all likely-hood dead, focused my attention immediately.

"Don't look so glum, anyone would think it was you wearing that uniform when it was hit," she added amused.

"I was wondering how they had managed to get the blood stain out."

That morning we stayed in close proximity to Hakim's tent. The reputation for desert hospitality was well deserved and we wanted for nothing that our comfortable rooms back in London could have provided. Despite this, I felt the anxiety in Pilgrim and watched her as she sat outside the tent looking out across the Arabian Sea. It was hard to believe so weighty a problem rested on our shoulders when the day was becoming so gloriously bright and warm. I knew she must feel it too, but I had prepared myself as best I could under the circumstances. I had my gun and my determination to stay alive; that comforted me. Besides, Cronus was mortal. That was all I needed to know.

Pilgrim had thrown a series of questions at Hakim after she had clambered back into the boat last night, all of which were related to the structure at the headland. 'How long had it been there? Who had seen it being installed? What, if anything, did anyone know of it?' Hakim's response had not been one of surprise. The structure had suddenly appeared one morning and was reported and investigated by the fisherman who had discovered it. When questioned, he had stated he had been fishing off the headland the day before and hadn't seen anything. As he had moored his boat in the cove on the opposite side of the beach for the night he hadn't heard anything either. The only puzzling piece of information he had given; was that no boat, ship or any other sea-worthy vessel had visited the headland that night. Hakim had shrugged his shoulders and could offer no explanation other than, the structure hadn't been any trouble and must have been put there by the government, who else? Everyone in the area, were simple fishing men; the most marginally sophisticated could be differentiated simply by the number of boats he owned. Good men living a simple life. Pilgrim had accepted the information at face value. I myself felt suspicious about the whole thing and stated as much. She hadn't said anything, just looked at me with a serious manner and put her hand on my shoulder as she passed on her way down to the shore. I took note that she had failed to mention the structure was a working signalling device. I joined her at the shoreline.

"Pennyweather must have built the signal tower from underneath the ground. Which means there must be other structures below it?" I suggested.

"But if that's the case, why haven't the local people noticed anything? Unless the tower is the tip-end, and the remainder of the structure is under water and reaches back to the island?"

"But that's impossible. I've looked at the map. That island has got to be at least sixty miles away!"

"Unlimited wealth and time," Pilgrim answered. "And it would be the perfect place for a man like Cronus."

I left her alone with her thoughts and returned inside the tent, but as the noon-day sun began to take its toll she soon joined me inside, complaining about the sand-flies at the shore's edge. We sat and talked. Hakim had taken his leave and promised to return later that day.

"All I can think about is getting to that island." she said seriously. "There are a series of two small atolls and then an island about sixty miles to the east of the headland."

"Can Hakim take us?"

"He's agreed to take us, but he wasn't happy about it. Before we go, Baxter, I should tell you; I don't have a good feeling about this."

"Thought about it, been there and accepted the consequences!"

"What I mean is, I don't normally feel fear," she added quietly.

"Then perhaps that's a good thing. The more dangerous the task, the higher the level of adrenalin. Let's hope you're just gearing up for the big one, right?"

Pilgrim had gone quite pale. Whatever feelings my words had conjured, the effect on her was visible. Her face had turned to marble and there was a distance in her eyes that made me distinctly uncomfortable, as if something was un-forgiven. I didn't want to move or say anything which might turn her attention toward me. I admit I was frightened, so I quietly waited for my cue. When she finally spoke her words were ragged with emotion and brokered neither contradiction nor questions.

244

"It's not the words we use, or our physical state, that convince people of what we know; it's the sounds we cannot keep from our lips."

I wasn't about to touch this conversation, I'd rather plunge my hand into molten lead. Whatever dangers Pilgrim perceived on that island, I would not allow her to face them alone.

"I can't be responsible for you out there, Baxter."

"It can't be any worse than the Cold Room."

The look she gave me convinced me it could get a lot worse. So what could be worse than death? I decided not to think about it.

"I exonerate you from all responsibility for my welfare," I stated solemnly.

She rose and began tying a turban around her head and then pulling over it a dark ankle length nondescript tunic and finished by tying it desert fashion. With that task completed she turned to me.

"Hakim will be back shortly and we should be ready."

I felt anxious to go and face whatever danger lay out there. I was prepared for it, whatever 'it' was, and I was determined to meet it on equal terms.

I had everything I thought we might need rolled up in a large cloth slung around my back and tied at the front. In truth it consisted of a pitiful group of items that even I didn't truly believe would have much impact if the need arose. Still, I was beginning to see the value of whatever little mental comfort I could summon, going a long way in bolstering my misgivings. As I strode down to the shore to

245

catch up with Pilgrim my heart and mind were set to whatever lay ahead and it momentarily struck me as odd, that I, trusting I was of sound mind, should put my life on the line for someone I had only met recently and barely knew. But then I considered the fact that people do form strong bonds with those they've shared a trauma with. All these unbidden thoughts flooded my conscious mind as we boarded Hakim's small, single-mast sailing boat. Pilgrim and I sat up front in the bow whilst Hakim held the tiller and deftly steered us off-shore and into open water, heading east toward the island. As the sun was still lashing its burning rays down, I thought how fitting the saying 'mad dogs and Englishmen go out in the noon-day sun'. Fortunately for us, as the boat cut through the water, the cool air was thrown up off the sea reminding me I was alive. I looked over the side to observe the teal furled waves topped with white froth that showed we were moving at a reasonable rate of knots. The wind was full in the sails, causing an occasional snap and with no other sailing vessel in sight, I glanced back at our leather-faced captain at the tiller. Our journey was, thank goodness, without incident, and if it had been for any other purpose, the whole experience would have constituted a most pleasant excursion. As it was, a tangled ball of worry began to tighten in the pit of my stomach. Pilgrim had sat quiet and motionless, allowing the sea air to tease tendrils of hair from under her drab headscarf. I couldn't begin to know what she might be thinking and as she never looked at me, it was my signal to leave her alone with her thoughts. There was a grim determination in the set of her shoulders and I worried about her state of mind that had been forged from years of conflict. What struck me unnervingly was that we had been in full sight for anyone to observe our departure. And our arrival at the island would definitely be noticed by its inhabitants. Within a few hours the island came into view. As we neared, it was apparent a single person whose silhouette stood at the shores edge was waiting, for no purpose other than our arrival.

CHAPTER THIRTEEN

I started at the beginning of this story attempting to convey to you that extraordinary things can happen to everyday people. But beginning this chapter and knowing what I have to write; even I, who was involved and a witness to it, can scarce believe that it's true. Therefore, I will lay it all before you as it happened to me.

We reached the shore quickly under that massive white billowed sail that was then quickly and unobtrusively wrapped and tied, forming the look of a large armed crane. Pilgrim hadn't looked at me or spoken a word, her whole being seemingly focused on the person on the beach. I knew I was out of my depth in these close-cut manoeuvres, where I couldn't be certain if we were ahead, or behind in this deadly game. It was not until that point that I fully realised my fate once again lay in my own hands. I decided adamantly that my life wouldn't be taken for free, I'd make them work for it.

Reaching the island shore, with its swath of caramel sand, dotted by bright green palm trees that leant over like tropical birthday candles stuck in by a child; Hakim jumped over the side of the boat into the shallow water and with the aid of the waves and a strength wholly belied by his physique, heaved up the bow onto the giving sand. Pilgrim threw off her tunic and scarf into the boat before we jumped off onto the beach. The sentinel, was a striking young woman, who moved forward to greet us. With an almost imperceptible nod of his head to her, Hakim pushed his boat back into the water and jumped back aboard. I looked anxiously at Pilgrim, realising we were now stranded.

The young woman was tall and approximately thirty years of age, with very pale luminescent skin. Her midnight black hair cut close to her long neck and verdigris eyes made for a stunning combination. As her gaze fell upon me, thoughts came unbidden flooding my mind, all of them foolish and thank God none of them salacious. I was convinced she knew what I was thinking. She seemed to be carved from stone but as Pilgrim moved forward with her hand outstretched, she gently smiled. Her tailored white linen trouser-suit with white flat closed shoes looked like a uniform and I made the assumption she had been sent as our escort. She introduced herself, whilst holding the gaze of Pilgrim.

"I am pleased to meet you, Neath A. Pilgrim. My name is Asteria and you are Mr. Henry Baxter. Welcome to the island. You are expected. Please follow me."

Without waiting for any reply she turned and began to walk up the sand path where we followed. It quickly became enveloped from above by tropical trees and shrubs with leaves the size of doormats. The canopy became so dense, the temperature dropped like a stone and I felt grateful for the reprieve from a merciless sun. During our ten minute hike, stepping over the gnarled roots that traversed our path, I was aware not a single bird could be heard or seen. The flashes of chartreuse green, where the sun illuminated the leaves from above, gradually became more frequent until the forest fell away behind us and we entered a clearing where hardy plants met sand. Before us, sloping up in front, were boulders nudged up against a barren landscape that appeared almost semi-volcanic with their deep crimson pumice-stone. However, standing in high relief behind it, was an imposing citadel that looked as if it had been hewn from the rock cliffs behind. The proportions of the construction were impressive, with columns sitting on ornately carved stone cushions. Moving slowly and deliberately forward and not looking back, our guide continued mounting the wide stone steps up to the main entrance. As we neared an imposing arched stone entrance I looked at Pilgrim quickly and she looked at me and smiled. The relief that swept through my body threatened to dissolve my reserve. I noticed she didn't miss a thing, as her eyes scoured the exterior walls, iron studded doorways and deserted paths swinging to the left and right, and not a single man or beast of burden in sight. I had expected to see someone, a guard even. If I had thought about it more clearly I would have concluded that either there was nothing of value to steal, or the fortress didn't need to be defended. If I had known what lay in wait for me behind those forbidding walls I would never have had the courage to enter.

We hesitated, before walking through the arch entrance.

Suddenly our escort stopped, with a slight tilt of her head, she turned to us.

"Is there a problem?" Asteria asked.

Pilgrim and I, looked at one another,

"We're surprised by the building," Pilgrim replied honestly.

Pilgrim's reply seemed to satisfy her curiosity and she continued forward. I knew we were both thinking the same thing. This girl didn't understand our amazement, which meant she was not socialised. We both became increasingly interested in her.

As we continued walking up the worn stone steps of the stronghold, we entered into a dark hallway that was, thankfully, many degrees cooler. Still without seeing another living soul, we were escorted out across a smaller courtyard and along a colonnade to a heavily studded door which had the remnants of red paint around the studs, hinting that it had once been painted a dark maroon. We stood still, as this slight woman pushed the door open into a great hall whose white marble floors reflected the tall columns and three story arches with a view over the turquoise Arabian Sea. The air was sweet with the scent of jasmine from an ancient plant winding up the external columns.

We were invited to sit at a large blue granite table with legs carved into sea serpents, with richly upholstered seats in a velvet ruby cloth with elaborate fringe-tassels hanging down from its cushions. Asteria offered us tea, which we readily accepted. The moment she had closed the door behind her, I turned to Pilgrim, asking, "What do you think?"

"What do I think? Theres something definitely strange about that girl," she pondered.

"Agreed."

"She doesn't seem to possess basic learned human attributes."

"What?"

"She doesn't behave like a normal human being, Baxter."

"I'm getting used to that," I answered dryly. My nerves were beginning to get the better of me as I saw Pilgrim lift an eyebrow in response to my nervous state.

"Do you think she's a robot?"

"Too many films Baxter. Try to hold your nerve."

"Okay then, is she an autonomous electromagnetic carbon based life form?"

"Difficult to say at this juncture."

Soon after the sound of confident footsteps could be heard approaching the outer-door and I held myself in readiness. Pilgrim said,

"Ah, this must be our host arriving, and it sounds as if they're not alone."

Walking in front of Asteria, who was carrying a tray, came two men and a woman, all wearing identical white linen suits. If my alarm bells had only jangled before, they were now pealing. For some unknown reason one of them appeared delighted to see us, that is to say; delighted to see Pilgrim. He virtually bounded over to her, all teeth and moustache, without any of the formal pleasantries I felt necessary in good etiquette.

"Neath, absolutely delighted to meet you. You don't mind me calling you, Neath, do you?" He quivered in suppressed excitement. His accent was not one I recognised. His expectation of our meeting was certainly greater than ours.

"As we've not been formally introduced, you may call me Pilgrim," she stated firmly and without warmth.

'Indeed.' I thought, straightening my shoulders.

The man revealed only the slightest flicker of disappointment which was quickly quashed by a toothy smile that bordered on the grotesque.

"Of course, where are my manners. I am Professor Tear from Rhitzig, Austria. I'm head of genetic research and development. Please allow me to introduce my colleagues, Professor Van de Lingen from Bassinhas in the Netherlands, where she was Chair of genome research for the European Council for population growth and management. Professor Van de Ligne heads our 'slice and a splice' laboratories here." He gave an involuntary laugh, to which no one responded. "And Professor Ashour, from Odessa Island, Antarctica. Professor Ashour is our driving and creational influence, plus he single-handedly completed his father's work in identifying, isolating and developing the self-actualising genome."

Professor Tear was a man in his late sixties of average height with typical male pattern baldness, small brown eyes and a mouth that was barely a gash across the bottom of his face. I knew with some surety those who forgot his name would only need to say, 'You know, the man with all the teeth and that unruly moustache'.

The way in which Professor Van de Ligne looked down her nose at us, confused me. She had tufts of flaxen hair, and what was left of it was kept short, she reminded me of a doll that had taken a particularly brutal haircut from a pre-schooler. Her colleague, Professor Ashour, was the odd one out, he looked as if he should be at school, well, university maybe; he looked so young. He had a mop of black hair, blue eyes and would have appeared almost normal, if he hadn't been part of the group. There was something collectively alarming about them and I dreaded to find out what it was.

Professor Ashour seemed particularly keen to strike up a conversation with Pilgrim, whilst the other two professors sat obediently in observance.

"So how did you find us all the way out here?" Professor Ashour asked excitedly, sounding almost out of breath.

When Pilgrim looked at him without answering, he continued with a smile on his face, like a comic whose first joke had bombed before a hostile crowd.

"It's not important how you found us. I suppose you must have a lot of questions?"

Pilgrim spoke, and with a measured gravity I have since come to recognise as the precursor to the 'duck and cover' scenario. I didn't look at her, I looked instead at the doubt that began registering on the faces of the professors, although none was shown by Asteria. The professors evidently knew something of Pilgrim.

"Where is Cronus?" Pilgrim asked pointedly.

They had each looked genuinely puzzled. If they didn't know about him, what did that mean?.

"Gideon?" I prompted.

Without saying anything, the flicker of recognition to the name registered on their faces. Professor Van de Ligne spoke up.

"Gideon, our head of operations, will be joining us shortly. Cronus, we all know of, but not as an actual person. Cronus is our founder and benefactor. The Cronus organisation funds all our research here."

Professor Ashour joined in.

"I appreciate you wanting to meet Gideon. Perhaps we can talk until he arrives, now that you're here and we have a chance to meet you."

He had opened his hand to Pilgrim and was obviously unaware of the emerging role he was about to play in all of this. It was like watching children first encounter fire.

"A chance to meet me? You were expecting me. Why do you believe I came here?" Pilgrim asked. I noted the blue of her eyes had intensified.

"But I thought?" Professor Ashour directed an anxious stare to Professor Tear. With puzzlement registering on Professor Tera's face, he raised his hand to halt further discussion. Looking at Pilgrim, he said.

"Please forgive us. The fact of the matter is, you form the corner stone of our theoretical research. It's true we've never met you, but we know a great deal about you. I've even written several papers on you. No one could have predicted if, and when, Mother Nature would bring you forth. I knew one day you would appear. I just can't quite believe…we would actually meet in my lifetime!" Professor Tear seemed exhausted by his words.

A desperate sense of fear gripped my chest like a steel girdle causing me to sweat.

Suddenly, Professor Van de Ligne's eyes widened in amazement and dread.

"You don't believe this is *Absu*? It can't be!" she uttered in a frightened voice. "Not here!" She was shaking her head and looking beseechingly at Professor Tear and Professor Ashour.

"Asteria has confirmed it," Professor Tear stated plainly.

Asteria made no gesture toward acknowledgment, or even interest.

Professor Van de Ligne's reserve had evaporated, her eyes darted back and forth, uncertainty writ large on her face.

"We can't have her here." She involuntarily edged away from Pilgrim.

Whatever she knew about Pilgrim it frightened her. What I knew about Pilgrim frightened me, but there was a big difference between me and our new acquaintances: Pilgrim and I were on the same side.

Professor Tear spoke up with a fixed smile. Asteria remained unmoved by the conversation.

"I apologise, Pilgrim: what must you think of us? It's just the theoretical probability of such an anomaly of nature occurring, is so fantastic, as to be almost unbelievable, and yet here you are, as my research has hinted at all along!"

"How can you possibly know anything about me?" she stated with an underlying tome of anger. "And I'm sorry to disappoint you, but I am not Absu, whoever she is."

Professor Tear answered, whilst trying to contain his excitement, which I feared would be the undoing of him.

"Absu, is Sumerian, for 'from the beginning'. It refers to the genetic code you carry. As I mentioned, I've written papers about you and I didn't even dare to hope you existed. Then of course you can imagine my surprise that you're female. All my research points toward a dominant gene carried in the male line. But its recessive, and I'm so overwhelmed, I don't know what to say." He leaned back in his chair, both elated and drained. I was half afraid he was going to cry.

Pilgrim studied him coldly.

He was in a nervous state of shock and excitement, as we watched him rein in his emotions. Regaining some control, he spoke quietly.

"I would very much like to ask you some questions, with your permission?"

The contemplative look Pilgrim gave the Professor made me believe she thought he was, at this juncture, mentally fragile, and so I wasn't surprised when she agreed to indulge his request and allow him to ask one question: with the proviso she ask some in return. He readily agreed, hunching forward with his hands clenched together.

"I believe I know what you are capable of: complete elemental control. Have you experienced this?"

"No," she replied, with a note of surprise in her voice. She glanced briefly at Professors Ashour and Van de Ligne, noticing their worried glances at Professor Tear.

"What is the goal of this facility?" Pilgrim asked.

"To create a Supreme Being in intellect and ability," Professor Tear answered sincerely.

He seemed tired but strangely satisfied as if he had completed a long and arduous journey and he sat contentedly in one of the chairs, his eyes fixed upon Pilgrim. All I could do, along with the others, was to watch and listen as this unnerving conversation unfolded. I felt exhilarated, scared out of my wits and helpless, all at the same time. I also acknowledged to myself that this moment would never come again and to absorb as much of it as I possibly could. Pilgrim seemed to ignore the fact she was the centre of attention and continued her line of questioning.

"Your work here, it involves genetic research? Absu, 'from the beginning,' explain."

Professor Tear answered before the others.

"Absu, in relation to our work, refers to the genetic strand that suddenly appeared over 4000 years ago in man, during the age of the Sumerians who named it. It was said to come from the heavens and mentally enlightened every being that carried it in their genes through generations; a sort of a fast- forward for part of the human race."

My curiosity got the better of me and I asked, "How did they identify the strand?"

"They knew a significant number of their race began showing signs of vastly increased mental intelligence. The elders believed it was divine intervention, a blessing on their race. Whereas before, they had lived a very basic and rudimentary life, in a single generation they began to write, use language more profitably, buildings became more sophisticated, food was farmed more efficiently, medicine became a core interest and as many of the inscriptions tell, life for their race began."

The room fell to a deathly quiet. Everyone's eyes were on Pilgrim. She looked at me with so much pain in her eyes I almost choked. Whatever she was feeling, Professor Tear's summation was invoking some form of recognition in her; as she asked slowly,

"To what areas does your research extend, identifying gene groups, growing genetic strings, human cloning, foetal research, foetal manipulation?" At the flicker of concern in their eyes, she continued, "I see. Hasn't anyone ever told you: these things are sacred?"

Professor Van de Ligne and Professor Ashour remained stoically quiet. They didn't appear shocked or remorseful, they were cautiously alert, but then their curiosity pushed the conversation forward.

Regaining some of their previous confidence, - they scrutinised Pilgrim's movements. Pilgrim had stood and was walking slowly forward facing the group as she called over Asteria, who obeyed.

Gently lifting Asteria's hand in hers, she turned it palm-up. Carefully and deliberately, with no resistance, or look of concern from Asteria, Pilgrim removed a delicate pen-knife from her pocket and before anyone could protest, she made a shallow cut across her palm. Asteria screamed in pain and snatched back her hand, staring wide-eyed and frightened at Pilgrim.

"I apologise, Asteria. I had to be certain."

Asteria clutched her hand to her chest where her blood was already beginning to stain the front of her tunic. Her face was one of hurt and confusion; yet she said nothing.

Professor Ashour, without taking his eyes from Pilgrim, ordered Asteria to the infirmary and to return promptly after. I was dismayed by the way Asteria was treated. It was blatantly apparent to me there was something special about her, ethereal almost, but she was spoken to like a serf. We all watched her exit. It was a most bizarre and shocking sight as she walked away with her hands at her sides, drops of blood spotting the floor, even opening the

259

door with the hand that was cut, before quickly pulling it away in pain and using the other.

As soon as she had left and closed the door behind her, an oppressive silence filled the room. I had absolutely no idea why Pilgrim had cut Asteria's palm.

"What is she, third gen, fourth gen?" Pilgrim demanded.

Professor Ashour spoke, clearly annoyed.

"You've ruined her. There is no way she will be able to survive this. You had no right to interfere. Thirty years of research gone! We thought you were more perceptive."

"Its because of my *perception* that I'm pleased to disappoint you."

I was scared by the pace things were moving, and I, like Pilgrim, had questions.

"Why won't she survive?" I asked.

"She won't survive purely because she can never fulfil the purpose they designed her for," Pilgrim replied for them.

Pilgrims detachment made me wary. A knot formed in my stomach, as I said, "They *designed* her for."

"Yes, designed. Asteria, in many ways is like you and me. With one *intentional* difference. She has been genetically engineered for a single purpose. I don't believe for one minute she is the finished product, too many flaws."

"But, she is human isn't she?"

"Yes, she is. In all ways that are visually necessary for her to assimilate into our current society, she conforms. It's her behaviour patterns that have been deliberately suppressed. She has never been exposed to the everyday human traits that make us able to function and survive in our world. She's the human equivalent of a tortoise on the Galapagos Islands. No fear, just function." Pilgrim stopped short, speaking slowly and deliberately to the three professors.

"You cannot claim ignorance or coercion for your actions. You will meet the full penalty for your destructive exploitation."

She was beginning to pace slowly back and forth, toward the outer walls of that cavernous room. She reminded me of a tiger in a cage, subconsciously evaluating her spatial boundary. Pilgrim continued.

"Asteria, named after the Titan goddess of necromancy and prophetic dreams." She was looking around her, touching the walls and continuing to talk, seemingly oblivious to our presence. I was not alone in feeling this wasn't going to end well. Just one look at the professors, their faces now masks of anxiety, reminded me they knew more about Pilgrim's abilities than evidently she did.

Professor Van de Ligne stepped forward, gaining Pilgrim's attention.

"Professor Ashour is correct. Asteria will not survive this," she stated solemnly.

"She may start asking a few impertinent questions, as her mind begins to assimilate the experience." Pilgrim stopped and observed them with a look of pure disgust. "You intend to kill her."

Professor Van de Ligne took an involuntary step back. It was Professor Tear's turn to step-in.

261

"I had no idea you were able to experience such depths of emotion."

Pilgrim stated menacingly, "The creator of my design made me more unique than you can possibly hope to imagine."

"And who do you believe your creator to be?" A man's voice rang out from the open door.

"Certainly not you, Cronus," Pilgrim answered, slowly turning to face him.

The man who confidently approached us was diminutive in stature, of approximately eighty years of age, with a few wisps of grey hair which lay in contrast to his honey complexion. He stood with a straight back in his white, full-length thobe, with a cool stare and a self-assured stance, which left me in no doubt he was a Titan. He spoke with a soft Arabic accent, "You are correct. But we aspire – we aspire," he said slowly, with a theatrical lift of his arm and turn of his hand. "We have yet to perfect the stability within the strands to sustain a full metamorphosis."

Professor Van de Ligne's question revealed her disbelief.

"But you are Gideon. Cronus is our benefactor."

"My former name was Gideon Imperator and is now held by another. I am Cronus."

He walked toward Pilgrim and stopped short as she stood her ground and stated, "You're here to kill me. I understand your reasoning and I fully accept you will. You know of course my successor has been groomed for the position for some time?" he explained.

"I doubt hes groomed his successor?" I emphasised.

The look of annoyance on his face bolstered my nerve.

"Do the other Titans know of your ambitions?" I demanded

"The Titans work collectively with a hive mentality, the goal of one is the goal of us all, Mr. Baxter."

Hearing him use my name left me feeling hollow, as if he'd claimed a piece of my soul. Looking back to Pilgrim, his fingertips meeting contemplatively, he asked, "It is difficult for us to understand why you wish to prevent us from attaining our goal?"

Pilgrim replied, "Then you have not learnt the importance of balance. Your organisation has allowed, promoted and has been directly responsible, for some of the most heinous crimes in history. You are the profiteers of human misery." Pilgrim stated frankly; her pupils now quite dilated, her hair fallen back from her face as she moved with an organic fluidity, "And with your latest weapon, the Drepáni: you cannot be allowed to continue."

"But you must realise *you* are here for *us*, not for *them*. You must know that." A tinge of desperation edged his words.

"You're wrong. Consider your reasoning. You believe this Absu was introduced after man had shown his hand. Sounds like a correction to me."

It was clear the whole situation was escalating, when suddenly Asteria returned. The almost vacant expression that had been in her eyes when we had first met, had changed markedly. She appeared unsure, but gave Pilgrim the slightest of nervous smiles.

Professor Van de Ligne gave Asteria a dismissive glance.

"You observe she is frightened of you." She turned, saying earnestly to Cronus, "We can't use her, it will taint all our research." Seemingly unaware of the imminent danger the rest of us were feeling, she added, "We would do best to go with the next one."

Asteria turned and spoke gently to the professors and Cronus.

"I am not frightened of Pilgrim. I have been expecting her. Neither, am I frightened of you. I am frightened of myself. I'm not sure why, but I feel it. You have asked me questions concerning my dreams over the years and I have answered them, but you failed to ask me the right questions."

Cronus said, "You were never designed for war. You have always been handled with care. You were our greatest achievement."

"Shouldn't that be, *we're* your greatest achievement. You neglected to observe a fundamental law governing every species on this planet, which you didn't calculate for, and couldn't eradicate, purely because you could not have foreseen Pilgrim coming so soon." She looked over at Pilgrim, who continued to pace.

"And what is that?" Professor Van de Ligne demanded with a quiver in her voice.

"Self-preservation," Asteria answered.

Professor Ashour stepped forward.

"What do you mean; we never asked you the right questions?"

"You should have asked me what I am. But because you considered me to be your own creation, you didn't. In your self-absorption you forget to take into account *your* origins. You never thought what had lain down and mapped your genetics, and in your design, would have anticipated and planned what your ultimate abilities and goals would be. You are only temporal beings."

I knew the professors and Cronus were in a great deal of danger. Not only did they have Pilgrim to contend with, but now Asteria, who despite her angelic looks and soft voice, was provoking that sense of self-preservation in me she had mentioned only seconds before. A sense of foreboding emanated from her, creating an intense energy in the air that caused my pulse to race. My heart was hammering so hard in my chest I could feel its rhythmic wave in my ears. They had tampered with the on-going evolution of human-kind and were about to experience a wrath that would be metered out by a being with a greater sense of survival and a far more dangerous arsenal.

All eyes turned to Asteria, she said, "I am the harbinger of your greatest fears, and Pilgrim has ignited that knowledge within me. If you try to run or harm me or mine, you will bring about your own destruction."

I watched in fascinated horror as her pupils dilated and beads of sweat broke out across her face. I didn't know if she was in control of herself or not. I felt the air move around me, causing hair and clothes to flutter. Suddenly, Pilgrim was at my side gently pulling on my arm. I carefully lifted myself from my chair allowing her to draw me back. Asteria's blind gaze fell upon us and then shifted onto the three professors and Cronus whose fate was written in horror and resignation upon their faces.

Asteria spoke softly, but every word rang against the walls.

"I see you all, your lives, your hopes, your dreams, and your deaths. I offer you no solace." Asteria was becoming caught up in the visions, and the depth of her experience was beginning to manifest itself in a dark purple haze that began to slowly swirl around her. "Come for you death then, if you seek it, I will not shield you from it."

Without warning the outer-door swung open to a man, who immediately fired a dart-gun catching Asteria in the shoulder. Pilgrim instantaneously swung about; in that split second everything within the room slowed. As her hair, billowed from her shoulders in slow motion, I experienced time evaporate.

Asteria's unconscious body hung eerily just above the floor. My whole being stilled as I recognised Pilgrim's influence. The air in the room was becoming so oppressively thick, my lungs stung as they fought for oxygen. The professors, the man who'd fired the dart, and Cronus remained standing, unable to move or speak.

At this point I couldn't move and I realised Pilgrim was no longer in control of herself. I witnessed that other part of her and saw its latent presence awakening in her face. When she spoke, her words echoed from a place far beyond our realm, from a distant time, eons ago.

"I have no pity for you, but I won't allow suffering."

We were all about to experience the dominion of a being both terrifying and just. I capped my fear and focused on taking shallow breaths: I meant to survive this. There was a static energy of such intensity in the atmosphere it crackled and spat against the interior of the room, causing objects to fracture and shatter. Massive swathes of light ebbed and flowed through the room. My eyes involuntarily moved to observe Pilgrim. My heart caught in my throat at the desolation that lay there. Levitating from the floor, her elbows at her sides, her hands and fingers splayed; her eyes began to mirror the stars whilst profound waves of loss and grief washed over me in such rapidity I succumbed and was drawn into their depths.

Through my disembodied view I witnessed her haloed in a blinding iridescent blue light as it began to radiate and pulse in intensity. My body had become an immovable shell and I was trapped inside and couldn't get away. I was forced to stand and witness the event. There was no morbid fascination on my part, no fear, just a tidal surge of mercy that crashed upon my mortal shore. As my mind threatened to collapse, I touched a plane of consciousness long forgotten as my thoughts melded with my soul resonating with that omnipresent manifestation which is Pilgrim.

My vision blurred and I couldn't be sure I remained conscious, but what I saw; I understood. I saw the outlines of Cronos and the professor's bodies quiver. Only Asteria's shape remained constant. My head felt tight and I couldn't be sure I was still alive, as I had no sense of myself. The outlines began to expand until their cohesiveness disintegrated and shot outwards leaving no trace. I watched the walls of the room ripple and shift as they too disintegrated. Pilgrims, form had become indiscernible as it was masked by a pure white light. As the structure of the building dissolved about us, there was a roaring in my head which was deafening. It was rage of such magnitude it scorched my soul. Just before I yielded, I saw Pilgrim coil and lash into an energy in the sky above, a luminescent sapphire emitting shards of light that cloaked the island beneath her. She rose rapidly, I knew my end had come; my last thought was of her; then with an intense ferocity she released a charge to the island. Its surge blinded me, chasing me into oblivion.

CHAPTER FOURTEEN

Many times since, I've tried to recall precisely what had happened. When I awoke, I found myself lying next to Pilgrim, on the hard earth where the citadel had once stood, now razed to the ground. It was night. Staying still and looking about me I saw the crumpled body of Asteria curled around the body of a young girl. The soft movement of her breathing filled me with relief. Then I heard Pilgrim whisper my name. Leaping to my feet, I ran over and scooped her up, cradling her in my arms. Her eyes remained closed. She didn't utter another word as I laid her down away from the scorched earth . I left her momentarily and checked on Asteria and her companion. It was a few minutes before Pilgrim came round and regained some of her strength.

Our experience was so far beyond words, none were said. As Asteria and the girl awoke huddling together, we rested and took stock of what had just occurred.

Later, after some hours and in a rare show of assurance, Pilgrim said magnanimously, she'd never met anyone who'd survived one of her more intense episodes and perhaps over time I would develop the ability to stay conscious.

"That minor change you experience, remind me to tell you about it one day," I said

No one else had survived to tell the tale.

We left the island by seaplane, with Asteria, and the young girl of about fourteen that could have passed as her daughter, the resemblance was so striking, but in actuality had to be her clone. We accompanied them as far as Egypt, where we landed at dawn in the port of Alexandria. The rising sun had thrown its shimmering light across the water, changing those azure ripples to silver and gold and I stood mesmerised by its beauty. The air was comfortably warm and sweet with the smell of orange blossom and vanilla intermingled with the distinct nutty aroma of heavily roasted coffee beans.

After Pilgrim and I had said our goodbyes, we watched as Asteria and the girl left on a sailing boat which gently slipped out of the harbour. I later learned Asteria had requested Pilgrim to find her a permanent home somewhere isolated. I didn't ask where; frankly I didn't want to know.

Pilgrim uttered those words which always put me in a good mood.

"Let's get something to eat!"

Instead of our usual hurry back to England, we took a more leisurely pace and mode of transport that afforded Pilgrim the time to recuperate by sleeping, sometimes for days at a time. Within two weeks we were back at L'améthyste, where I was greeted by name at the door. The feeling of belonging somewhere reminded me we couldn't stay there forever, as much as I'd have liked to, and I voiced as much to Pilgrim. She had murmured something unintelligible.

I'd been surprised when on our first evening back having dressed for dinner, Pilgrim entered our living room wearing a pair of jeans, a thick sweater and was in the process of donning a woollen hat, coat and gloves. I said, "You're going out? Wait, I'll change."

Before I could start toward my bedroom, she'd stopped me stating she was going to be away for three days, maybe more. She'd suggested I should get some practice in with the Major and had promptly left. I had skulked back to my bedroom and undressed, ordering room-service in the process. I knew she could look after herself, well most of the time. The thing that bothered me, after some soul-searching, was that I was feeling left-out of whatever adventure she was now having. I decided to contact Major Coal in the morning and set up some lessons. I had reached a decision on my vice, not that I considered it as such; I was going to become an expert marksman.

Pilgrim returned five long days after, looking emaciated and sporting a large bruise traversing from her right temple and finishing across her brow.

"What the hell happened?" I demanded. The bruise suggested Pilgrim had been unable to defend herself and been hurt by her opponent.

"It's my own fault. I walked into an iron bar hanging overhead in a cellar." She winced as she touched the angry, dark purple bruise.

"And what were you doing in a cellar?"

"I was hiding, if you must know!"

"Here's the deal; I pour us a large glass of red and you tell me all about it?"

"Done!"

"Good!"

"Is your marksmanship improving?" she asked as I made my way to the bar and pulled the cork from a bottle of Chateau Neuf de Pape.

"I'd like to think so, but you'll not distract me as easily as that. Well?" I asked pointedly, handing over a generous glass of wine with more legs on it than a centipede.

"When I left you that day, I intended to visit an old friend of mine, Hansford."

"Ah, so that's the 'H'!" I lifted up my finger in revelation.

"Yes, that's the 'H'. Hansford has been very helpful to me in the past with obtaining and supplying information not readily available even through altruistic channels."

"MI6, of course."

"When we left the island, I thought a quick check on a couple of loose-ends, just to tidy things up."

"You don't expect the Titans to be intimidated or influenced by you, given the fact they cannot be certain of your abilities?"

"Thank you for your vote of confidence, Baxter, but I carry the Absu."

"You know delusional vanity is never pretty." I teased.

"For your information, my intention is to slow them down in any way I can, it also lets them know, I know what they're up to and I won't allow it."

"So perhaps they do know what you are?"

"I'm not sure. This Absu thing; the Professors' interpretation of it doesn't match my feelings. Sure, I know about me." She seemed almost embarrassed. "I feel like an integral part of everything around me, but that's not all, I also feel, at times, 'off-planet.'"

"Off-planet?"

"You know when you're not plugged into the everyday life - you know the whole society thing, everyday thing, you know, more 'off planet'," she nudged encouragingly.

"Actually yes, I get the general idea, having survived one of your more interesting episodes. But technically the off-planet thing could be the Absu?"

"The Professor's conclusions were all theoretical, and as they're not around to confirm I exist, then it's all a matter of speculation, isn't it?"

Neither of us believed that.

"You must have shown up on something?" I replied, warily.

"Maybe, but who's to say what it was, or if the rest of the Titans knew what Cronus was up to. I'm not underestimating them, Baxter, but neither am I over-estimating them. They might know I exist on paper. Proof of what exists inside me is something else. Surely, if they knew they would have followed me my whole life, or I'd be dead, or at least imprisoned somewhere. We know Cronus was seeking to supplant the human-race. Do they know he was trying to create some kind of Supreme Being? If they do, they're harking back to the *myth* of the Titans, when there were humans, super-humans and gods. That confirms how insane they are."

I had been listening avidly to what she had to say.

"Do we know for certain there were no super-humans alive in the sixth century B.C?" I postulated.

"Don't you start."

"Maybe they're just trying to bring back a blood-line that is almost extinct."

"You mean like the Gloucestershire Old Spot pig!" she answered with derision.

"No, seriously, have you thought about it?" I asked.

"Yes, of course I have. But strangely enough, I couldn't get past the genocide, torture and physical cruelty to meet their own selfish ends, part."

Standing up, she moved over to the bar and poured herself another glass, returning with the bottle to refill mine.

"We've thrown down the gauntlet Baxter. It's unlikely they'll pick it up. The N.E.G will be useless to them now they know I'd obliterate them if they used it."

"I agree, they wouldn't be that stupid. But they'll want answers."

"All they want is the Absu, and to control it."

"Do you think they know about Asteria and her companion surviving?" I asked. "Maybe you should put yourself in a box and go into storage?" I added light-heartedly.

Her lack of an immediate response caused me to look up.

"If things do get tough, I might just do that." She threw over the silver snuff box containing the Red Pearl.

274

"You can store that for a start." Laughing at the look of shock on my face she said, "now back to that cellar."

It had turned out Pilgrim had been determined to locate the company responsible for supplying the island, hence finding herself in the cellar of a powerful politician, with nothing to show for her endeavours other than an enormous bruise. She had hoped, in turn, the trail would lead her to another Titan, but the trail had eventually gone cold. Unfortunately for us, our use of the seaplane provided by Hansford to extract us off the island; had inadvertently tipped them off. A rookie mistake – but hey, we're not perfect. Frankly, I just wanted to get the hell out of there.

My prediction of the Titan's surveillance was confirmed earlier than I expected. The day after we'd returned to L'améthyste, a letter arrived with a wax-seal depicting the profile of a winged angel kneeling with its head resting on the hilt of a sword. Unnervingly, it was addressed to both of us. I choose to open it, and seeing a card inside, used the fabric of my cuff to extract it. I read the note quickly and relayed the message to Pilgrim who was now sat in one of the recessed reception chairs.

"It's an invitation," I remarked cautiously.

"Let me guess. It's from Alalngar Okeanos Uni."

I exhaled deeply before continuing, "how could you possibly know that?"

"I've thought about the most probable areas of control for our notorious twelve and it seems I've got at least one right."

"Don't you mean eleven?"

"Not for much longer."

"You don't think it's a little unusual to receive an invitation from a Titan?"

"I believe it's unprecedented. Mr Uni holds the position as head of the Diocesan Chancery," Pilgrim replied with aplomb.

"And that means what exactly?"

"The Diocesan Chancery is the most influential branch of all written documents used in the official governance of religion."

"I thought the Titans didn't believe in God?"

"What made you think that? It's what 'God' represents that they believe in. Besides, how do you harness a large proportion of one of the greatest forces on earth?"

"You mean man?" I answered.

"Correction, our species."

"When you say 'our species', you mean what exactly?"

"Baxter, I had a mother and a father just like you. It wasn't an immaculate conception. If this Absu thing is to be believed, like I said, I'm just a fast forwarded version. Although it is interesting I'm here and now."

"Let's not go there, and I was just checking on the whole parental thing," I said nonchalantly.

I returned to the invitation.

"We are invited to meet him or her, at Largo Park, tomorrow at five o'clock." I looked at Pilgrim. "What do you think?"

"I think forewarned is forearmed. Let's make sure we're on time and prepared. This should be good. Make sure to take your gun."

"And what are you going to take?"

"This!" she stated triumphantly.

Held in Pilgrim's palm was a black leather baton which, with one sharp outward flick of her wrist, shot a telescopic blade.

"My new sword. I have several others, but for the purposes of tomorrow I believe this one will suffice."

Pressing a button in the handle the blade retracted as quickly as it had appeared.

"I wouldn't have thought you were in need of such toys," I quipped.

"Evidently my more intense skills take a toll. I can recover more quickly when I'm not forced to use them."

"Point taken, incidentally our new mode of transport has been delivered."

It was with some difficulty the following day that we were finally able to locate Largo Park, in our custom made, off-road Morgan.

Pilgrim had been impressed, asking how we'd managed to jumped to the front of a three year queue.

"I have my *interesting* friends," I confirmed.

"Just a minor point but how do you intend to drive this fine automobile, when you don't know how?"

I held my breath.

"Take care of that will you?" she smiled.

"At the first opportunity."

The reason Largo Park didn't appear on any maps was because it hadn't been officially registered for over five decades. Largo Park is in fact a very large derelict and crumbling mansion set on private land of over forty acres. We reached the high wrought-iron gates that had only recently been pushed open, leaving deep semi-circular grooves through the built-up earth.

The drive up to the house was potted with holes, weeds and the occasional dead branch that had fallen long ago and now disintegrated under our tyres. Looming ahead, sprawled along some considerable length, lay the remains of Largo Hall. What had once been a magnificent house with turrets, a clock tower and belfry, along with numerous chimneys standing in high relief, now stood balefully abandoned and in ruins. I looked up at the darkening sky flecked with the first twinkling stars and the silver curve of the moon. Moving slowly ahead, we passed a line of abandoned bee-hives, some rotted back to the earth with a few sat battered and worn, with the final remnants of white paint on their dislodged roofs. As we neared, we saw the most extraordinary sight; a shuttered horse-drawn coach with a black pair standing to attention, and a liveried coachman atop. Nothing surprised me these days. Slowing down and pulling over to the further side of the circular drive, I tapped Pilgrim's arm and pointed up to one of the chimneys. Threading through the air ascended tendrils of smoke.

"But the place is completely derelict," I remarked. "Look over there, the roof is missing and see the branches of that tree poking out through the window."

I felt for the gun in my shoulder-holster under my jacket and felt somewhat comforted.

"We're expected. Let's go in and find the source of that fire," Pilgrim urged with purpose.

Walking past the coach, with no acknowledgement from its driver, I noticed the horse blinkers carried the same seal that had embossed the invitation.

We entered the hall through a large stone entrance whose date of fifteen-hundred-and-sixty, was carved and worn in stone above the door. Stepping over the weather-beaten threshold into the cathedral like foyer, we trod carefully, across fragments of stained-glass lying scattered at our feet. There was silence between us as we picked our way forward through piles of damp leaves. A single battered doll's head covered in cobwebs, which had been placed many years prior, lay on the edge of a worm eaten console.

The interior was ultimate decay, with parts of its architecture barely recognisable. Black sooted mould climbed from the floorboards, up the cracked walls and spread across the ceiling like the elongated fingers of a wizened hand. Traversing the only passable walkway through to the heart of the house, we navigated past broken plaster and caught a glimpse of the ancient stone underneath.

Eventually we entered a large cavernous hall, with its wall of broken windows oddly latched shut. A frail and elderly gentleman sat stooped in a wheelchair, whilst his middle-aged companion, seated in a high back winged chair, in front of a monumental stone fireplace with a roaring fire in its raised grate, looked up. After the perfunctory introductions, I remained very much on my guard. Pilgrim mirrored my demeanour. The man sat next to the fire, stood in one fluid movement walking a few paces toward us. He spoke with the well-clipped vowels.

"Ms. Pilgrim, Mr. Baxter, thank you for accepting my invitation to meet. May I introduce Mr. Pennyweather, and I am Mr. Alalngar Okeanos Uni."

"Otherwise, known as Okeanos; a Titan." I interjected.

He gave the slightest inclination of his head in acknowledgement.

Mr Pennyweather, sat shrivelled and pale, his knees and waist covered by a large blanket. On his head rested a Homburg and his gloved hands were placed in a large fur muffler. Despite his considerably advanced years, his eyes were bright and alert. Okeanos was dressed impeccably. His dark hair curled at his shoulders and his Bowler and black leather gloves now rested on the ancient fire-mantel. His hands were soft and white, and more easily associated with a young girl than a man.

During his introduction, Mr Pennyweather occasionally would murmur something and give a half smile, to which Okeanos responded by providing an explanation.

"Mr. Pennyweather has very little hearing. Put your hand up occasionally when he smiles at you and that will be more than enough for him. Won't it, Ancient P." Okeanos, patted his shoulder affectionately.

His congenial affability didn't fool me. There was a coldness in his eyes that couldn't be misinterpreted.

"You've invited us here; we would therefore be obliged if you could explain your unusual request," Pilgrim stated civilly.

He moved to his chair and began to pull it toward the fire. The evening had enveloped the antiquated pile and the unexpected appearance of the coachman, who quietly and efficiently began to place large lit candles around the immediate vicinity of the fireplace, indicated a longer meeting than we'd anticipated. Bringing odd decrepit chairs in from other areas of the house for us, the coachman gave a respectful nod to his employer and left. Now we were as comfortable as we could hope to be under the circumstances.

"I have invited you here, Ms. Pilgrim, because I too have my weaknesses and despite your *accomplishments*, I would not dream of your visit being unaccompanied. Mr. Baxter." He gave me a precipitate nod.

"I am your weakness?" Pilgrim asked.

"More specifically, what you represent," he responded softly. "I was elected to meet with you, to see if we can reach a mutual agreement that will allow us all to co-exist peacefully on this planet."

"I doubt that, especially after Mrs Cotterill and Dr Bonnin," I rasped, shocked at his nerve.

"Mrs Cotterill's death was regrettable and the original order entirely lost in translation. You may rest assured those responsible are no longer alive," he stated dismissively.

"And Dr Bonnin?" I demanded.

"We have used apothecaries for millennia. Dr Bonnin will join a distinguished, if not unwitting line."

281

His clinical analysis was grating. I asked, "As Okeanos, ruler of water, Mr. Pennyweather must have come in rather handy as your subterranean engineer," I postulated.

"Yes, although he was my predecessors."

"I find it odd, as a Titan, that you could be so sentimental regarding a member of staff," I said.

There was a pause as Okeanos stared at me coldly with a hint of annoyance in his eyes. I continued, "Unless hes more than that?"

Instead of replying to my question, he turned to Pilgrim asking, "You have not answered my question and time is precious to me," he said gravely.

Pilgrim observed, "In mythology, Okeanos never went to war with the other Titans. He stood apart from those of his factioned order. You've taken a considerable risk coming here, but I don' believe its for our benefit."

"You're correct. What you represent is the culmination of eons of work and sacrifice. We are in sight of the end of our quest. Thousands of years of selective manipulation to take us back to what we once were. I'm proposing your compliance...nothing more. The entire procedure would take less than a minute with our technology."

"I'm not the one you're seeking, Okeanos," Pilgrim stated.

There was a distance in her eyes, I found unnerving and I was reminded of our situation by the cold, hard steel sheathed in my holster.

"You're certain?" He betrayed the first trace of emotion in his voice.

"I am. If the Titans continue to pursue this line I will annihilate you all," Pilgrim answered resolutely.

There wasn't the slightest flicker of fear passing Okeanos features. Ancient P, had since fallen asleep in his chair. The wind outside was beginning to pick up and blow through the broken windows causing some of the candles to gutter and smoke.

"I do not doubt our goal. You have only to look about you at the homogenous mass that have so little purpose, and therefore, so little right to life," Okeanos added with emotion.

"You're delusional," I countered. "You don't know the people of the Earth. When was the last time you came off your privileged pedestal to see who it is that is actually making the world turn?"

"Your ignorance and romanticism is predictable Mr. Baxter, given your limited intellect."

"Baxter is right on some levels. Your dogma is skewed. It's no longer able to achieve its end without bringing about its own destruction," Pilgrim warned.

"Then why are *you* here? You are prophesised. You are moving toward your ascendancy," he added with conviction.

"I believe I'm here to stop you. Your avarice to create a Supreme Being is flawed and your doctrine manipulated to achieve it. I don't believe I am prophesised. My presence on earth at this time, is ordained by a higher order then yours."

Okeanos, shook his head slowly and smiled, saying, "Then I thank you for your time." He lowered his head in mock deference before continuing, "I shall be industrious with the years I have remaining and be mindful of my legacy. Let us agree to go our separate ways."

"Your organisation makes that request impossible," Pilgrim warned.

"Then we shall just have to wait until you die of; shall we be generous and say, natural causes?" he smiled.

"You could try, any other means, but I wouldn't recommend it." Pilgrims eyes began to dilate, as she added with conviction, "If I identify the Titan's hand in anything questionable, I will seek each of you out, including your successors, and end this."

Despite every physical attribute that identified him as a gentleman, I knew he couldn't be further from that station. His very existence made my flesh crawl. There was something malevolent behind his eyes that caused my breathing to shallow. And he confirmed my suspicions by saying,

"I should warn you concerning that 'beau gosse', he is scheduled for termination."

"If hes touched, it would be regrettable," Pilgrim answered, matching his menace.

The atmosphere in the room had become rigid in its implacability.

"Its time for us to go," I suggested to Pilgrim. Fortunately, she took my recommendation.

"You'd better hope we never meet again." Pilgrim turned on her heel.

I followed her lead leaping over debris whilst trying to catch up with her.

Driving away from Largo Park, I asked worriedly, "Who is beau gosse?"

"Beau gosse, is the French for, 'handsome young man.' He was talking about 'H'."

"Thank god for that. I thought he meant me?"

The following overcast day found Pilgrim and me in a contemplative mood and I didn't want to be the one that said it; but I was exhausted and longed for a bit of peace and quiet. More importantly I needed time to assimilate everything that had happened. The thought of another round of anything approaching what we had been through made me feel weakened and ill.

"Baxter, I thought you'd stored this," Pilgrim asked seriously.

She handed me the silver snuff-box containing the red pearl.

"Shouldn't we give this to the authorities?"

"It's safer with us. Its our insurance."

"I should think after your warning, they'll keep a very low profile." It was a hopeful remark.

"They'll certainly need to be more creative. I don't want to devote any more time to them. Besides I have something far more important I want you to take a look at."

So it was on a rainy afternoon with a charcoal sky, which leant down to graze the tops of the buildings; we left London behind and travelled to the southwest of England, to the coast of Devon. We disembarked at Exeter St

David's train station which was bustling with commuters. Students with weighty backpacks and those on their day excursions from the rural villages at its outskirts stomped toward the exit. It was a bit of a squash on the platform as we funnelled past the coffee-shop amongst the throng. Having almost shunted an old lady selling flowers from a basket, Pilgrim declined the posy she offered, but dropped a few coins in her hand all the same.

As I'd been informed we were to be met; I had mistakenly envisaged the usual car. Instead, we exited the station, crossed the car-park and walked toward a tall thoughtful looking man in a dark suit leaning up against a serious car. As we neared, I instantly recognised him as the person who I'd seen exiting the house at Bow Lane, so long ago. He was in his early mid-fifties and certainly fit. I unconsciously sucked in my gut and straightened myself up. We slowed as we neared, prompting him to say,

"About, bloody time."

"Oh, quit whining. I don't know how people work with you."

Walking straight up to him, Pilgrim planted a kiss firmly on his cheek. To which he responded by lifting her hand and placing a tender kiss upon her inner wrist. I wasn't quite sure where to put myself and surprisingly, neither was Pilgrim. This had been a purely primal gesture on his part that identified Pilgrim was his. Hiding her embarrassment, she quickly turned to me and made the introduction.

"Baxter, this is Hansford, MI6, a valuable *friend*," she verbally underlined. He gave her a wolfish grin. She bit back tiredly, "And in complete contrast to the sobriety of you. Hansford, this is Baxter."

It did cross my mind, how much Hansford knew of Pilgrim's true nature? I automatically extended my hand which he shook slowly and deliberately. I was so glad he wasn't perfect. 'Not perfect', I can work with, 'perfect', I've got no time for. Addressing me, and to make sure Pilgrim heard as she opened the passenger door, he issued a warning.

"Careful, Baxter, she can get you into all sorts of trouble."

As I placed our cases into the boot and closed it, I looked him in the eye and replied, "I know!"

As I opened the rear passenger door, Pilgrim asked, "Baxter, would you mind sitting in the front, I'm really tired and I'm hoping to get forty-winks?"

"Certainly, no problem," I replied.

Before I could hold the door open for her, Hansford had claimed it, and was helping her into the back.

"Care to explain to me where that bruise come from."

"I clouted it against an iron railing, not very smart."

It suddenly struck me she had been gone for five days! I gave her a questioning look, as she ducked into the car. I caught her glare not to say anything. I knew the question I was would ask her later.

Hansford stepped around to the driver's door and slid behind the wheel. As we drove from the car-park, he looked into his rear view mirror.

"So, how was Africa?"

"We learnt a lot," before she quickly added, "actually it turned out to be quite informative, and thank-you for all your help."

"No problem, anything I can do to help the criminal classes."

"Really Hansford, you shouldn't joke like that, you'll put Baxter off."

At this point, I had discovered an important fact about Pilgrim and Hansford; they each thought a great deal more of one another than they were willing to admit. Hansford, must have been observing me out of the corner of his eye.

"I think Baxters way beyond that point. You won't be put-off, will you, Baxter?"

"No, I will not be put-off. Incidentally, I have no romantic intentions toward Pilgrim; just as long as we're clear on that."

The atmosphere in the car became electrified and I worried in case I had gone too far.

"I can see why hes valuable to you and I know he'll keep an eye on you; won't you Baxter?"

It was more of a command than an enquiry.

"Most definitely," I answered.

"I've updated Chandler. He requests the pleasure of your company, once you've taken a breath," Hansford stated, back in business mode.

As Pilgrim nodded-off in the back and eventually lay slumped across the seat, my years of only speaking when spoken to, kept me quiet for the remainder of our journey.

Hansford didn't seem to want to talk; so I was left with my thoughts and wondering where on earth we were going.

The roads gradually became more narrow, from the motorway to the dual carriage way, to just a single hedge-rowed lane. The remainder of our journey took us to the small village of Merrelmare on the east Devon coast. Its appointment couldn't have been more idyllic. Nestled between the lush vibrant green hills, it looked out onto a vista of open slate-blue sea, with its horseshoe stone port below and a few fishing boats swaying listlessly side to side on the incoming tide.

We took a sharp left, where I noticed a weather beaten sign reading, 'Merrelmare House'. A long gravel drive took us up to a large Edwardian house. Standing to attention at its entrance, stood an older man in dark-green tweeds and what I took to be his smiling wife, clad in bright pink wellingtons, a yellow knitted jumper and a long silver plait of hair. As she relinquished his arm, she stepped forward to greet us.

Hansford made the introductions for Mr. and Mrs. Flint. He, formally of Scotland Yard, and now both retired to live in Devon, to serve as the new custodians of Merrelmare House. Once we had alighted and our suitcases had been whisked inside by Mr. Flint; Mrs. Flint bobbed around like an old mother-hen. She spoke with a strong Devonshire accent.

"You'll be absolutely famished I know. So I've got a lovely cottage-pie in the oven with fresh veg right off the farm. Apple pie and clotted cream for dessert, so bring your appetite with you."

She vanished in through the front-door, no doubt to follow that string back to the kitchen.

I looked questioningly at Pilgrim. She had looked away, and I felt she was hiding something. It hadn't immediately struck me that the house was far too big for just the two of them, until Pilgrim turned to me upon reaching the lobby and said, "Well, what do you think?"

"I think, it's staggeringly charming," I stated agreeably, adding, "We're staying here for the weekend?"

"I thought permanently, as a base, away from London; somewhere to relax, somewhere safe. What do you think?"

Pilgrim didn't need my approval, or anyone else's for that matter, but I was humbled that she'd asked.

"I think it's perfect," I stated honestly.

"Good, because we've bought it," she said hurriedly.

My elation was quickly smothered by regret, as I remembered poor Mrs. Cotterill. Pilgrim read my thoughts.

"The Flints can take care of themselves. Mr. Flint was head of CID with the Metropolitan Police Force, and Mrs. Flint, well, she's a local. She was born just down the road and knows this place like the back of her hand. They can't be happier than to be here."

Pilgrim seemed to be very anxious for me to like them and I did, but she was keeping something from me, and I wondered what it was, until she again, seemed to pick-up on my thoughts.

"Fair enough. Mrs. Flint is a *little* eccentric, but eccentric *good*, not eccentric bad."

"If that's all it is, and they can look after themselves, then I'm in. From the looks of things we'll have our pick of rooms." I was actually quite pleased at the prospect of a large apartment with a view of the Devon coast.

The grand lobby had a staircase that wouldn't have been out of place in L'améthyste. With original oak-panelling the general atmosphere of the house was one of warmth and security. I could smell the aroma of a real wood-fire and walked toward one of the reception rooms. No fire there, but the largest aquarium I had ever seen spanned the length of the wall. It was very impressive and the movement of its water caused me to take a closer look. I jumped at Pilgrim's voice behind me.

"It's a sea wave aquarium for a rather special resident," she explained.

"I've never seen anything like it."

As if on cue, Mrs. Flint entered and bustled up to us.

"You've met the General, then?" she asked expectantly.

I looked questioningly at Pilgrim, who did nothing other than turn back to the aquarium with a raised brow and disconcerted look on her face.

"Eh, no, actually ... I haven't," I answered.

Tapping the glass front and sliding back a hatch door on the top of the aquarium, she dropped a bristle covered crab leg into the water, which immediately sank to the bottom. Peering with fascinated apprehension at the rocks and seaweed along its length, I waited for another sign of life. I missed it at first; it wasn't until an enormous black claw came into view that I hesitantly took a step back, and watched aghast as the largest lobster I had ever seen came into view. With one deft move he'd swiped up the crab-leg and headed back into the recesses of the tank. I was so shocked I didn't know quite what to say, other than the obvious.

"He's a big fellow!"

"That's the General. Rescued `im off a fishing boat that came in to `arbour in 1969. I spent a month's wages to buy him, and he was big then! Told the skipper, no one `al buy him; too big to be tasty; so I got `im and `es been with us these forty years. Mr. Flint `ad to recess the tank several feet into the next room, `es gotten so big. I've written `im in my will. When I die, `es to be taken out to sea and put back. Well, I better go. Dinner will be ready, in a few shakes of a lambs tail!"

When I could be sure she was out of ear-shot, I turned to Pilgrim, who pre-emptied my thoughts.

"Good eccentric!" she smiled.

Gathering in the red-room we stood at a vast oval table, where sat on the whitest linen tablecloth, lay a silver tray with five Champagne flutes on it. Mr. Flint entered and catching a nod from his wife popped open a bottle of chilled champagne and began to fill the glasses.

Hansford had taken off outside somewhere, and now returned with what I could only describe as a large black woolly bear, with a coat the colour of sloes. We were informed by Hansford; it was in actuality, a dog. With its muscular broad shoulders reaching mid-thigh, we all took a precautionary step back. Hansford explained proudly, "He's a Bouvier de Flandres, they're bred for herding and protecting cattle against packs of wolves. I thought he'd make a good guard-dog for you." He was clearly pleased with his choice.

Pilgrim stated with a look of dismay on her face, "I can't look after him. I can barely look after myself!"

Hansford said, "Always me, me, me, isn't it. As it happens, *Boo*, is for the house. He's military trained and has seen his share of action in Afghanistan. Shot on two separate occasions, weren't you boy, and still dragged a soldier to safety." He gave the enormous hound a rub behind the ears.

"Boo?" Pilgrim said, looking at Hansford in disbelief.

Hearing his name mentioned with such distain, caused Boo to walk over to Pilgrim and nudge her forcefully back.

"You see, he's not scared of anything!" Hansford added admiringly.

"I am not picking up after that dog," Pilgrim stated flatly.

"Quit your whining. Boo is toilet trained. Although I recommend he use the outside toilet," he said contemplatively, adding, "I'm told he can be a bit wiffy at times."

"Why would anyone call a dog, Boo?" Pilgrim asked

In an attempt to dispel the sight of Boo sat on the outside toilet, I quickly diverted my thoughts, and immediately asked, "You know Pilgrim, I've been thinking about your middle initial, 'A', what does it stand for?"

"Not sure," she said startled, adding, "the registrar left it as, A."

"Seems rather odd," I queried, "You don't think your name is an anagram for Athena, Goddess of War," I stated, before I could stop myself.

She shot me a puzzled glance, but said nothing, as she laughed it off. I noticed Hansford wasn't laughing.

"Raise your glasses, please," Mr. Flint commanded.

"Baxter, why don't you propose a toast?" Pilgrim prompted.

I couldn't think of anything other to say than,

"Here's to Pilgrim, so glad you're a freak and not a monster!"

At this she genuinely burst out laughing.

After which, the stilted toast became 'The Freak!'

EPILOGUE

It was some months after that life returned somewhat back to normal. I had spent the week cataloguing at the Vault, whilst Pilgrim had brought new items in for storage. Pilgrim's five day sabbatical had included a meeting at the Natural History museum in London, in regards to part of a new exhibit entitled, Cleopatra. She had been reluctant to share with me the item for storage, as not even the Egyptian antiquarians knew of it.

Our evenings had been spent relaxing at L'améthyste while we were in town. It wasn't that I hadn't frequently thought about our run-in with the Titans, because I had. I suppose our mind does what it can to allow us to resume a day-to-day life. I'm not sure what I feel we're entitled to, especially given our line of work, but our privacy became the first casualty.

We'd been sat quietly after a hard day's work discussing the final details needed before we headed back down to Devon. A waiter had approached us carrying a salver, which he offered to Pilgrim. On the salver lay a buttonhole bouquet of flowers with a business card. Taking the card she read the only word embossed on it and handed it to me.

Deliberately leaving the flowers on the salver, she thanked the waiter, and he turned and left taking them with him.

The embossed word 'Cronus' was stamped on the card.

"What does it mean?" I asked.

"It is the language of flowers, Baxter. The flowers on the salver were Monkshead. They were sent in medieval times as a warning that, 'a deadly foe is coming'. It means the successor to Gideon Imperator, is now in place. There is now a new Titan and this Cronus is a woman."

"How can you be sure?"

"Because she offered me Monkshead before; at Exeter train station."

Printed in Poland
by Amazon Fulfillment
Poland Sp. z o.o., Wrocław